# Out of the Night and into the Dark

*Out of the Night and into the Dark*

Published by The Conrad Press in the United Kingdom 2020

Tel: +44(0)1227 472 874
www.theconradpress.com
info@theconradpress.com

ISBN 978-1-913567-06-4

Typesetting and Cover Design by:
Charlotte Mouncey, www.bookstyle.co.uk

The Conrad Press logo was designed by Maria Priestley.

Printed and bound in Great Britain
by Clays Ltd, Elcograf S.p.A.

# Out of the Night and into the Dark

Kathryn Cowling

# May 1939

## I

## JOYCE – FOURTEEN YEARS OLD

Even through the summer months, when it was pleasantly warm, my house was still freezing cold. It used to smell of a mixture of boiled cabbage and mould and had done for as long as I could remember. When I was younger, I used to think my mother was lazy because she didn't clean our house like my friends' mums cleaned theirs. As time went by, however, I began to realise that she was different to other mothers. Sometimes she would just sit on one of the rickety chairs at the kitchen table and cry.

I used to hold her hand and try to find out what was wrong with her but, in the end, I gave up trying and maybe even caring. I would look up at her and watch as she just shook her head, with an ever-tragic expression on her face, and then she would start to sob woefully. When this happened I would go out to play because I had no idea what to say to her.

My best friend was Mabel Johnson and she lived next door to me but her house was so much nicer than mine was. I don't know how I would have survived without Mabel and her family. Their house was awash with warmth and laughter. I loved being there. Mabel's mum was a plump, jolly lady who always seemed to be smiling and was the total opposite of my mother. She used to say:

'Be kind to your mother, child, she's been through a lot has Beryl.'

I did try but my mother seemed to be locked in her own world where no one else lived. My father reminded me of a shadow. He came home from work at the same time every night and cooked tea for me and Mum, until I was old enough to relieve him of the chore. He said very little and spent his evenings with his nose buried in the newspaper before going to bed. When he headed upstairs, Mother used to jump up from her seat and totter up after him like a duckling following its parent.

I never heard them have a conversation with each other and they rarely spoke to me. Even though I got little acknowledgement from either parent I never lacked for anything materially. I was well fed and it didn't matter that my clothes were second-hand, they were adequate for my needs and I had nothing to complain about. Four doors up from me lived the East family. There were four sons and two daughters and they ran around the street barefoot. Their clothes were nothing but rags.

Oddly though, they always seemed happy enough even if they looked as though they were starving. Sometimes the children would ask me if I had any spare food, I always obliged. Their mother and father were just as inadequately dressed and underfed but they also seemed happy enough so I shouldn't complain. I had everything I needed.

By the time I was ten or eleven years old most of the household chores fell on my shoulders. I began to do everything that needed to be done around the house and eventually managed to rid it of the stink and make it a more pleasant place to live in. Occasionally my father would smile a kind of half smile at me, when he came in from work, and smelled the tea cooking. He would tell me I was a good girl. This made me happy. He was acknowledging that I existed.

In September of that year, Mabel told me one day, as we walked to school, that we were at war with Germany. I didn't really know what that meant but Mabel didn't seem bothered so I thought nothing of it. We lived in a small terrace about ten miles from Plymouth docks. Nothing much happened around here and I assumed that wouldn't change.

Sadly, I was very wrong. I came to find out that Hitler liked to drop as many bombs on the docks as he could. This was because he wanted to try and stop any ships bringing supplies to England or sailing to other countries for them. I had really hoped that Plymouth docks were far too small and insignificant for Hitler to bother about.

A few weeks after Mabel had told me about the war I came home from school and found my father sitting in the kitchen. He was dressed like a soldier. He told me he had enlisted because it was his duty to fight in the war against Hitler. It was the most words I had ever heard him say at one time. I asked him how long he would be gone but he just shook his head and said 'as long as it takes' then he stood up, slung a bag over his shoulder and walked out the door and up the narrow street.

I stood and watched him go until he was out of sight. I sighed as it struck me that I would miss him a lot and I hoped he would come home soon. He, at least, gave me some words of recognition which was more than my mother did.

After he left Mum seemed to retreat even further into her

shell. She barely noticed when I returned home from school with a gas mask under my arm. She nibbled away at the food I gave her and got thinner by the month. Mabel's mum used to pop in and say:

'Beryl, you've got to snap out of this, it's doing no good to anyone!'

It didn't help, my mother continued with her semi-existence. I was due to leave school in a few weeks' time and had no idea what I wanted to do. I supposed I could work in one of the local factories but that was not very appealing. I lived near a bustling city so there were a variety of jobs to be had. Mabel had set her heart on becoming a typist and her parents were paying for her training. I quite fancied that too but when I asked my mother if I could do the same but she just stared at me.

The sweet shop on the corner of my street had put a notice in the window asking for an assistant. I liked the idea of working in a sweet shop and because it was within walking distance I wouldn't have to shell out for bus fare. One day, after school, I put on my smartest dress and walked into the shop. I was oddly nervous about asking Mrs Purvis if she would consider me for the job. I had known her for as long as I could remember and had never felt anxious in front of her before but it seemed different now I was here and needing employment.

However, she soon put me at my ease. She showed me how to balance the sweets on the large iron scales using different weights. I was then shown how to work the till. When she asked me to ring in an amount myself I found it very easy and left the shop half an hour later after being told the job was mine. It was now Friday and I wasn't required to start working until the following Monday. Mrs Purvis's previous assistant had left to work in a munitions factory but was working until she started her new job on the Monday. This meant I had the whole weekend in front of me to enjoy.

I skipped home and found my mother in her usual place. She was sitting in one of the tatty arm chairs staring into the fire. There were no flames in the hearth and barely any heat coming out of it. I quickly grabbed the poker and began to prod the fire back to life. When a couple of small flames started to form I quickly shoved some kindling on them until the fire eventually began to spring to life, illuminating and heating the kitchen at the same time. I then added a few nuggets of coal and the room was warm in no time at all.

Mother didn't move the whole time I knelt at the hearth teasing the fire back to life. I told her about my new job but she just stared into the grate as the tiny flames started to lick up at the back of the fireplace and disappear up the chimney. She showed no outward acknowledgement of what I had said. I sighed and set about cooking the tea on the Aga oven that dominated one wall of the room.

As usual, Mother had done no shopping so trying to make a palatable meal with the ingredients I had was no mean feat. Suddenly a siren began to wail. It was now about six months since Mabel had informed me that we were at war and it was a chilly March day in 1940. The noise sounded like a cat in pain and I was startled and a little unsure what we were supposed to do.

Mabel had told me that her dad was preparing the basement for them to go down into in case of an air raid; I guessed the siren meant that an attack from the air was imminent. I couldn't think what else it could be. I wasn't absolutely sure how to get into our basement but I knew I had to try, and quickly. Hastily I turned off the hob and turned to face my mother, she hadn't moved an inch. I knelt in front of her and looked her directly in the eye. It seemed to unnerve her a little.

'Where's the basement, Mum, we need to get down there, the Germans are coming to drop bombs on us,' I hoped that wasn't true but I needed my mother to realise the urgency of the situation. She began to tremble and lifted her arm and pointed to the cupboard under the stairs.

I raced to it and pulled the door open. It was packed solid with household items. The ironing-board and clothes-horse were stacked against one wall. Old curtains and bedding were pushed against the far end. Mother's shopping bag on wheels, which I had never seen her use, was partially blocking the door-way and there were old shoes, boots and an array of gardening equipment taking up the rest of the space. I called back to her and told her it was full. She said nothing so I ran back into the kitchen. She hadn't moved but there were tears sliding down her cheeks.

For the first time in my life I felt a smidgen of compassion for the pathetic life she lived. I realised that she must have some emotions because she was obviously feeling frightened, her tears told me this. I raced over, knelt in front of her and wrapped my arms around her waist then I buried my face in her lap. I felt a prickly sensation rush through me when I felt the weight of her hand on the back of my head and for some inexplicable reason I wanted to cry, I didn't though.

When I heard an ominous droning sound coming from some way in the distance I wasn't sure, at first, what it was. When

I realised, I was instantly terrified. The noise was the sound of countless planes flying in the sky and the fact that the air raid siren had sounded made me realise that they were enemy aircraft. I clung tightly on to my mother as the noise got louder and louder. It was the most terrifying sound I had ever heard.

In the distance I could hear screeching sounds as the shells fell and explosions when they hit the ground. I prayed to God to make the Germans keep bombing where they were and not head towards us. My prayers were partially answered. One explosion shook our house so badly that dust sprinkled down from the ceiling and I heard the sound of glass breaking. I could no longer stop my tears. The terror I was feeling paralysed me on the spot that I was in.

I briefly wandered if it was God's plan for Mother and me to die together and get to know each other in the next life. I have no idea how long the raid lasted because at some point, I must have fallen asleep. When I awoke, all was silent and Mother had her arms around my shoulders. I shook myself awake. My body ached when I tried to move it because I had been in one spot for so long. I stiffly pulled myself into a standing position, trying not to wake Mother as I did so.

I looked out of the window and saw it was now pitch black outside. The attack had started just as the daylight had begun to disappear. Mother remained asleep. I went into the kitchen and put the kettle on the hob. The half-cooked food was now a congealed mess and I was no longer hungry. I put some loose tea leaves in the teapot then poured us both a cup of tea. I shook Mother awake and handed a cup and saucer to her. She seemed startled and unaware of where she was.

I explained that we had been caught up in an air raid but

that we had been lucky and there was only a small window broken at the back of the house and that was the extent of the damage, apart from everything being covered in a film of dust. Mother nodded, then turned and began staring into the dying embers once more. I sighed. For a short time, during the air raid, my mother had seemed human and had shown me love in the form of her hand on the back of my head; now it seemed as though the shutters were down once more and I was back where I had always been, alone.

# 2

The day after the first raid I went next door and asked Mabel's dad if he would help me find the cellar in our house. He promised he would pop in after work and I thanked him and then continued with my journey to the shops. At the crossroads at the far end of the road some men were working on what looked like a corrugated iron shed and I stopped to look. Soon, a small crowd had gathered. I listened as the women gossiped and found out that it was actually an air raid shelter and that this was where we should go when the siren rang out.

I looked at the flimsy structure and didn't fancy spending a minute in it let alone an hour or a night. I hoped my home actually had a cellar. In the distance I could see strange silver objects bouncing in the clouds. They were tethered to the ground but I couldn't see what they were tied to. The butcher told me they were barrage balloons. Their purpose was to thwart any enemy planes, I wasn't sure how that would work but I'm sure whoever put them there would know.

Mabel's dad located the trapdoor to the cellar at the bottom of our stairs. It was covered by a homemade rug and nailed shut so there would have been no chance of Mother and me taking shelter there even if I had managed to find it. When we finally managed to prise it open, the sudden gush of air caused a cloud of dust to shoot out which covered us both from head to toe. We brushed ourselves off and I followed Mr Johnson, Mabel's dad, and his torch down the uneven steps.

I think I may have read too many story books because I was

convinced the dead bodies of our ancestors would be strewn around the concrete floor with macabre wounds and staring eyes, but the cellar was completely empty. Mr Johnson swung the beam of the torch around every corner of the room and found a light switch. There was no bulb in place for it to work but at least that meant I wouldn't have to traipse down here with torches or candles once we had sorted that minor problem out.

Over the next few days, Mabel, Mrs Johnson and I made the cellar as habitable as a concrete box could have been. The small bulb did not make a huge impact in illuminating the room but once our eyes became accustomed to the dimness we could see well enough. I scraped the walls with a wire sweeping brush until there was no loose dust or plaster then did the same with the floor. I gathered a few clippie mats from around the house and placed them in the cellar along with two chairs from the back parlour.

Mrs Johnson advised me to put some books or magazines in the cellar in case the raid was a long one. She also told me to have a bag always ready in case of an attack. In it, I was to put the ration books which mother and I had been issued with a few months previously, any important documents such as birth certificates and insurance policies and any precious family photos. I did all this and once I had finished I felt a little more in control of the precarious situation we found ourselves in. This did not actually quell my fear when I thought of the next bombardment but it did give me a modicum of comfort.

# 3

I tugged the collar of my coat up and pulled it tightly around my neck. The raids continued as the year progressed and I was glad of the protection of the cellar. The walk from the sweet shop where I worked to my home was only a short one but it was a bitter cold December evening. It was barely six o'clock but it was pitch black and I could scarcely make out the shapes of the houses in our street. The government had decreed that the country must go into black-out mode throughout the hours of darkness and any citizen inadvertently showing any small chink of light would be fined or imprisoned if it happened on a regular basis.

I understood their reasoning but struggled with the practicalities of the situation. I owned a small torch but tended to save this for emergency situations as Mr Johnson had told me that batteries would be hard to come by if the war dragged on. He seemed to know a lot about what might happen and I was grateful for his advice. As I felt my way along the familiar street I felt a small crowd of butterflies flutter in my stomach with excitement.

It was the day before Christmas Eve and regardless of my cold and uncaring upbringing I loved the joy of the season. The usual array of coloured lights that were normally on display in the shops, were sadly missing, due to the blackout, but I still saw several Christmas trees standing proudly in front of my neighbour's windows. They were all decorated with strings of tinsel and tiny brittle balls. I had managed to get hold of a small chicken for our own Christmas dinner and Mrs Johnson had made an extra small Christmas pudding, way back in October, for Mother and me.

I was really looking forward to my two whole days off, Christmas and Boxing Day, and to some time to myself. I reached the end of the street and pushed my front door open. I shouted hello to my mother as I dumped my coat, scarf and gloves on the bannister then headed up the narrow passage-way towards the kitchen. I suppressed a sigh because I knew what would greet me. Mother would, as always, be staring into the dying embers, totally unaware of what was going on around her.

To my surprise, I pushed the door aside and saw a roaring fire in the grate. It radiated a wonderful amount of heat and I stood and enjoyed it, just for a moment. I allowed the warmth to caress my freezing face. I smelt a delicious aroma and turned to see what it was. Sitting at the kitchen table, looking very handsome and proud was my father.

I cannot describe my joy at seeing him and I ran over and hugged him from behind. He was immediately embarrassed by this unwelcome gesture of love but I didn't care, I was just happy to have someone else in the house. Mother's mood often dragged me down with her and I had to fight within myself to remain cheerful and upbeat.

The wonderful smell was coming from the three plates of fish and chips sitting on the kitchen table. This was a real treat and I thanked my father for buying it. Usually after spending hours on my feet in the shop I then had to come home and cook for Mother and me. Pulling back the chair and sitting down I began to tuck into the meal. Once I was done, I got up and put the kettle on the hob and made us all a cup of tea. I was sure that my father smiled at me as I put his in front of him but it might have been all in my mind.

As we slept that night the air raid siren whirred into action warning us all of imminent danger. I hurriedly pulled myself out of bed and yelled to my mother and father. I quickly made some tea for the flask and grabbed the bag of our necessary items. I also picked up a loaf of bread, a knife and some butter in case the raid turned out to be a long one. Once, I was in the cellar, I switched on the small bulb and lit the paraffin heater. Our shelter was not the warmest of places and even worse at this time of year.

My father and mother followed me in and Father pulled down the hatch while I helped Mother into her chair. Then we had a dilemma, there were only two chairs and three people. This predicament was solved by Father hauling Mother out of her chair and sitting in it himself, he then pulled her onto his lap. I found it utterly strange seeing the two of them sitting so closely and intimately. I had never seen them as much as hold hands before but I liked what I saw.

Soon the noise of aircraft sounded in the distance and I prayed to God that my name was not on any of Hitler's bombs. Each time an explosion sounded I trembled violently but was constantly trying to still myself so I wouldn't upset Mother. At one point Father leant towards me and patted my hand, this small act of kindness almost brought tears to my eyes and I wished he was home all the time to take care of us. At some point through the long night I poured us all a cup of tea and buttered some bread for anyone who wanted it.

Most of the incendiaries seemed to be falling some distance away and for that I was grateful. I eventually dropped off to sleep in my chair only to be woken by my father who told me that the 'all clear' had sounded and that it was safe to go back to bed. I thanked him and walked stiffly back up the stairs and climbed into bed. After half an hour, I realised I was not going to get any sleep so I rose and went down into the kitchen.

It was an hour before I needed to start work so I decided I would have a leisurely breakfast of porridge. I looked around and was glad to see that our house had suffered no damage in this raid. Father joined me about ten minutes later and we ate our breakfast and drank our tea in companionable silence.

When we had eaten, I asked him how long his leave was, and he explained that he had to go back to his regiment on Boxing Day. He told me that a lot of soldiers had been given leave and he believed that the government had plans for its newly enlisted army. It probably meant being sent abroad but he had no idea where. That was why he was lucky enough to be home for Christmas.

I told him to make sure he looked after himself when he did return to his unit. I then stood up to go and rouse Mother from her sleep. Father also stood up and he pushed me back down in the chair and said he would see to Mother while I had another cup of tea. I told him I could get used to this treatment and smiled widely at him. He winked back at me.

At the shop, I told Mrs Purvis, excitedly about my father's unexpected home coming and she was delighted for me. She went through a door at the back of the shop and came back with bottle of sherry which she insisted we drink with our Christmas dinner the following day. I bought some pipe tobacco and a pair of socks as a present for my father and when I finished my shift that day I felt much happier than I usually did.

Having my father home meant that I would not arrive home to a cold, soulless house and have to put a meal together while I was dead on my feet. It was astounding how such tiny things, like walking into a warm room and smelling food cooking could lift my spirits so enormously. Dad was cooking eggs and bacon in the frying pan when I got home. They smelt delicious and soon my mouth was watering.

While he was busy I slipped upstairs and hastily wrapped Dad's Christmas present. I then put it at the foot of the tiny Christmas tree that stood in the corner of the room. I had bought the tree at the market for a bargain price because no one else wanted it due to its lack of height and spindly appearance. I liked it though.

That evening, the three of us, Mum, Dad and me sat drinking hot cups of cocoa around a glowing fire. It was one of the most magical times I could remember. My father actually talked. He told us about his basic training and the very good friends he had made at the army base. He explained that they had been through such a lot together already that he believed they would be pals for life. This was a new side to my father that I had never seen but liked instantly. It seemed to me that he, being out amongst the human race had actually turned him into a member of it.

Living with my mother must have been dragging him under as much as it wore me down. It was as though she was a hidden rip tide in a glassy sea and once your feet got caught, there was no rising above the surface. I assumed she couldn't help the way she was but a tiny part of me fervently wished she was not so egocentric and self-absorbed. If she could have just made a tiny effort, life would have been so much happier and more relaxed.

Father and I tidied the house together before we went to bed that evening. I was delighted he was there and hadn't realised quite how much I had been dreading the festive season with just my mother. Mabel's parents had asked us to join them but I'm sure I heard a sigh of relief when I politely refused. I was quite sure that my mother would happily suck the joy out of Christmas for the family next door and they were too kind for me to allow her to do that. For that reason, I had resigned myself to a miserable Christmas but now Father was home.

Christmas day was my favourite day. Although our past Christmases were quiet I always had presents under the tree and enjoyed a delicious lunch with my parents. Traditionally, Father would visit the pub after the meal and I would go next door and play with Mabel so Mother was free to sail away on her ship of misery where I believed she was quite happy to go.

There was a sharp nip in the air as I pushed back my bedclothes that wonderful Christmas morning. I squealed as my toes touched the linoleum rather than the tiny rug by my bed, the floor was as cold as a frozen lake. I slipped my feet into my thread bare slippers then pulled a thick woollen cardigan around me. I pulled back the curtains and looked onto the street below. It was yet to awake and looked very beautiful in the early morning light.

Intricate white patterns of frost wound their ways around the windows and doors as a solitary cloud floated across the dark blue sky. The orange light from the street lamps threw macabre light patterns across the narrow road and a tiny robin stood on the window sill opposite. His puffed up redbreast was proudly lifted then the tiny face and beak looked skywards and he flew away. I heard a noise coming from downstairs and hurriedly washed and dressed myself.

Looking in on Mother, I could see she was still fast asleep but Father's side of the bed was empty. I left Mother to her slumber. Who knows? She may have found some solace for her misery in her dreams so who was I disturb that? I walked, once more, into the warmth of the kitchen. The fire was burning brightly in the grate. I sat in one of the easy chairs to the left of the fireplace then turned to see my father with his back to me. He seemed to be fiddling with something so I crept nearer for a closer look.

As I did this he turned and I saw a wooden box, set in the middle of the sideboard. It had a grill of some type on one side and four large black knobs on the other.

'Merry Christmas love, this is for you, I know how lonely it can be living with your mother so I thought this might help.'

I peered closely and was quite sure I seen a picture of some-thing like it in an old copy of *Woman's Own* magazine which Mabel's mum had given to me. I gasped when I realised what it was.

'It's a wireless, oh Dad, switch it on,' I begged.

He twiddled the knobs a few times and messed about with a separate bit of the equipment by the side, I think he said it was called an accumulator but I couldn't be sure. I was totally fascinated and bemused as I watched him trying to tune the box in. Then, suddenly it was as if the whole room was illuminated by sound of the clear and precise voice of Frank Sinatra, singing out of the instrument. I could not hide my astonishment and my father laughed and told me he had felt exactly the same when he had heard the music for the first time.

I simply couldn't work out where the sound could possibly be coming from and how it was transmitted into our kitchen but I didn't care. This was the very best present I had ever had and I rushed over and hugged my father tightly. To my utter joy the embrace was returned and that made my whole day perfect, even though it had only just begun.

A small cloud darkened the mood in the room, ever so slightly, when my mother shuffled in. To me, it felt like her presence had broken the magical bond that had formed between me and my dad. Mother sat in one of the armchairs by the fire and even she, who was moved by absolutely nothing, couldn't help but stare at the strange contraption sitting on the dusty wooden sideboard. I could almost feel her confusion as the song 'Moonlight Sonata' finished and was quickly replaced by 'Don't Sit Under The Apple Tree With Anyone Else But Me'.

To my utter astonishment my father took me in his arms and began to twirl me around the room, I couldn't help but giggle; this was fast turning out to be the best day in my whole life. After the song had finished the News came on and we decided we would listen to it later in case it put a dampener on the day. With the war the raging around us, there was rarely any good news from the newsreader. Dad showed me how to switch the wireless off and on and how to tune it in when needed. We then prepared breakfast together.

As the three of us began to eat, I heard Mother mumble something and I asked her to repeat what she had said as I didn't catch it the first time. She said it again, just a little louder, between tiny, bird-like, mouthfuls of food.

'I don't want it in the house,' she whispered, looking directly at the wireless.

I am ashamed to say that at the particular point in my life any modicum of love I had ever tried to feel for this miserable woman disintegrated and I actually began to hate her. To me, it seemed, she wanted everyone's life to be as joyless and downright wretched as hers and a spark of anger flared up inside me at the injustice of her statement.

'Oh yes, Mother! Why the hell should anyone bring any cheer into this bloody mausoleum! Perish the bloody thought that we could sit and listen to programmes together and enjoy a tune or two, no let's just sit here and bask in your pitiful bloody misery until we're all as old, bitter and twisted as you are!'

The sting on my cheek from my father's hand shocked me out of my outburst and I sat back down on my chair and held my face, I had not even realised that I had stood up. My father looked a little guilty and ill at ease and told me I was not to speak to my mother like that. I mumbled an apology and began to gather up the breakfast plates.

My mother had now ruined everything. She had blackened the shiny polish of the day like soot on a copper kettle and inside I seethed with the injustice of what had happened. I couldn't believe how she could change the harmonious atmosphere in a second without explanation or acknowledgement. I washed the dishes in the deep sink in the scullery while fighting back the tears that threatened to engulf me. When I returned to the kitchen, the wireless was gone and there was just a square mark in the dust stood where it had once stood.

Father was sitting in one of the tatty armchairs, reading his paper and mother was, as usual staring into the dancing flames. Her hands were folded in her lap and I felt as though I could quite cheerfully shove her smug face into the fire. I didn't actually know if her expression was actually self-satisfied. To me, it just felt that way because of the raging anger that was coursing through by body and threatening to billow out through my ears in a trail of steam.

The day dragged. We all exchanged presents in an awkward silence and ate our Christmas dinner in the same way. I was happy to escape next door for an hour in the afternoon and voiced my anger to Mabel about my mother. My dear friend hugged me as I cried and tried to bolster my spirits by saying that I wouldn't have to stay at home forever and when I moved out and met a husband I could buy my own wireless and there was nothing my bloody mother could do about.

This little chat cheered me somewhat and, when I returned home for the evening meal, the atmosphere between my father and I was less stilted. We drank some of the sherry Mrs Purvis had given us and it made my cheeks glow. When Mother went to bed, Father and I played cards and I really wished that we still had the wireless to listen to. I think my father felt the same way but his loyalty to Mother meant that he had to bend to her wishes, regardless of the way I felt. While he was home, Dad managed to get hold of some glass to replace the broken window, from the bombing raid a few months earlier, and I helped him fit it. It brought some much-needed light into the room.

It was with a heavy heart that I waved my father off the next day and I stood watching until he had disappeared from my view. A wave of loneliness overcame me that was so strong it took my breath away. I could hardly drag myself back into the house. I longed to run after my father but knew I couldn't. I wished I could go with him. I was always afraid my mother would slowly draw the life out of me as she had with him. With great reluctance I turned and walked into the house. The unseen pull to flee seemed so real it was as though an invisible pair of hands was dragging me backwards.

Mother was sitting in her usual spot with eyes fixated on the hearth but not really looking at anything. The hatred I felt for this pitiful woman was so intense it scared me. I turned and walked back down the narrow passageway adjacent to our stairs and retrieved my coat, hat and gloves from the bannister. I shoved my arms in the sleeves as quickly as I could. As I pulled my gloves over my fingers I heard my mother whine.

'Joyce, where are you going?'

Her voice gave wings to my heels and I flew up the road, running as fast as I could until I reached the outskirts of the town. Once I had reached the grassy fields surrounded by the tall hedgerows I slowed my pace a little to catch my breath. I came across several large boulders strewn around a glassy stream. It looked like a giant man had simply picked them up, thrown them in the air, and watched as they landed at will.

I sat down, close to the running water. I watched as the tiny stream travelled down the slight hillside winding its way around the tiny rocks. The graphite grey sky was dotted with cotton wool clouds as seagulls soared gracefully above. They squawked and screeched their presence continuously and I would have given anything to swap places with one of these creatures and be able to fly away and never return.

The gloom of the day threatened to overcome me and

the thought of spending the next however many years living with my mother frightened me. I knew that I could not stay out forever and sometime later I trudged home and began to mentally prepare myself for it being just Mother and me in the house. Being home made me feel, as I imagined, the Great Houdini did, when he was trapped in a tank of water upside down. He was unable to breathe and was chained and blind-folded and continuously fought to escape. This was how I felt and I prayed to God that one day I would stop feeling so entombed and desperate.

# 4

Christmas seemed a lifetime away and I felt like I had aged years in the previous six weeks. The continuous bombing raids made me feel as though my nerves constantly jangled and I longed for someone to take care of me and comfort me as the bombs dropped around us. I came to realise that the German pilots were not hugely accurate and sometimes dropped their weapons miles from the docks and onto the population below.

Mr Johnson said that all the Germans were Nazis and had no regard for human life so we must protect ourselves as best we could. He gave me a couple of tin helmets and told me and Mother to wear them when there was a raid going on. He explained that it would offer just a little more protection from falling masonry or glass. I wished that Mr Johnson was my dad and that I could spend the frightening times in their cellar with him but I knew he had his own family to take care of. I was grateful for any little thing he did for us. I thought him a very kind man.

I got a few letters from my dad during this period and although they were upbeat and chatty I couldn't really work out exactly where he was or if he was in any danger so I tried not to think about it. The warmth of the winter sun stroked my face and caressed my bare arms as I walked home from the shop on this warm February day. Children played hopscotch and hoopla in the street and I had a sudden longing to be a child once more and be free of the burden of caring for my mother.

I slowed up a little, quite involuntarily, as I approached

home. I would much rather have been out in the fresh air than cooped up with my miserable mother. I felt someone tugging at my skirt and turned to see a young boy, about twelve years old, standing behind me holding out a brown envelope.

'Telegram for you missus,' he announced before remounting his bicycle and pedalling off towards the far end of the street.

I looked at the letter and saw that it was addressed to my mother so I shoved it in the pocket of my blue dress and continued my journey up the street. I noticed a few sudden movements behind the twitching curtains of my neighbour's homes and some sixth sense told me that all was not well but I didn't know why. I had just reached my front door when Mrs Johnson, Mabel's mum, came out of her door and grasped both my hands. I looked at her with a mixture of confusion and dismay. The lines on her forehead and the sadness in her eyes told me that something was troubling her.

'I saw the telegram boy, Joyce, show me the letter love,' she said.

I took the crumpled correspondence from my pocket and handed it to her. She then opened my front door and led me inside. I turned back around. I was definitely now sure that the people in my street were looking at me from behind their net curtains and I began to feel scared; something was not right and I needed to what was happening, what did everyone in the street seem to know apart from me? A lone seagull suddenly screeched loudly and angrily in the sky above me and a deep feeling of foreboding overwhelmed me.

Once we were inside the house, I filled the kettle and put in on the hob. I then turned and watched as Mrs Johnson knelt in front of my mother and handed her the brown envelope.

Shadows seemed to be dancing around the room but I knew it must be my imagination; the windows were too small to allow any in. Time seemed to stop as my mother slowly opened the letter and began to read. I started when my mother emitted a sound not dissimilar to the seagull I had heard earlier.

She then began to rock in her chair then began shake her head wildly from side to side. I was unaccustomed to this behaviour and at a bit of a loss as what to do. I turned and spooned some tea into the teapot, added hot water and stirred. I then poured three cups of tea and added a dash of milk to each. I handed a cup to Mrs Johnson and attempted to hand one to my mother. As I leant close, however, she lunged forward and knocked the cup sideways. It went flying across the room and smashed onto the hearth. Mrs Johnson held my mother tightly.

'Go and fetch the doctor Joyce love, tell him it's urgent.'

Without question I did as I was told and almost ran straight into Mr Johnson as he walked home from work. I told him Mother was ill and I was fetching the doctor. He dropped his work bag into his small front garden then headed into ours.

The receptionist was sitting in the small dark outer office of the surgery when I pushed the door open and raced in. I explained that Mother was gravely ill. She rang a bell and Doctor Smythe appeared from the back room already carrying his medical bag as though he already knew what was wrong with Mother.

The doctor and I raced the small distance back home. As we grew closer I could hear Mother's piercing screams down the street. Dr Smythe entered first and I followed. I had no idea why I felt so bewildered and scared. Mr and Mrs Johnson were physically holding Mother down when I walked into the room.

It seemed like a totally surreal situation to me.

Mother seemed to have gained some outward strength and was almost escaping from my neighbours who were fighting to hold her down. Both were lying across Mother's writhing body and yelling her to calm down. She wasn't listening. It was not until the doctor jabbed a needle into the top of her leg that her agitation began to subside. I watched as she stopped moving and looked at her as she became completely still like a deflated balloon.

The doctor mumbled something to my neighbours and between the two of them they hoisted Mother up and carried her upstairs to her bedroom. Mr Johnson came down first and quickly pulled me into his arms. Although I was a little embarrassed at this unusual act of affection I quite liked the warm safeness of his embrace. Mrs Johnson appeared next and was dabbing at the side of her eyes with a small, white handkerchief. She then told me that Mother would be fine until the next morning and that I knew where she was if I needed her.

The Johnson's and the doctor then shuffled out of the house talking in muted conversation and I couldn't hear what they were saying. I was unsure what to do. I noticed the broken cup in the hearth and went to fetch a sweeping brush to tidy it away. I did this and shovelled the broken crockery into the fireside bin. I then squeezed the water out of a damp cloth in the scullery and washed the tea from the wallpaper before it stained it.

It was as I stood up, once my chore was finished, that I noticed the crumpled letter behind the bin. I retrieved it and smoothed out the creases and began to read;

*To Mrs Beryl Dean*
*It is with deep regret that we must inform you of the death*
*of Private Matthew Dean. He was killed in action bravely*
*defending his comrades and Britain will always be grateful*
*for his part in the war.*

*Colonel Henry Armstrong*

I didn't know how long I stood looking at the letter or when
the tears began to fall. All I knew was that my father was dead.
I realised then that I loved him and always had done. I felt an
overwhelming sorrow for the cards he had been dealt in his
life. Being married to Mother had not been easy but he stood
by her and never contemplated leaving. In my head, that was
braver than shooting at a distant enemy in the hope they'd be
killed first.

# 5

I sat in the armchair to the left of the fire and immediately smelled the familiar odour of my dad's tobacco smoke. I longed to feel his strong arms around me. I thought back to when he twirled me around, to the lively tune, on Christmas Day and I thanked God for the memory. I now believed that the man, the one who swung me around to the music on the radio, was the person my father would have been if he hadn't been suffocated by my mother's misery.

I went upstairs. Mother was lying on the bed with her head lolling to one side. Tears fell continuously from her unfocussed eyes. Instantly, I could tell that she was totally locked in her own misery and would not show a scrap of consideration for me. The realisation came to me that this was all my mother did. The only person she thought about was herself and her suffering. She didn't give mine a second thought. I knew then that I hated her and I always would. I closed her bedroom door and walked back down the stairs.

As I reached the bottom step, the front door opened and Mabel rushed in. She pulled me into her arms and rubbed my back. She told me how terribly sorry she was and what a lovely man my father was. I held onto her and cried until it felt as though there were no tears left then we walked into the front room. She made us a cup of tea. She sat and listened and I felt much lighter than I had done when she first came. She allowed me to cry, be angry and to talk about everything my dad meant to me.

When she left I locked up the house. I picked up the photo of my father in his army uniform. It stood proudly in the centre of the mantelpiece. He was smiling broadly and I felt my heart constrict when I realised that I would never see him smile again. I didn't think I would get much sleep that night but my emotions must have exhausted me because I was asleep almost immediately my head hit the pillow. I dreamed that my father had come home and we were dancing once more.

Waking up the following morning bought the grief back afresh but this time I kept my emotions in check and began my daily routine. It was a warm day so I left the hearth unlit but re- kindled the fire in the Aga to make tea. I took a cup up to mother. She was sleeping now, breathing softly and peacefully and I felt pity for the nightmare she would have to face when she awoke. I left her tea on her bedside table.

The walk to work seemed to take longer than usual this morning but I wasn't sure why. It seemed as though my legs were heavier than they ordinarily were and that my head was full of cotton wool.

I was aware of the sympathetic looks coming in my direction from the people I had lived close to all my life. It annoyed me. I neither asked for nor wanted their pity. One of the smallest children from the East family barrelled out of their house and almost ran into the side of me. I put my hands out to stop the little girl from sending me sprawling, she stopped and I saw that it was Josie, who was around seven years old.

'Oh Joycie I'm proper sorry to hear about your daddy, he was a lovely man, he always used to give me a penny.' She wrapped her arms around my waist and I clung onto her. I enjoyed feeling the warmth of another human being.

I looked down and saw tears running down her grubby face. I took out my hanky and wiped them away. I then thanked her and told her to pop into the shop later and I'd give her a few sweeties. She walked away clutching my hanky in her hand and I continued with my journey.

The street was exactly the same as it had always been. The pavements were grey and there was dirt in between the paving stones. The narrow road was dotted with pot holes and over-flowing drains, the same as it always was but today it seemed different. I had never noticed quite how filthy the buildings were and the raucous squawking of the seagulls seemed to penetrate through to my brain like it had never done before.

I used to think the net curtains that hung in most of the windows were white but I was wrong. They were all a horrible yellow-brown colour and most were dotted with holes and pulls. The whole street seemed to have changed. It was no longer vibrant and colourful. The people, my neighbours, were not smiling anymore or chatting, they all looked miserable and withdrawn. It was as though a giant hand had swiped the colour out of the world and sprinkled it with grey, powdered dust.

The shop bell clanged loudly as I entered. Mrs Purvis was sweeping the shop floor and looked visibly startled when I walked in.

'I didn't expect you today love, what with the terrible thing that happened with your dad, how's your Mum managing?'

I looked into the kindly face of my employer and tried to smile but my features didn't move.

'Might as well work, there's not much else I can do and Mother is coping as normal,' I replied.

I then took off my woolly hat and began to weigh ounces

of sweets into bags. This was to ensure we were ready for the dinner time rush of school children who always came in for their sherbet lemons, strawberry bonbons or mint imperials. Each child had a different preference and I knew pretty much what each one would buy when they came into the shop.

Concentrating on weighing the confectionary took my mind of the jabbing sadness that stabbed at my heart as though trying to remind me of what at happened, as if I needed reminding that my dad was dead and I would never see his face again. Getting hold of a good stock these days was also difficult due to the government having introduced sweet rationing in January this year.

I looked around and realised that the shop was looking a little empty. Mrs Purvis had tried to cover the gaps using advertising cards but the premises still looked decidedly lacking and a lot less colourful from when I first began working there.

The day flew by surprisingly quickly and before I knew it I was heading back up the road towards home. I had no idea what mood I would find Mother in but I really wished I didn't have to put up with her. As I got close to home my step slowed to almost a stop and for some unknown reason, I had never done it before, I knocked on the door of the Johnson's house and walked in. Mrs Johnson was standing at the stove stirring a giant pot of stew and my mouth watered at the smell.

'Hello my love, how's your mum? Still sleeping I expect, the doctor gave her a good dose,' she said, asking and answering her own question at the same time. I nodded but I didn't know why I didn't simply tell her the truth.

'Mabel will be home any minute, stay and have some tea with us, I don't suppose your mum will be eating much anyway, it's a sad time for Beryl, she really loved your dad.'

I thanked her and said I would love to. She seemed to forget that I loved my dad too and I was suffering his loss but her focus seemed to be on my mother's sorrow. Mabel's three younger sisters all raced into the room declaring that they were starving, all at the same time. They pulled out chairs then sat at the table eagerly awaiting their tea. Mabel and her sisters all looked like they were carved from the same piece of rock. They were all strikingly similar to look at; the only difference was they got smaller, like a set of Russian dolls.

Mrs Johnson began to spoon dollops of stew into bowls with a metal ladle then began laying them in front of us one by one. Mr Johnson came home from work and sat at the head of table then remarked about how good the food smelt. I grabbed my spoon and began to tuck into the delicious meal. There was not much meat, due to rationing but it was thick with vegetables from Mr Johnson's allotment. Fluffy, white dumplings sat on top of the thick gravy and I couldn't remember when I last tasted a meal so good.

Mabel, me and her sisters played snakes and ladders after the meal and, as usual, I found the longest snake on the board and ended up right near the bottom while Mabel found all the ladders and won three games in row. Around eight o'clock, Mrs Johnson said I'd better get home to check on Mother. I knew she was right but I couldn't hide the reluctance in my eyes as I pulled the chair back and thanked the Johnson family for a lovely evening. I so wanted to be a part of a family like theirs.

Mrs Johnson hugged me before I left and told me my mother would soon be her old self. I don't know why she thought that would cheer me up but I thanked her again anyway. I walked the short distance home and pulled the key through the letter box and let myself in. The difference between this house and Mabel's was totally depressing. My home was as cold as a fridge while a fire burned brightly in the grate next door.

# 6

I wanted to be anywhere but home but I know I had to go there. Mabel's house was so full of laughter while mine was as quiet as a graveyard and about as homely. I entered my house and walked quietly up the narrow passage, to ensure I would not disturb mother, then went into the kitchen and put the kettle on the hob. While I waited for it to boil, I prepared the porridge for tomorrow's breakfast.

I made two cups of tea then headed upstairs to take one to Mother. I pushed open the door and softly called her name. The room was as black as pitch and there was a strange, nauseating smell emanating from it. I fumbled for the light switch and flicked it on. The bulb was fairly dim but I could see the shape of Mother's body lying under her blankets. Her eyes were open and her skin was the colour of lint.

One of her arms was outside of the covers and hung limply over the side of the bed. Her wrist was cut wide open. I could see the sinews and veins inside her arm. On the floor was a pool of blood the size of tractor wheel. I felt the teacup fall from my hand and heard it smash on the floor. The tea splattered across the room and mingled with Mother's blood.

Also on the floor was my father's cut throat razor and a picture of my parents on their wedding day. I had never seen it before. I couldn't believe how young and carefree Mum and Dad looked. I wondered why the hand of fate had turned them into old grey people so early on in life. I gazed at my mother. The deep lines that were always etched across her brow were now smooth. Her mouth was hanging open and her tongue lolled out of one side.

I moved closer and lay my mother's arm under the blankets, then I touched her face. Her skin felt waxy and cold. I shivered as I thought I felt the touch of her hand on the back of my head, like she had done on the night of the air raid, but I knew that I couldn't have. My mother was dead.

I let the tears roll shamelessly down my cheeks when I thought what could have been if only she could have shed her cloak of misery. We could have comforted each other and helped one another come to terms with the loss of my father. Maybe, we could have had the relationship shared by other mothers and daughters? Now I would never know.

The sight of so much blood sickened me. I covered her face with the sheet and walked downstairs. I sipped at my own tea which was now lukewarm. A startling realisation washed over me like a tsunami. I now realised that I was totally alone in the world and had absolutely no one. When I had finished my drink, I walked back to next door. Mabel opened the door and was surprised to see me back.

'Mother's dead,' I told her with no outward show of emotion.

Mabel's mouth dropped open and she started yelling for her own mother. The next few hours went by in a haze of activity. Mr and Mrs Johnson raced next door. Mabel's dad was hiking up his braces as he barged passed me with Mrs Johnson in hot pursuit. Mabel just stood watching them. I pushed gently passed her and walked into her cosy front room. I sat in a vacant armchair and nestled in its warmth and comfort.

At one point I heard the clang of the ambulance bell and wondered what the urgency was. Mother was dead, it was too late. I pondered if I had gone home straight from work if I could have saved her but then dismissed this thought from my mind. Her arm was almost severed at the wrist so death must have come quickly. I was worried because I felt no sorrow at all at her passing, just relief. It was as though a giant millstone had been lifted off my neck and I was so light it felt like I would float up to the ceiling.

At some point Mabel's parents came into the room. Her mother eyes were red rimmed and full of tears. I wanted to comfort her but didn't know how to. She sat opposite me and Mr Johnson came in with a tray of cups of tea for us. I loved the taste of tea; it always made life feel that little bit better. Mrs Johnson began to talk.

'Your mother wasn't always the way she was you know, I've known her since junior school and we spent most of our days giggling back then,'

Her eyes had a faraway look in them as though she had gone back down the years and was with my mother once more. I couldn't imagine, for a moment, that my mother had once been a giggly school girl;

'Before she had you, she lost three babies, all boys, all born too early to live in this world, with each death Beryl died a little inside and she couldn't shake the misery out of herself. She told me that all her three boys were born perfect in every way and how warm they were when she held them then how quickly they went cold. The doctor told her it would do her no good seeing the babies but Beryl insisted, saying that just because they were born dead; it didn't mean they never existed. I think the doctor was right, she should never have held those baby boys,' Mrs Johnson finished, as a tear slid down her work-worn cheek.

I felt sorry that my mother had lost her children but I wished she had loved me more. I remembered the years I had spent, as a tiny girl, doing everything in my power to make her notice me but she didn't. I guessed she loved the dead babies more. That night I slept on the Johnson's sofa. It was a small two-seater that was shabby and threadbare. It was not long enough for me to stretch my body out so I woke in the night because of the pain in my cramped legs.

I sat up and pulled the blanket around me. The room was cold now that the fire had been banked down and was no longer cosy. As my eyes grew more used to the darkness I could see the odd shapes of furniture dotted around the room. The large side board that stood against one wall took on the form of a grotesque monster and the fireplace seemed like a giant open mouth waiting to swallow me whole.

I was afraid. I was barely fifteen years old and had no idea what would happen to me. My wages from the sweet shop would not be enough to cover the rent let alone buy coal and food. How would I survive? I couldn't stay with Mabel's family for ever. Their house was too small. Mabel and her sisters slept in one room in a double bed and her parents slept in the other. I was quite sure that if I spent too long sleeping on the sofa my legs would become deformed and twisted but I had nowhere else to go.

The enormity of my situation hit me like a thunderclap and I felt angry and alone. I hated my parents for abandoning and not caring about me enough to stay alive. I was too old to go to a children's home. When an orphaned child reached fifteen, he or she was thrust out into the world to cope on their own.

I didn't realise that I was crying until my tears rolled down my face and into my mouth. This made me even angrier because I couldn't see what good crying would be.

I was still sitting pondering when the sky lightened and dawn arrived. I got up and walked towards the window. Pulling the curtain aside I gasped. The sky was a cacophony of beautiful colours and the sight made me feel glad inside. I heard a noise and turned to see Mrs Johnson walk into the room.

She had curlers in her hair and was wearing an old worn dressing gown with a rope belt over a Winceyette night dress. She walked over to me and pulled me into arms. I adored the feeling of her embrace. The warmth of her body was like a comforting blanket enveloping me and making me feel safe. I held on as long as I could until she gently eased me towards the sofa and we both sat down, she still held onto my hand and began to speak.

'Joyce, my love, I know you must be wandering what's going to happen to you and I think I might be able to help,' she nodded as she spoke and I was immediately interested in what she had to say,

'I have an older brother who lives in Bristol who is in need of someone to keep his house tidy, I can call him from the telephone box on the corner if you like? I know he's got someone a bit older in mind since his last housekeeper left but I can tell him all about you. I know you're only fifteen but you have had to be an adult most of your life and I know that you are quite capable of running a home, what do you say?'

I sat and pondered for a moment. I didn't fancy looking after an old man in a strange house and an even stranger city but what else was there for me?

'That would be great Mrs Johnson; could you give him a ring and ask him if he'll take me on? I'd be really grateful.' I told her,

'Of course I will lovey, he's a lovely man, his name's Albert Farthing and I always hoped that one day he would marry but he's over forty now so I doubt it will happen, I hate the thought of him being lonely, as soon as we've had a nice cup of tea and a bit of breakfast I'll go to the phone box but right now I need a wash and to put some clothes on, I don't think the neighbours would appreciate me wandering up the street in my night wear,' she said then walked back out of the room and upstairs once more.

I think she was trying to make light of the situation with her little joke about going outside in her dressing gown but I couldn't laugh because I felt as though nothing would be light ever again. It seemed to me that my life would now be forever shrouded in darkness. I would be at the beck and call of a grumpy old man with no friends to talk to or a life to call my own. My misery weighed so heavily, it seemed to be pushing my body towards the ground. I sighed and began to prepare myself for the day ahead and whatever the future decided to throw at me.

# 7

Less than a week later I found myself sitting on a train heading for Bristol. Everything had happened so quickly that it all seemed to float by in a daze. The Johnson family helped me clear my home. The furniture was old and shabby and there was nothing much to sell so most of the stuff was carted off to the second-hand shop. The proprietor wasn't hugely impressed with the stuff but I think he took it out of pity. I now had a small carpet bag that held all my worldly goods. It contained a few bits of clothing, a couple of photos of my parents and a small amount of toiletries.

My final week's wages paid for my train fare but left me virtually penniless. Mrs Johnson had given me some sandwiches for my lunch and a bottle of cold tea. I looked out of the train window and before long the rolling countryside had vanished and was replaced with concrete buildings. I felt frightened and alone and longed to feel the comforting arms of Mrs Johnson wrapping me in an embrace.

I couldn't eat the sandwiches because my stomach was so churned up at the thought of what was ahead of me. The tea, though, was refreshing and delicious. It helped moisten my dry mouth. Before I knew it, the guard was yelling that we had arrived at *Temple Meads* station. I felt the urge to crawl under my seat and stay there until the train took me back to the cosy warmth of the Johnson's little house but I knew I couldn't.

I picked up my luggage and walked along the narrow alley between the seats. The train door was already open so I stepped down onto the crowded platform. I had no idea who I was looking for and was terrified. Tears threatened but I kept them at bay, I knew they would be of no help whatsoever. I gazed around the mass of faces and caught sight of a gentleman holding up a piece of cardboard with my name on it. I gulped and waved then walked over to him.

'Hello Mr Farthing, I'm Joyce Dean,' I said, trying to control the quiver in my voice but not really succeeding.

'Hello, my dear, please call me Bertie,' he replied and a smiled a warm welcoming smile that made me feel better almost instantly.

'Come with me, I've got the car parked outside, give me your bag.' He said as he simultaneously pulled it from my hand.

I followed him from the station. I kept as close to him as I could because I was terrified that if I lost sight of him, amongst this throng of humanity, I would never find him again. I could hardly believe that there could be so many people in one small place. In my little world, the small little town near Plymouth where I had travelled from, I knew everyone and we were all the same colour.

I scanned the various faces. Some were very dark brown and others were just slightly tanned. I saw a Chinese or Japanese couple hurry pass and was fascinated. I had seen pictures of them in the comic books I read but had never seen a real foreign individual. Every person seemed to be in a rush. I heard the train hoot and the station master shout that the vehicle was leaving once more. I had the urge to turn and run after it and scream, take me home, but I carried on following Mr Farthing.

Finally the crowd thinned a little. I felt a little less panicky now that I was not crammed amongst human bodies like a sardine in a tin. Mr Farthing took some keys from his pocket and opened the boot of a large, shiny, blue car and put my carpet bag inside. He closed it, then indicated to me to get in the passenger seat, which I did. Inside the vehicle smelled of leather and polish. The driver's door opened and Mr Farthing climbed in.

I was absolutely dumbfounded. I didn't know anyone who owned a car and never thought I would actually have the chance to ride in one. I looked at the dials on the dashboard at the front and watched as the key was turned in the ignition and after a few attempts, it spluttered into life. I didn't realise that I was grinning widely as we drove out onto the road and past the milling pedestrians.

'You like her?' Mr Farthing asked as he too grinned widely,

'I love her,' I gushed, 'I've never seen anything as beautiful in the whole world.'

He laughed 'She's a 1934 Austin 10/4, I got her a few years ago and she's my pride and joy,' he explained, then leaned forward and turned a dial. First I heard a crackling sound then the melodious voice of Gracie fields singing ' *we'll meet again*' rang out over the airwaves.

I was shocked to the core and also fascinated. I laughed loudly and began to sing along and so did Mr Farthing. By the time he pulled up outside some houses on the outskirts of Bristol, I felt as though I had known him all my life.

He was a tall man who carried himself proud and straight. His hair was silver and slicked back with *Brylcream* and he had a parting at one side. There was a small kink running through it and he reminded me of Bing Crosby. I watched as he walked around the vehicle and pulled opened the passenger door. I felt like a royal princess as I swung my legs around and climbed out. I noticed the intense blue colour of his eyes that were speckled with tiny grey flecks.

I followed him a little way up the road until we were standing in front of a large, granite-built property. It had small forward-facing garden with iron railings surrounding it. There was a little rose tree in the centre in full bloom. The bright red colour of the flowers was beautiful as was the wonderful aroma coming from the plant. I watched as he pushed open the heavy, iron gate and then I followed him up the short pathway.

He turned his key in the lock then pushed the door open. Standing to one side, he gestured that I should enter. The house smelt much the same as the car. It was a mixture of polish and leather but I could also smell a hint of lavender.

'Well, here we are, I'll show you to your room and let you get settled in then we'll go through the list of things I need you to do for me, your wages will be £8, 6s,5d a week. Your working day will start at 6am and finish at 6pm and you will have Sundays off,' He explained as we walked up the plush, carpeted staircase.

I gasped, that was almost three times what I was earning at the sweetshop and it would be all my own money. I wouldn't have to give the lion's share to Mother. I felt like my heart was singing inside as I imagined what I could buy with my first lot of wages. I felt as wealthy as a king. Mr Farthing opened the first door, along the landing, and I followed him into the room.

He put my bag on the bed then told me to come down to his study when I had unpacked. I knew this wouldn't take long as I had few possessions apart from my ration book and my family photos. He explained where his study was then walked out pulling the door behind him.

I sat down gently on the bed and wandered if someone was playing a terrible trick on me. For the last week I had imagined spending the rest of my days with a miserable, ugly old man in a cold, dark house that lacked comfort and warmth. Instead, I found myself in a luxurious home that I could only have dreamed of living in. My room had a large bay window that looked down onto the quiet street below. It was decorated beautifully. Pink roses adorned the wall paper and the heavy velvet curtains were tied back form either side of the window and they matched the wall paper.

The whole place was somewhere that I imagined only the very rich would live in. The Johnson's cosy, little house was always clean and tidy but it was a total comparison to this large, spacious house. I wondered how Mrs Johnson had landed in a small terraced house and her brother lived here. The single bed was high with an iron bedstead. There were two plump pillows and a candlewick bedstead cover and, at least, four blankets underneath.

Never in my life had I known such luxury. A large wooden wardrobe stood against one wall with a matching dressing table on the other. They were both a shiny walnut colour and the dressing table had a little stool in front of it. When I sat on it I could see my reflection in the three sided vanity mirror that stood on top it. I could see that my complexion was fairly pale and my cheekbones jutted out. I could do with gaining weight.

The past week had been so busy I barely had time to think, let alone eat. It felt like, for the first time in my life, some-thing good had happened to me and I really wished my father was alive so I could tell him all about my good fortune. I unpacked my few belongs and walked back down the stairs. I felt like laughing out loud making whooping noises but I contained myself.

I found the study and knocked quietly on the door.

'Enter,' I heard a voice say and pushed the door slowly open.

Mr Farthing was sitting behind a large desk. It had a leather top and looked very old but tough. He was sitting on a leather chair that he spun round when I walked into the room. He had his back to the window behind him and the desk was covered in an array of drawings or plans, I wasn't sure which.

'Ah, come and sit down Joyce,' Mr Farthing said as he pointed at the chair on the opposite side of the desk, I did as I was told.

'Now, Joyce, my previous housekeeper has abandoned me to go and work in the munitions factory up the road, apparently she earns more money and works less hours but there you go.' He stopped talking and pushed some tobacco into a small wooden pipe. He struck a *Swan Vesta* match and once he had packed the tobacco into the clay bowl he lit it. I loved the oak like smell the enveloped the room. I watched as he puffed away and a contented expression washed over his face.

'Basically Joyce, I'm a sad case, I've never managed to do a thing for myself even though I've always lived alone, Mrs Larkin, my previous housekeeper, has left instructions in the kitchen on how to work the many gadgets in there as I've no idea how to even boil an egg. I work mainly from home, I need you to tend to my basic needs, cooking meals, laundry, keeping the house clean and any other task I feel needs tackling, I know you're only fifteen but my dear sister tells me you have an old head on your young shoulders and you've been running a home virtually since you could walk,'

I smiled and nodded.

'My mother was unwell through most of her life so all of the chores were left to me, my father helped as best he could until he joined the army then it was just me and Mother for a while,'

I hadn't realised a tear had slid down my cheek when I mentioned my father and hastily swiped it away but Mr Farthing was on his feet in an instant, putting a comforting arm around my shoulder.

'Lilly, my sister, told me that you had lost both your parents recently, don't be afraid to cry Joyce, it's nature's way of healing a saddened heart,' he said as he pulled a crisp, white handkerchief from his trouser pocket and handed it to me.

I thanked him and dabbed at my eyes. I could smell the sweet sandalwood scent of his aftershave. His hanky smelled of Persil washing powder and reminded me of Mrs Johnson's washing as it whirled around on the clothesline. That was one thing they had in common, I think it was the only thing. Mrs Johnson was a short, dumpy lady with thick set limbs and a no nonsense outlook on life. Mr Farthing was tall and lithe. It seemed to me that his mind was permanently elsewhere.

'Now, I need to get on with my work, you wander round and get acquainted with the place, I sincerely hope Mrs Larkin has left decent instructions in the kitchen, otherwise neither of us will eat or have any clean clothes,' he finished and smiled the broadest most handsome smile I had ever seen. Small wrinkles appeared at the side of his eyes and mouth; they made him look distinguished and important.

'What job do you do, Mr Farthing?' I asked curiously.

'I'm an architect,' Joyce, 'before the war I designed houses for the wealthy, now I work for the government on secret projects I'm not allowed to talk about, I also write a bit of poetry although I'm not terribly good at it,'

'I wouldn't ever be anywhere near clever enough to become an architect but I do like poetry and I'm sure yours is very good,' I said as I stood up, 'I'll leave you to get on with your work, what time would you like your evening meal and do you have an groceries in the kitchen?'

'I'd like dinner at six o'clock please, but I'm afraid there is no food in the house, the shops are in walking distance and you'll find a basket in the larder in the kitchen, also in the kitchen is a jar on the mantelpiece that contains my ration book and the housekeeping money, there should be plenty there so I'll leave you to it.' I smiled at him, nodded obediently then left the room.

To me it felt as though I had been transported to Utopia. I walked around the house, starting with the upstairs. There were five large bedrooms. Mr Farthing's was the largest. I guessed this was his room because there were clothes strewn around the floor and toiletries on the dressing table. The bed was unmade and three dirty cups were scattered around his bedside table along with some used plates. The other four rooms were empty apart from the furniture.

I set about tidying Mr Farthing's room and wondered to myself how anyone could be so messy. I stripped the bed and went in search of some clean sheets. I found some inside a large, luxurious cupboard in the bathroom. Never in my life had I seen such a room. At home, the toilet was at the end of the garden and we bathed in a tin tub that hung on the wall in the scullery when the room was not being used.

If we needed to go to the toilet at night, we did it in small bucket on the landing that I emptied each morning. This bathroom took my breath away. A large enamel bath dominated the centre of the room, standing regally on its four clawed feet. The toilet and the cistern above were in one corner of the room and the chain hung down beside with an ornately decorated handle. In the other corner were a sink and the cupboard where I found the sheets and pillow cases.

I returned to the bedroom and made up the bed. I then set about picking up the various bits of clothing thrown carelessly around the room. If I deemed them clean, I put them on the wooden hangers in the wardrobe, anything dirty I piled on top of the sheets and made my way down to the kitchen with the bundle of laundry. I also picked up all the dirty crockery and wiped down the furniture.

I found the kitchen at the end of a long corridor at the back of the house. This was another immense room with a large wooden table standing directly in the centre. Most of the rooms in this house were almost the size of the whole ground floor of the little cottage where I had once lived. There was a huge cooking range standing against the far wall which was as shiny as a new pin.

I started to put the dirty washing in the sink when my eye was caught by a strange contraption in the scullery. I wandered over and read the note on top of it. Apparently it was called a twin tub and it washed the clothes automatically. I read the instructions then placed the laundry in one side of the machine.

Re-reading the directions, I took the Persil washing powder from above the shelf and sprinkled it on the clothes. I switched on the twin tub and gaped in amazement as the contraption filled with water and the clothes began swirling around, quickly I pushed the lid down and giggled, what would they think of next?

I found the shopping basket where Mr Farthing had said it would be then I lifted the housekeeping jar down from the mantelpiece. I looked inside and couldn't remember ever seeing so many ten shilling notes in one place. I took one of the notes and some change along with Mr Farthing's and my ration book and put them in the little purse Mabel had given me as a going away present.

When I got my first week's wages I meant to buy some writing paper and write to her, we both promised to correspond at least once a week when we had said our tearful good bye on the station platform. The day was still warm but I fetched my cardigan anyway and walked out of the back door and through a narrow alleyway at the side of the house. I looked left then right to try and decide which way the shops were.

To the left of me, in the near distance, I was sure I saw the familiar red and white awning that was usually erected above a butcher's shop so I turned and began to walk in that direction. It was a beautiful day in late February 1941. Although there was a war on Bristol was quiet and peaceful with everyone going about their business as usual. Birds floated above in the cloudless blue sky as the sun tried its best to shine.

I had guessed correctly and entered the butcher's shop. The man behind the counter wore an apron that was decorated in the same colours as the outdoor awning and a straw hat was perched on his head. He was rotund and had his shirt sleeves rolled up as far as they would go.

'What can I get for you, madam?' he asked.

'Have you got any beef skirt?' I enquired, then I placed the two ration books on the counter. Meat had been rationed since the beginning of this year so it was *hit or miss* on what we could buy these days.

'Only for my prettiest customer,' he smiled and began to hack a slab of meat off the joint on the chopping board behind him. As he did so, he asked me about myself and where I was living. I told him about Albert Farthing and my job there.

'Couldn't meet a nicer man than Albert Farthing, he's a proper gent, shame he never married but I think he's far too set in his ways to take the plunge now, say hello to him for me will you, we often have a pint together at the Golden Lion but I haven't seen him for a bit'. The butcher finished what he was doing and handed me my parcel of meat.

I promised I would and proceeded with my journey. I stocked up on carrots, onions, turnips and leeks at the green grocers as these items were yet to be rationed and could bulk out a meal that may be a little lacking in meat. Then I crossed over the road to the bakery. I bought some bread then went to the shop next door and bought a bag of flour and some baking powder. Finally, I went to the dairy and bought a pat of butter and a bottle of milk. Again these items were still freely available. The basket weighed a ton and I was glad the house wasn't too far away.

Once I was back in the kitchen, I mixed the flour and butter together to make pastry. I then chopped the onions and turnip up and cut the meat into tiny chunks. I rolled out the pastry, placed the filling in it and added some parsley that was hung up in the kitchen and sprinkled on some salt and pepper that I found on a shelf in the scullery. I then pulled one half of the pastry over the other and crimped the sides to make two perfect pasties.

I put them in the oven to cook then went to attend to the laundry. Again, after carefully studying the instructions I took the wet washing out of one side of the twin tub and dropped it into the other. I took the rubber lid and placed over the sopping clothing and turned it on. The machine began so spin so fast I thought it might actually take off, thankfully it didn't and once it had finished, it came to an abrupt standstill and the loud noise ceased.

I removed the rubber cover and pulled the clothes out, I was astounded to find them almost dry. As evening was approaching I decided not to hang them on the outside line but to put them on a wooden clothes hanger above me instead. There was a pulley to lower it down and once I had laid the washing over it, I hoisted it back up again. The warmth from the stove would have it dry in no time. I was happy with the amount of work I had manged to get done in such a short time.

Just before six o'clock I knocked on the study door and asked Mr Farthing where he would like to eat his dinner. He stated that he would like it in the dining room and would very much like me to join him. I thanked him, said that would be lovely and that dinner would be ready at six. I found the dining room and saw that this was one of the smaller rooms in the house. The dining table was highly polished and seated four people. A sideboard at the far wall had three drawers that contained the cutlery. On the shelves in the cupboard below was a collection of bottles of alcohol.

I placed the cutlery on the table and went to the kitchen. The aroma of the pasties cooking was making my mouth water and

I couldn't wait to get stuck in. I realised that this was the first time I had actually felt hungry in days. I put the food on the plates and carried them back to the dining room. Mr Farthing was in there already and he had placed two wine glasses on the table and was proceeding to pour liquid into both of them.

I was a little excited. I had never tried wine before and I hoped that I would like it. We sat down and I was surprised that Mr Farthing began to eat immediately without saying grace but it did not bother me unduly.

'My word, Joyce, this is absolutely delicious, did your mother teach you to cook?' he asked in between mouthfuls, I smiled.

'Actually it was your sister who taught me, she has been far much more of a mother to me than my own and I love her dearly,' I replied.

'Lilly is a good woman and I adore her, I'm very pleased that she sent you to me Joyce, I have a lady who comes in every morning to work as my secretary, her name is Mrs Everton, I think we are all going to get on awfully well together,' He raised his glass and I did the same and we clinked them gently together.

I loved the sweet taste of the amber liquid as it slid down my throat and silently thanked God and Mrs Johnson for bringing me to this wonderful house. The day that had begun with so much trepidation and sorrow had ended in the total opposite way. I could now see a bright light shining at the end of my once dark tunnel and I knew that I would enjoy every single hour that I worked for this wonderful man.

# 8

I rose bright and early the next morning. At first I didn't realise where I was then my eyes grew accustomed to the light and I realised whose house I was in. I swung my legs out of the bed and walked towards the large bay window. Pulling open the heavy curtains, I gazed at the street below. Because of the early hour, it was quite empty. Trees lined either side and shook gently in the soft breeze. Their giant roots seemed to be trying to claw their way out of the pavement below and large cracks were appearing in the concrete

I dressed and went down to the kitchen. My first task was to make Mr Farthing's breakfast. He told me he was an early riser and liked a poached egg on toast with a cup of tea. I padded down to the kitchen and began to prepare his food. As I waited, I pulled open the wooden back door and allowed the cool, refreshing air into the kitchen. There were only two small windows in the room and a tall concrete wall stood behind them so the light was limited. I guessed the large oven kept it warm in the winter and the bright lightbulb kept it light.

Once the meal was made I walked up two narrow stairs and along the corridor then knocked on the study door. I entered when I heard Mr Farthing shout. He was sitting behind his desk with the sunlight shining through the window behind him, making it seem like he had a halo around his head. His hair was dishevelled and un-brushed and he was wearing pyjamas. He cleared his papers to one side so I could place the tray of food on his desk.

I smiled as I said good morning. He looked tired. There was stubble growing on his chin and lip and I wondered if he had been up all night. I asked him if there was anything particular that he needed doing today but he shook his head in a disinterested way and said he was happy to leave everything in my capable hands. I stepped outside and as I was pulling the study door behind me, the front door opened.

I watched as a tall, thin woman walked in and pushed the door shut behind her. She was wearing all black and I guessed she was around her mid-forties. There were still a few streaks of black in her hair but it was mainly grey and pulled back into a tight bun at the nape of her neck. Everything about her seemed pointed. From her nose and chin to her narrow shoulders and pointed shoes. She turned around and looked at me.

'And who might you be?' she enquired and I noticed her nose wrinkle slightly as if she had just caught a bad smell.

'Um, I'm Joyce… Joyce Dean, Mr Farthing's new housekeeper,' I explained, swallowing deeply and feeling strangely nervous.

'Umph!' Was all she said as she shoved past me and pushed open the study door.

I watched as she transformed herself immediately once she was in the room with Mr Farthing. A beaming smile dominated her face and softened the angles of her nose and chin. She bid her employer a cheery good morning before asking him if he would like a cup of tea. Before I could hear the answer to her question the door was shut loudly and abruptly. I shrugged and walked back to the kitchen to begin my daily chores.

I dusted the unused rooms then went through the kitchen cupboards to see what food actually was in them. Mr Farthing was correct, there was very little and I would need to stock up the larder if I was going to continue cooking him decent meals. There were no herbs or spices apart from the sprig of parsley I had used the day before. I had found the large cellar of salt and pot of pepper so I wouldn't need to buy these. Once I had compiled my shopping list, I reached for the basket on the shelf and turned and headed for the back door.

I started violently. Mrs Everton was standing directly in front of me, I hadn't even heard her enter the room, let alone get this close to me.

'I know your type,' she hissed as she put her hands on her hips and pushed her bony face towards mine.

She didn't frighten me. For too long I'd had to put up with my miserable, self-pitying mother and Mrs Everton reminded me of her. Both had the bitter lines of self-injustice carved into their nasty faces.

'And what type is that then, Mrs Everton?' I spat, leaning forwards and shoving my face right in front of hers.

She seemed flustered for a moment as though she thought I might be upset by her obvious hostility then looked taken aback because I wasn't, she huffed and puffed.

'No respect, these days,' she finally managed to say while shaking her head from side to side.

'And what respect do you think I owe you, Mrs Everton? I don't know you and now we've met and I certainly don't want to get to know you,' I finished and then, pushing her aside, I walked out of the door into the sunshine. I couldn't help but chuckle to myself as I heard her say;

'Well, cheeky little bitch!'

I didn't care what she thought of me. I knew from bitter experience that some people in this world only lived to cause misery for others. I saw that the minute Mrs Everton stepped through the front door. I would not let her cast a shadow on my day or indeed my life. I hummed quietly to myself as I continued onto the shops.

By the time I had arrived back at around three o'clock, Mrs Everton had left. I knew this because her thin jacket was no longer hung on the coat peg by the front door. I put the shopping on the side and walked towards the study and knocked on the door. Pushing it open, I peered around it.

'Would you like a cup of tea, Mr Farthing?' I asked.

'Yes please Joyce dear,' he cleared his throat, 'have you been upsetting Mrs Everton?' He enquired as he raised an eyebrow and I could see the hint of a smile on his lips.

'No, Mr Farthing,' I replied as I walked further into the room, 'she seems to have taken a dislike to me, that's all.'

'Take no notice of the woman, Joyce, she lost her fiancé, Herbert, in the Great War, even though it was more than twenty years ago, she still wears black, in his memory, and talks about him as though he was here only yesterday,'

'I'm sorry for her, Mr Farthing, but there's no need to take it out on other people, I will try to be kinder to you if you would like me to,' I finished, trying to placate my employer.

'Best to just keep out of her way where possible Joyce, she was only a couple of years older than you when Herbert died, I can only assume your youth and vibrancy offends her some way but she is a very good secretary and I wouldn't like to lose her,'

'As you wish Mr Farthing, I will make every effort to be nice to her, tea?'

'Yes please, thank you Joyce,' he smiled and I pulled the door closed behind me.

I couldn't help thinking what a cheek it was for miserable Mrs Everton to go tittle- tattling to Mr Farthing about me when she was the one who was rude to me. I would definitely avoid the woman where possible. I was happy to let her absorb herself in her own misery and ignore the beauty that surrounded her. It would eat away at her until she was left on her own with no one to blame but herself.

# 9

The chilly winter days had now left us and were replaced by the warm march winds. The blue skies were now filled with colourful birds who had returned to sunnier climates. I didn't really notice the warmer weather. I only knew that this was the happiest I had been in my whole life.

I looked forward to the evening meals I shared with Mr Farthing. I liked nothing more than watching his face as it became animated when he talked about a certain project he was working on. He would never divulge too much information as the government had banned its employees from talking about their work. I felt privileged that he talked to me about it as much as he did.

I was glad to be home on this particular evening because the temperature had dropped and it was a little colder than the previous day. I should have put a cardigan on under my thin coat but the falling temperature had crept up on me and caught me unawares. As I walked through the back door, into the kitchen, I was enveloped in a wall of warmth and bathed in a shower of light. I loved this house. It was cosy and homely and I liked nothing more than keeping it in pristine condition and making sure Mr Farthing had everything he needed.

I came to realise, during our evening chats, that Mr farthing was a little lonely and was glad to have someone to talk to. I began the evening meal, humming away to myself in the process. As I turned to unhook a saucepan from the shelf above me, I saw her. Mrs Everton was standing in the corner of the room. I had no idea how long she had been there; she'd usually left by this time so I didn't have the misfortune of bumping into her.

'You think you've got him just where you want him, don't you? She snarled as her bird-like eyes turned into small slits.

'Hello Mrs Everton, would you like a cup of tea? I asked deliberately ignoring the animosity in her voice. I didn't really know what she was talking about.

'You can stick your bloody tea, I'll make sure he gets rid of you girl, I know your type,'

'What type is that then, Mrs Everton?' I asked as I set about peeling the potatoes.

She walked towards me and I turned and stood my ground.

'A bloody harlot, intent on snaring herself a sugar dad....'

She stopped abruptly and almost jumped out of her skin as Mr Farthing entered.

'Hello Mrs Everton, it's not often I find you in the kitchen, I thought you left ages ago?' he enquired

She spluttered a little then smiled widely.

'I thought I'd come down and see if young Joyce wanted a hand, it's a lot for a young girl to take on, running a home as big as this, isn't that right Joyce?' she looked at me with pleading eyes.

'Yes, that's right, Mr Farthing,' I answered.

'That's very kind of you, Mrs Everton, but I can assure you young Joyce is more than capable, now let me see you out.' He held out his hand, gesturing towards the door and the passage that would lead outside.

I watched her shuffle away in front of him and sighed. Why was it that some people were intent on trying to rain vitriol down onto others? I had never said or done anything to make the horrible woman dislike me so much. I really couldn't understand what her problem was. I quickly put the old hag's face out of my mind and continued to prepare the meal.

Meat was in short supply at the moment so I made a Homity pie that I would serve with boiled potatoes and carrots. I'd made it once before and Mr Farthing declared it was the most delicious food he had ever tasted. I went into the dining room and pulled the heavy, brocade curtains together. I set the table for two and poked the fire in the grate. The room became warm, cosy and inviting.

I was very much looking forward to the food. The aroma wafting from the kitchen was making me feel very hungry. Fifteen minutes later, we were both sitting at the table tucking into the hearty meal. Neither of us spoke until we had finished eating then we both grinned at each other.

'My goodness, Joyce, that was nectar from the Gods,' he said then had a small sip of wine; I smiled then rose and picked up the plates and carried them into the kitchen. I returned a short time later with two bowls of apple crumble and custard. Housewives were encouraged to make a crumble rather than a pie because the former needed a lot less butter. I think I actually enjoyed it more as it was a lot less stodgy.

I leant over Mr Farthing's shoulder and put the pudding in front of him. As I did so, my sleeve caught his wine glass and we both went to grab it at once. My hand caught it first and then it was enveloped by Mr Farthing's. His hand was soft and silky, not like any other man's hand. All the men I knew, like Mr Johnson and my father were labouring men and their hands were roughened by a life time of toil. Mr Farthing's was as soft as a satin glove.

When his hand touched mine, it felt as though an electric shock had raced up through my arm making me quiver, not in pain but with a delicious pleasure which puzzled me a little. I steadied the wine glass then sat down to eat my own food but found, rather surprisingly, that I was no longer hungry. Since I had started working for Mr Farthing a few weeks previously, I couldn't get enough of the wonderful meals I was able to make but now I found I had no appetite at all.

Usually, I really enjoyed my cooking. My gaunt appearance had disappeared and my cheeks were round, rosy and full. There was no sign of the bones that jaunted out when I first arrived. The butcher's boy had said as much the last time I was in the shop and I had blushed and giggled. For the first time since we began eating dinner together the conversation was a little stilted and I had no idea why. I looked towards Mr Farthing and he too seemed to be playing with his food rather than eating it.

The awkward silence was broken abruptly and terrifying by the wail of the air raid siren. This was the first time this had happened since I'd arrived at this house and I was momentarily nonplussed. When I was out shopping I had noticed that the children were returning from the countryside where they had been evacuated to at the start of the war. Everyone had gossiped about this being a 'phoney war'. Now, I saw them on the playing field and in the shops. This made me think the chances of an attack were slight.

I felt better knowing that the children had returned home. The streets were far too quiet when they were away. At this time, however, there were more important things to think about. I remembered the government leaflets telling us to keep to a bag of essentials ready in case of an air raid. I recalled when my mother was still alive that this included ration books, family photos and any important documents. They also advised us to keep a flask ready for use and food, in case the raid was a long one.

When I first arrived, all this was in place. Now the ration books were in the pot in the kitchen and any photos and documents were in our bedrooms or sideboard drawers. I didn't know if I should grab them or race to the safety of the cellar. The decision was taken away from when Mr Farthing grasped my hand and began pulling me, behind him, towards the cellar door which was under the stairs. I quickly followed, feeling bewildered and scared.

Before he had a chance to close the door behind him, I heard the burr of approaching aircraft and I was absolutely terrified. The last time I had sat out a raid was with my mum and dad. The presence of my father helped quell the terror I was feeling; now my heart was racing and I felt as though I couldn't breathe. We hurried down the narrow concrete stairs then Mr Farthing pushed open a second door. It was a wide, heavy door which he bolted securely behind us. Hearing the bolt slide into place made me feel comfortable and safe.

I stood in the darkness listening to my employer scrabble around for the light switch and when he did the darkness was suddenly dispelled and the large room was illuminated. I looked around. I had never been in this room before. Luckily we had not had any need to use it. I could hear the growl of enemy aircraft approaching. The closer they got the louder the noise became. I didn't know I was trembling until I felt Mr

Farthing's arms around me.

'It's ok, Joyce, we're safe as houses here,' he soothed.

'I didn't pack an air raid bag or bring the ration books and everything we're supposed to,' I told him as I pressed my face into his chest.

'It's too late to worry about that now Joyce, we're just going to have to sit it out,' he replied.

I stayed, swamped and safe in his warm embrace. I could hear his heart beating gently in his chest. His arms were strong. The smell of his familiar sandalwood aftershave comforted me and I clung to him. I looked up into his face and saw him looking down into mine. His vibrant blue eyes were full of tenderness and concern. Without realising I was doing it, I found myself softly brushing his lips with mine. Butterflies danced around my stomach although I didn't know why.

Mr Farthing kissed me back. His tongue began probing my mouth; I did the same to him. The passionate kisses were making me feel dizzy and my head was spinning with pleasure. I clung onto him then felt his hand slide inside my blouse. His touch felt wonderful and I sighed with happiness. When his fingers touched my bare breast, I almost screamed in delight.

'Are you sure Joyce?' Mr Farthing whispered huskily in my ear.

His hot breath on my face and ear made me tingle inside and I knew that I was more than certain. I whispered to him that I was definitely sure. I couldn't wait for what was to come.

He led me towards the corner of the room and began lifting the cushions off an old sofa and began arranging them on the floor. I watched with impatient anticipation. He then turned and held out his hand and I reached for his. He kissed me once more then began to unbutton my blouse, gently and slowly. He bent down and kissed my chest and breasts. I had never felt such a wonderful sensation.

He undressed me then pushed me down on the cushions and lay next to me when he was naked himself. I felt his hand slid inside my thigh and lifted myself towards him. When I felt his fingers slide inside me, I gasped.

'I love you Mr Farthing, please don't stop what you're doing,'

'I think you should call me Bertie, Joyce,' he laughed and continued.

I stroked his body as he did mine. The hairs on his chest were soft and his arms and shoulders were muscly and manly. He asked me again if I was sure and I insisted I was. He climbed on top of me and pushed my legs apart with his own. I looked into his beautiful face and cupped it with my hands. I opened my legs wider and felt a sharp pain as he pushed himself in me.

I squealed loudly then the pain was replaced by a sensation I can only describe as heavenly. With each thrust an injection of pure ecstasy raced through my body and I was sure I'd die if he stopped what he was doing. I was moaning loudly now and thrusting myself at him and begging him not stop. Bertie was saying over and over again how much he loved me and going faster and faster.

I was screaming with unadulterated desire. Then we came together and his thrusting slowed. My whole body was tingling, as though an electric shock had gone right through me but there was no pain, only pleasure. It took a while for me to get my breath back then suddenly I became embarrassed at my nakedness. Bertie seemed to realise this and pulled a blanket off the sofa and covered us both up.

I lay with my head on his chest, still feeling light-headed and wondrously satisfied. I thought if I died right now it wouldn't matter because I had experienced the most exquisite desire ever. It felt as though a whole new entity had taken over my body and made it throb with joy.

'Any regrets, Joyce darling?'

'None whatsoever,' I replied, 'that was the most beautiful experience of my life, I have never felt anything like it ever before,'

Bertie kissed me softly, then passionately and we made love once more. I couldn't get enough of his virile body and wrapped my legs tightly around his back as I begged for more. When the all clear sounded it felt to me as though something alien had intruded into our private world. I wanted to stay in the cellar, lying on the cushions with Bertie forever. I didn't want to stop making love with him ever.

I think Bertie felt the same because neither he nor I moved. We just lay together revelling in our closeness and shared ecstasy then Bertie spoke.

'I'm forty-two, Joyce, far too old to be making love to a fifteen-year-old girl,' he sighed.

'I may be fifteen years old but in my head I feel a lot older, I've had to grow up quicker than most people and cannot ever remember feeling like a child,' I replied.

'It's also illegal, you know that, don't you Joyce?' he asked as he pulled me close to him.

'I'll be sixteen next May,' I told him, 'that's only a few months away then it will be legal.'

'I know that, Joyce, but there are also the moral consequences of a middle-aged man bedding a fifteen-year-old girl.

I don't think my bosses or any of my colleagues would be happy about it.'

'Well bugger them and bugger the legal rubbish, do you want to be with me?' I sat up, pulling the blanket over my breasts and turned to look at him. He smiled,

'That's fine then, no one needs to know, it'll be our delightful secret,' I told him then began kissing his warm, soft lips once more.

## 10

The raid had caused a lot of damage. As I walked to the shops the following day, I could not hide my horror at all the destruction around me. The attack had started at about seven o'clock the previous evening. The lady in the greengrocers told me how fires began raging within an hour and the emergency services were struggling to control them. Her husband, she informed me, worked as an *ARP* warden and saw it all first hand.

Bristol Museum had taken a direct hit to one side and looked to be in a sorry state. Castle Park had been heavily bombed. St Peters Hospital had been destroyed and four of Bristol beautiful old churches had been badly damaged. It was heart-breaking to witness the devastation to homes and lives. I watched as housewives scrabbled around their demolished houses searching for any few precious possessions that may have survived.

The women from the *WVS* and the Royal Voluntary Corps all helped as soon as they were given the all clear that the buildings were safe. I was happy when I saw someone find some photos or a pair of shoes from the wreckage of their homes, at least they had something from their old lives to hang onto and treasure. I learned that two hundred and seven people had been killed that night with hundreds injured and thousands of homes destroyed.

I felt guilty that I was walking around in a bubble of joy when so many others had suffered so much. I decided I would pop into the council offices and volunteer to do some fire watching duties. At least then I would be doing something to help with the war effort. My last port of call was the butcher's shop. I hoped to get some sausages to put with mashed potatoes for tea later on that day.

The shop bell clanged nosily as I walked into the empty shop. Les, the butcher's assistant was behind the counter. I asked him what meat there was to be had and he held up a skinned rabbit and said that was all he could offer me. I thanked him. It was better than no meat at all and I could make a tasty stew. Once he had wrapped in paper, I handed over the ration books then placed my shopping into my basket.

Les handed me back our ration books then asked me if I would like to go to the cinema with him the following Saturday. I thought for a minute then said that would be very nice. The last time I had been to the cinema was with Mabel and that was before I moved to Bristol and I loved a good film. I told Les I would meet him outside the Regal Cinema at quarter to six that evening, fifteen minutes before the start of the main film. I told him I would love to watch *A Window in London.* It was a thriller starring Michael Redgrave and Patricia Roc and I liked both the actors.

I walked the short journey back home and stepped into the warm kitchen. I put the shopping away and began to make a cup of coffee for Bertie and tea for Miss Everton. I knocked on the study door then pushed it open with my bottom. I handed Bertie his drink and he gave me the smallest of winks. I turned to see Miss Everton staring directly at us. I was quite sure that woman was a witch; she always had an evil glint in her bird-like eyes that sometimes unnerved me.

I set about my chores. Earlier in the day I had been down

to the cellar and made it more comfortable in case we should be caught in another air raid. As I rearranged the cushions, I felt a delicious ripple run up through my body when I remembered the night before. I also made sure that a bag was packed with emergency provisions and important documents as instructed by the government. I felt a little better now that I was more prepared.

That evening, as we ate dinner, I told Bertie about my date with Les and he told me he was very glad. He said he didn't like a young girl like me being cooped up in this house all the time. I told him that there was nothing I liked better.

Our lives continued as did the war. In the evenings Bertie and I were a couple. The blackout curtains allowed us unspoiled privacy to live as we wanted. In the daytimes, I reverted back to calling Bertie, Mr Farthing. I think this chapter of my life was one of the happiest I could remember. I'm not sure if it was luck or divine intervention but I never found myself pregnant. Sometimes I longed to feel a new life growing inside me, other times I was glad there wasn't because I wanted it to be just Bertie and me.

Being with him made me feel like a whole person, like something of me was missing before I met him and I'm sure he felt the same because he wrote this poem for me;

*Joyce*
*All my life I have been looking for someone*
*A lost piece of jigsaw or the answer I couldn't find*
*Every day I longed for something*
*Just out of my reach, hidden away or left behind*
*Then I saw your beautiful face and I knew*

*The missing part of my life was you*
*Xxxxx*

Those few short lines meant the whole world to me and I knew I would treasure them forever. I enjoyed going to the cinema with Les, he was a friendly chap with a cheeky smile. It became a regular Saturday night outing. Les always complimented me on my clothes or hair and insisted on not only paying for the cinema but also buying me a small box of chocolates with his ration. Of course, I always shared them with him.

Les explained that he had been turned down when he tried to enlist because he was deaf in one ear. He told me how bitterly disappointed he was and how he hated watching his mates go off to fight in a war that he was not allowed to. He did his bit by fire watching and other jobs but he longed to be in the thick of it. My application had been turned down because I wasn't yet sixteen and that was the minimum age, Les was seventeen.

In the last air raid Les had also volunteered to be a messenger boy. He told me how he rode his bike between different *Command* centres to let anyone that needed to know what was going on in other parts of the town. I thought this was extremely brave and I told him so. I explained how terrified I felt during an attack even when I was safe in the cellar. Riding his bicycle out in the open air with bombs falling everywhere must have taken enormous courage and I told him I was very proud. He smiled his wide boyish smile and asked me if I would be 'his girl'.

I didn't want to be harsh but I explained that I didn't want to be anyone's 'girl' and couldn't we should just stay as we were. He seemed to except this. The one bugbear was his wondering hands. When we were watching a film he would casually drape his arm around my shoulder then let it fall a little lower so his hand brushed my breast. I always swatted him away immediately and he would just grin.

His immature attempt at romance amused me but I didn't show it. I knew the only man I would ever love was Bertie Farthing and I constantly told Les that I didn't want to get serious with anyone. Still, he would try and kiss me as soon as the lights, at the movies, went out. More than a few times I had to tell him to stop or our Saturday outings would end. He would just grin and nod. I hoped, at some point, he would find himself a girlfriend who was the same mental age as him, not someone with an older woman's head, like me.

# 11

In March it was Bertie's birthday and I made it as special as I could for him. I bought him his favourite sandalwood aftershave and some silk handkerchiefs. He also bought me a present which made me giggle. I told him he was the only one who should get presents but he insisted that I deserved some too. Bertie gave me a beautiful emerald necklace with matching earrings and somehow managed to get hold of some silk stockings. The day was magical. We feasted on roasted goose and I made Bertie a birthday cake. I couldn't get hold of any icing sugar but I did manage to decorate with a few cherries and a candle. It didn't matter, we had everything we could possibly want in life and I thanked God for it every single day.

I loved it when the warmer weather danced on the horizon. I longed for the time when the birds would return and fill the skies with their melodies. Barrage balloons hoovered below the clouds like giant beacons of hope. Bertie and I had decided that we would get married when the war ended. We had talked about our future at length and decided that we would remain in Bristol.

I dreamt of a beautiful white wedding where Mr Johnson would give me away and Mabel and her sisters would be my bridesmaids. The very thought made me glow inwardly. Les had asked about my family and I told about the loss of my parents and how I considered the Johnson to be my family. I showed him some of the letters I received on a weekly basis from Mabel and he agreed we sounded more like sisters than best friends.

It was the first week of April when our perfect world caved in. There had been an air raid the evening before and Bertie and I had snuggled together on the cushions in the cellar making love. I was no longer shy about my body and felt as though Bertie and I fitted together like two solid silver spoons. The doorbell rang around lunchtime, the following day, and I rushed to answer it. I was slightly puzzled because we weren't expecting visitors.

I pulled it open and was overjoyed to see Mrs Johnson standing on the doorstep. I pulled her into my arms and hugged her tightly at the same time as expressing how lovely it was to see her. I noticed that she seemed a little stiff and ill at ease but had no idea why. She followed me down to the kitchen where I made us both a cup of tea. Once she had drunk it she explained that she needed to speak to her brother urgently.

I nodded and went to get Bertie. He smiled also when I told him who our visitor was and then he told Miss Everton to take the rest of the day off. She didn't look too happy about this until Bertie told her that her wages would be paid in full. That seemed to pacify her a little and she left. Bertie asked me to bring Mrs Johnson into the drawing room, which I did. As she walked in Bertie strolled over and pulled her into a tight embrace.

'Lilly, this is wonderful, why didn't you tell us you were coming? He said. 'We could have arranged some entertainment,' he finished then looked puzzled at the sight of his sister's face.

Mrs Johnson looked nervous and upset and I caught hold her hand. I hoped nothing bad had happened to Mr Johnson or the rest of the family. I couldn't bear for these wonderful people to suffer anything terrible. They were as good as my kin to me and I loved them all very much. Mrs Johnson cleared her throat then reached into her navy blue hand bag. She handed a letter to Bertie. His face turned into a muddy shade of grey as he passed the letter to me, it said;

*Dear Mrs Johnson,*
*This is a friendly letter to let you know that your brother is a dirty old man. He's having it off with his fifteen-year-old housekeeper and I don't think that is rite.*
*From a friend.*

I sunk down onto the sofa. The shock of reading the letter felt like someone had punched me in the stomach.

'Surely you don't believe this nonsense Lilly? Bertie enquired, looking directly into his older sister's eyes.

'What am I supposed to believe when someone sends me this?' Mrs Johnson shouted, 'WHAT IS IT I'M SUPPOSED TO BELIEVE!'

'Well the truth for a start!' Bertie bellowed back, ' the type of people who write letters like these are deranged, I have never treated Joyce with anything but respect, she has been a Godsend to me and organised this house better than any previous house-keeper I've had, how can you believe this poisonous drivel?'

I watched Mrs Johnson grope her way to a chair and sit heavily on it. She seemed to be wrestling with her thoughts then she spoke.

'I'm sorry Albert but getting this,' she waved the letter around, 'fair knocked the stuffing out of me, Joyce is like my own daughter and I couldn't live with myself if I thought someone was taking advantage of her but you're right, I shouldn't have jumped to conclusions and believed a perfect stranger, can you forgive me?'

The poor lady was crying by the time she had finished speaking and both Bertie and I rushed over to her, I held her hand while Bertie hugged her.

'Off course I forgive you Lilly dear, there's nothing to forgive, the war work I do makes me a target for potential blackmailers so maybe whoever wrote that rubbish thought they could get some money out of me, please Lilly, dry your eyes and I'll get Joyce here to make up the spare bed for you,' he finished

'Thank you Albert but no, I need to get straight back, Mr Johnson is out most evenings doing his bit for the war and Mabel's joined an evening first aid class so there will be no one at home to watch the young ones,' she turned to me.

'I'm so sorry Joyce, I don't what I was thinking, racing up here with a bee in my bonnet, you are looking so much better than the pale, thin girl I saw off on the train, you're growing into quite a bobby dazzler,' she said and smiled widely.

'Please don't apologise Mrs Johnson, it must have been an awful shock, are you sure you won't stay, I'm sure Mabel would give up her class for one evening,'

'No thank you Joyce, Mabel already does enough babysitting when I'm at the WI or my knitting circle, I like her to get out and do her own thing when she can.'

I nodded and listened as Bertie insisted on driving her back to the station. Once they had both left I picked up the letter that Mrs Johnson had left on the coffee table. The obvious culprit, to me, was Miss Everton but I knew what her handwriting was like. It was neat and precise while the letter-writers' words were large and untidy with lots of unnecessary loops. Also, Miss Everton was a conscientious secretary and a good speller. The sender had spelt 'right' as 'rite'.

I waited anxiously for Bertie to return and as soon as I heard his key turn in the lock I rushed out to meet him. Once the door was closed firmly behind him we fell into each other's arms and held each other tightly. I knew that Bertie felt the same way as me, violated and intruded upon by someone who wanted to hurt us both badly, finally I spoke.

'The obvious person who would write such a letter is Miss Everton but I know this isn't her handwriting, do you think she might have disguised it?'

'I know Miss Everton took an instant dislike to you but I don't think that even she would stoop as low as to write such a letter and, lower too, to write in a way that would not lead me to suspect her,' Bertie replied.

'What do we do?' I asked tearfully.

'This,' he replied, 'he struck a match and burnt the letter then threw it into the grate, 'whoever wrote this has not caused the damage he or she hoped so we carry as normal my darling but we must be extra vigilant that none of the tradesmen, who deliver our wares, have an inkling of what is going on between the two of us. Once this wretched war is over we'll get married then maybe move to Australia or America and start afresh, what do you say?'

I smiled and said.

'I say roll on the end of this bloody war,' Bertie poured us both a drink and then resumed his work while I went to the kitchen to prepare our evening meal. I still felt threatened and frightened but tried not to think about, there was nothing I could do so there was no point dwelling on it.

We carried on our covert, joyous life before the carpet was dragged from beneath us once more, shocking us both to the core. It was the twenty ninth of April and it was a beautiful day. The sun was beaming down from a cloudless sky and it was comfortably warm as I walked towards the shops. I spoke cheerfully to my neighbours, who I now considered friends as I passed them in the street, and just enjoyed the happiness of everyday living.

I saved the butchers as the last stop as I wanted to ask Les what film he wanted to watch the following evening. It had dawned on me that we always watched what I wanted to see so I decided it was only fair to give Les a choice. There were two customers in front of me so I waited in the queue, wishing I was outside in the fresh air rather than stuck in the stuffy shop. My wait was rewarded with four sausages and four rashers of bacon. I thanked Les and he said he'd do anything for his best girl.

I handed him the ration books and he passed them back. I turned to walk out of the shop and he called me back and said he would like to watch a comedy called '*All at Sea*' at the cinema. I nodded, I wasn't particularly fond of those kinds of films but I had asked Les to choose. He asked me if I would do him a favour and drop a note into the letterbox at the end of the road. Apparently a person had offered to pay them extra in return for more rations. Les had written to tell him that this was illegal and he would have the same as everyone else. I agreed to deliver it for him.

I thought exactly the same as he did. Why should one individual get extra food just because they had enough money to pay for it? We should all be pulling together until the war was over, not trying to make ourselves better off than the next person. Les handed me the note and asked me to wait while he got a stamp and an envelope.

My curiosity got the better of me and I felt the urge to find out who this unpatriotic person was. I unfolded the letter and looked. I was not surprised to see that it was a wealthy land-owner who lived in a massive house on the outskirts of Bristol who had made the request. I tutted, the well-to-do always seemed to have a sense of entitlement. It was as though their wealth put them apart from us ordinary citizens. Well, at least this one was about to be put in his place.

Then I stopped and stared at the letter in my hand and my mouth dropped open. The realisation hit me like a freight train and I struggled to believe the obvious conclusion. The writing on the letter was spidery and over looped and dotted with spelling imperfections. It was the same writing on the poison pen letter that Mrs Johnson had received. Les walked back into the shop. The expression on my face told him I knew, he frowned deeply then spat,

'What did you bloody expect me to do?' He put his hands on hips, 'I heard that miserable old bag, Everton, whispering to her sister that you and Farthing were 'having it off', she thought I was deaf but she was talking on my good side and I heard every bloody word, you lead me on before swatting me away like I'm some troublesome fly then go home to sleep with that dirty old bastard!'

I stood, momentarily stunned, then I stumbled backwards out of the shop. I grabbed my basket with both hands and began to run home. I heard Les calling my name behind me but I didn't stop. By the time I reached home, I was shaking from head to toe. I put my basket on the kitchen table and lowered myself down onto a chair. I waited until my heart beat slowed and my trembling stopped. I could see still Les's ugly face, in my mind, yelling at me. I couldn't believe he had done such a nasty thing.

I got up and walked towards the study and knocked gently. It was some seconds before Bertie shouted 'come in'. I pushed open the door and saw Bertie with his head in his hands. He was obviously upset. He looked up and ran his hand through his thick, grey hair then held up a letter. I stepped forward and began to read;

*Dear Mr Farthing*
*It has come to our attention that you are conducting an*
*illicit affair with an underage girl. In these troubled times we*
*cannot allow any of our operatives to put themselves at risk*
*of blackmail or fall foul of the law. This is the reason that we*
*are posting you to Inverness to continue your work there. The*
*post is for you only and you will begin a week from now.*

My trembling returned. I dropped the paper onto the desk. Then I could feel Bertie's arms around me and I clung onto him. There were no words to be said, we both knew how we felt.

'I'll come to Inverness, after the war,' I sobbed, Bertie squeezed me tighter,

'I'll never love anyone but you Bertie, no one will be able to keep us apart,'

'I love you too my darling Joyce and you're right, as soon as you're old enough, we'll be together again,' He said and kissed me passionately, I smiled.

'I'll go and cook us a meal, we've still got to eat,' I said, a lot more brightly than I actually felt.

That evening, as we sat down to dinner, Bertie slid a piece of paper towards me. I read;

*Broken*
*Two lives ripped apart,*
*Two souls broken*
*The pain of a separated heart*
*True love stolen*
*I will think of you constantly*
*And know that my pain*
*Will someday be over*
*And we'll be together again xxx*

I raced over to him and held him tightly to me.

'Lots of couples have been separated by the war, we're no different than them,' I told Bertie as I sat back down and began to eat my meal.

Bertie looked up and nodded but I could see the sadness behind his eyes. I hated Les for what he had done and I vowed never to go near the shop again. I never wanted to clap eyes on his stupid face ever again. I still couldn't believe he would do such an underhand thing as writing to Mrs Johnson. He must have mentally saved her address when I showed him my letters from Mabel.

His deviousness was actually frightening but I decided against telling Bertie who had written the letter. I didn't want him to get in any more trouble if he decided to go and give Les a good hiding, although I wished he would. I looked at

Bertie's beautifully sculptured face and knew that I would never love anyone as much as I loved him. It would be hard being apart but I could do it, knowing that one day we would be together again.

Living in this house with the wonderful man who had become my soulmate was more than I could ever wish for and I thanked God every day for bringing us together. Before I met Bertie, it felt as though I was drifting through life with no purpose or direction. It was as though he was the anchor that steadied me and made me feel safe. We had just finished our meal when the air raid siren screeched into life.

I quickly gathered up the crockery and put it in the kitchen sink whilst Bertie boiled the kettle and made a flask of tea. Together we quickly put what our ration books in our emergency net bag and headed down into the cellar. Bertie groped for the light switch and I waited for the blessed bulb to work. The darkness seemed to suffocate me. Just as the room became illuminated I felt a wind hurtle behind us, then a vibrant blue flash, so bright it almost blinded me, flooded the place. The next thing I recalled was being hurled across the room with a force so strong there was simply nothing I could do about it then blackness enveloped me.

# 12

The smell of burning wood was penetrating through my numbed senses. It was a strong acrid smell that began to make my eyes sting. I opened them and saw nothing; just pitch blackness pressing down on top of me. I tried to move my body but couldn't, something was on top of me making any type of movement impossible.

'Bertie,' I croaked as I felt hot tears slide down my cheeks, 'are you there?'

I've heard people say that the 'silence is deafening' many times as I was growing up but I never really understood what that meant until now. It was as though the quietness was screaming into my ears. I sniffed and began to sob.

'Bertie, where are you!' I cried, 'please answer me, I'm frightened,'

I felt a slight movement to the left of me.

'I'm here my darling, don't be frightened,' Bertie whispered.

'But I am, I can't help it, what's happened to us?'

'We wasted too much time coming down into the cellar, I think, we've been caught up in an explosion but help will be here soon Joyce darling, I promise,' Bertie finished then he began to make an awful wheezing sound.

'Bertie!' I screamed at the top of my voice.

'It's all right darling, I'm here, got a bit of dust in my throat, don't worry,'

'Can you hold my hand please, Bertie, it feels like the darkness is choking me.'

I waited a while then I felt the tip of Bertie's fingers touch mine. This small connection made me feel less alone. The room seemed to be trying to swallow me up whole.

'I can't wait until we're married, Bertie,' I said.

'Me neither sweet Joyce but the time will fly by and then we'll be together once more, I love you, Joyce, I now know my life was empty until I met you, you have made me the happiest man on earth and I'll always love you darling,'

'Don't talk as though you're saying goodbye, please, I can't bear it,' I sobbed.

'Not goodbye my sweet girl, just adieu, until we meet again,' he mumbled.

I called his name over and over; my screams seemed to reverberate around the room but Bertie didn't answer. I began to feel cold. The left side of my body seemed to have lost all feeling then blackness washed over me.

I'm getting married. The lights are the brightest I've ever seen. Heavenly music is ringing out all around sung by voices as pure as angels. My father is walking me down the aisle. His smile is almost as bright at the lights. I wonder if my mother is here but I doubt it; then I spot her, sitting on the very front pew. As I approach her she turns to look at me. I am utterly astonished. She too has one of the sunniest smiles I've ever seen across her unlined face.

She looks completely different. Happiness is oozing from her pores and I feel tears pricking at the corners of my eyes. These are tears of joy. I look ahead and see Bertie. He turns to look at me and I am spellbound in an emotion of pure ecstasy. He is wearing his best suit and looks so handsome that my heart swells with pride. I have never felt so wholeheartedly contented in my whole life. I know that I will never again feel the same elation as I'm feeling right now.

It's as though Christmas, Easter and my birthday have all come at once. A thousand colourful fireworks are exploding in the night sky. Showers of light cascade down from above and the angelic voices sing louder. I know I will never come to such a wondrous place again. I'm so close to Bertie that I can almost touch him. I can smell his Sandalwood aftershave and pipe smoke. We smile at each other and I know that this is the moment I was born for.

The lights start to flicker as I stand next to him. I'm confused because the lights are stars. I can feel a force tugging at me, pulling me away from Bertie. I turn and my mother is standing next to me. She is now the way I remember her, old, haggard and full of self- pity. My dad falls to the ground. He is clutching his stomach and blood is spilling from a wound. I want to help him but before I can move, he disappears like raindrops drying up in the sun.

I am screaming to Bertie. I beg him to help me. The louder I scream the further away he gets. My emotional pain is now replaced by a physical pain so intense it feels as though my whole body is on fire. Such is the depth of my agony I want to rip my head off my torso to stop the hurt pulsating through me. Somewhere in the distance I can hear a bell ringing and a man's voice telling me that I'll be ok. I wonder if it's Bertie, I hope it is. I can endure as much discomfort as is necessary as long as Bertie is ok. The blackness envelops me once more and I am happy to be free of the tortuous pain.

When I open my eyes, I start to blink rapidly. The whiteness around me seems so bright it feels like its blinding me and is such a steep contrast from the dreadful blackness I previously endured. I squint and whimper. One side of my body is wracked with pain and I'm frightened. I can hear distorted sounds but they make no sense. Eventually, the black blobs I am trying to focus on begin to take shape and I can see that they are people. One approaches me and I can feel her breath on my face as she leans down towards me.

I can smell carbolic soap and I find it strangely comforting. I start to cry, I don't know why but I can't stop myself. I ask for my mum although I know she is dead. I feel a soft hand gently rubbing my cheek; I want to lift my hand and clutch at whoever is touching me but no part of my body seems to work. The person wipes my tears with her hanky and whispers that I am ok and in the best hands. I want to believe her but I don't.

The days seem to pass in a haze of pain and discomfort. One side of my body refuses to move and I have no idea who the people are that dance around me at different times of the day and night. They puff my pillows and feed me. They help me with the most intimate of tasks but I don't know their names. Another bright, sunny day dawns but this one is a little different. My mind feels less confused and I realise that I am in hospital.

I am lying in a long room with lines of cots down each side. Nurses go from bed to bed wearing their crisp, starched uniforms smiling and chatting. I wait until one approaches my bed.

'How is my employer, Mr Farthing?' I asked the nurse as she leaned across my bed and straightened the already straight blanket, she turns to me and smiles.

She seems very young. Her almost black hair is scarped stiffly behind her cap and she has bright blue eyes that shine when they catch the sunlight through the windows.

'I'm sorry lovey, your Mr Farthing is dead, poor man, he was killed instantly, the moment the bomb hit the house.'

She grasped my hand and looked into my eyes.

'You're very lucky to be alive, the explosion caught the whole left side of your body, you've got lots of broken bones but, in time, you'll mend, we'll take care of you I...'

Her voice started to become distorted then quiet. I can hear the noise of a creature sounding in so much pain I want to run to whoever it is and gather them in my arms. The sound of the distressed screaming I can hear is palpable and frightening. The young nurse's face has changed, now she is shouting too. I am surrounded by a doctor and several other medical staff. Their mouths are all opening and shutting but I don't know what they're saying then I am enveloped in blissful nothingness.

# 13

I am no longer in the hospital. One week ago I was discharged and driven by ambulance to a convalescent home in Clifton, on the edge of the Downs. The building used to be a hotel but now the government has requisitioned it and turned it into hospital for soldiers and civilians suffering from long term injuries. The blast that killed Bertie almost killed me too. The left side of my body was entirely crushed. My shoulder, arm, ribs, hip, leg and foot were all badly broken. My body will take time to mend.

It is now early May. I have already spent three weeks in the hospital and I have no idea how long I will spend here. I am sitting in a wheelchair in the grounds of the hospital. I am snuggly tucked in so I won't catch cold and someone comes to check on me about every half an hour. Sometimes they bring a cup of tea and sometimes a meal. I do as I am told.

I can see the Clifton Bridge in the distance stretched across two islands. That is my eventual destination. I will clamber over the railings and allow myself to fall into Bertie's waiting arms then we will be together for ever. I believe I am on some form of pain medication because my mind feels fuzzy, as though there is a blanket wrapped around my brain. My face and head escaped injury and I am told that I should feel lucky because of that. There are many disfigured patients sitting in the grounds near me but the sight of them doesn't alarm me.

I watch as their loved ones come to visit them and realise that the scars don't change how they feel about their injured relatives. I would rather be ugly and scarred and have Bertie alive. The acute loneliness I have felt since I arrived here feels like someone is constantly sticking pins in my heart. I always ask to sit out of the way so none of the other inmates will feel the need to talk to me. I have no longing to talk or be spoken to. I just want to sit and think about Bertie and everything he meant to me.

I feel as though my whole future has been ripped away from me and my heart feels as hard as stone. I function because I am told to but I do not feel alive. A cooling breeze rustles around my face as I look up and see a familiar figure walking towards me. Something stirs inside of me when I see her. For the first time since the blast, I feel a smidgen of hope that I am not entirely alone in the world. I watch the comforting, homely figure of Mrs Johnson stride purposefully towards me. She is carrying a shoebox tied with string. The sight of the woman who has been more than a mother to me makes me want to cry but I swallow my tears and wait.

A nurse is following her and I watch as she unfolds a chair beside me for Mrs Johnson to sit on. I know who the nurse is because she goes out of her way to be friendly to me, her name is Nurse Mellor and she looks to be around her mid-twenties in age. She always has a sunny outlook on life and I know that if things were different we could have become friends. She asks Mrs Johnson and me if we would like a cup of tea, Mrs Johnson shakes her head then turns to me as nurse Mellor walks away.

'How could you do it Joyce, how could you lie to me, I've treated you like my own daughter since you were a little nipper and you do this, I know there was something going on between you and my brother, I've read his poems,' she said as she patted

92

the shoebox to indicate they were inside.

'I didn't lie to you Mrs Johnson; I told you that your brother had treated me with kindness and respect because that's what he did,'

I realised that this was the first time I had spoken in weeks and my voice sounded gravelly and unfamiliar.

'You told me there was nothing go on and I believed you, you made me feel like I had a grubby mind and I can't forgive either of you for that,' Mrs Johnson finished as she dabbed at her eyes with a small handkerchief, ' I don't want you to have anything to do with my Mabel, young girls of fifteen do not have affairs with middle-age men, it's disgusting and illegal,' she hissed as she glared at me as though I was some specimen she didn't recognise. She then shoved the shoebox onto my lap. I grabbed it with my good hand to stop it falling to the floor.

I watched her walk quickly away as though she wanted to put as much distance between us as she could in case my badness would infect her. Now I was truly alone. The only family I had ever known had washed their hands of me and the way I felt was both startling and terrifying. The thought that there was not a person in this world who would miss me when I died made feel as trivial as the grime on the side of the building.

My left arm is no longer in plaster, it is just held in a sling. I slide the box onto Mrs Johnson's vacated chair with my right hand then pull at the string bow with my fingers. Lifting the lid off I peer inside and my heart constricts. The first thing I see is the emerald jewellery that Bertie bought me. I long to wear the earrings, once more, if only to see the pride in my lover's eyes as he looks at me. Bertie's poems and our ration books are also nestled in the box along with our birth certificates.

I replace the lid and decide that I will take the box with me when I leave this life.

The time drags as I count the days until my death. My arm is now almost healed and I now sit inside and view my world through the window. The sky is light grey and the clouds hang above me like ominous spectres waiting for me to join them. A cold wind whistles outside and squeezes in through the cracks in the old building. The coldness does not affect me. I'm just killing time.

Nurse Mellor spends long periods of time talking to me but I cannot find a voice to speak back. A kindly doctor in a white coat often sits opposite to me and asks me what I will do when I leave the convalescent home. What can I tell him? How can I explain that my life ended when Bertie's did and that I can see no future for myself? All I can see ahead is bleakness and sorrow stretching forwards and an unbearable sadness that will eventually eat me whole.

I can see compassion on his face but I can't tell him how I feel. I think that if I start to explain, the force of my deep-rooted sorrow will come crashing to the surface and drive me mad. I don't want to spend the rest of my days in mental asylum, I want to be with Bertie but how could I expect anyone to understand that. Nurse Mellor was constantly telling me how lucky I was to be alive.

I know that I should be grateful to have my life but I'm not. It's not a life without Bertie, just a hollow and meaningless existence. Many thousands of innocents, including young children, have been killed in this war and I am alive. I would gladly give my life for anyone who wanted it. It is sinful to crave death and not thank God for saving me but I know, now, that there is no God. If there was he would not inflict such monstrous agony upon me?

I feel as though He is gloating at me. I had sinned by sleeping with a man who I was not married to and my punishment was to be kept alive to spend the rest of my life repenting. I intended to create my own destiny. As my broken body mends I started to feel excitement that soon I could leave this place and this life. Nothing could be worse than how I am feeling now. If there was nothing after death, then that was fine. I preferred nothingness to pain.

Nurse Mellor came to talk to me and informed me that I would be discharged in a week's time. For the first time in days I felt a tinge of happiness, not much time to wait now. She said she had a friend who would like to visit me and would I mind? I looked at her then turned to look out of the window. It was now nearing the end of May and cold weather seems reluctant to leave. The greyness of the day makes me feel at one with the world, it reflected how I was feeling inside.

Nurse Mellor returned followed by a slightly built lady. She was holding a pie dish wrapped in muslin and nurse Mellor introduced her.

'This is Susan, Joyce dear, Susan Bromley, she's a regular visitor to the hospital and most of us would give our right hand for one of her apple pies, would you like a slice?'

I looked at Susan, the pie and then nurse Mellor. Susan looked like a nice lady but it was too late for me to start making friends. My life in this world was finished. I turned and looked out of the window. Rain started to pour down and splatter all over the window panes. It grew fiercer and water flew across the grounds like metal poles stabbing at the grass. I liked it.

The weather seemed angry and so was I. It was as though it knew how I was feeling inside and was commiserating with me.

I turned around. Susan was sitting opposite me. On a small table beside us were two slices of apple pie on saucers. Susan picked hers up and took a bite out of it. I watched as her eyes closed as she enjoyed the deliciousness of the food. It made me want to eat my slice but what was the point? I am so close to the end that I can almost feel it. Susan finished her food then turned to me as she wiped the crumbs from her lips.

'I bet you'll be glad to get out of here,' she said as she picked up my plate and offered me the food.

I turned once more to gaze out of the window. The rain had stopped and a bright ball of sunshine was trying to peek out from behind one of the cobalt grey clouds. I watched as the vivid colours of a rainbow arched in the distance, framing the scene. I was angry once more. I needed the dark greyness and pouring, thunderous rain drops to help me do what I had to do. The violet edge of the rainbow seemed to be smiling at me. I scowled at it.

The sun made a bigger effort to push its way out from behind the cloud. I watched as the rain ceased altogether and the rainbow vanished. I turned to where Susan had been sitting but she was no longer there. I didn't hear her leave and was surprised to see her seat empty.

I turned and looked at the slice of apple pie. It looked delicious. I picked it up and bit into the soft, flaky pastry. It melted in my mouth and the warm sweet apple dripped down my throat and tasted like nectar. I could see why everyone would fight for a slice of it. It was one of the loveliest things I had ever eaten. I brushed the crumbs from my lips and put the empty plate down beside me. It struck me, fearfully, that I really enjoyed it. For so many months I had functioned without feeling, tasting or caring and I was content with that.

I didn't want to enjoy anything in this life ever again. Bertie was dead and, to me, any enjoyment I felt would be a depravity that would make my lover think I did not care but I did. I love him so much it's as though an iron belt tightens around my chest when I think of him. Sometimes the tightness of it made me struggle for breath and I wondered if Bertie was coming to rescue me.

I never ever want to feel happiness in this life; it would be an affront to Bertie's memory. I turn, once more, to gaze out of the window. The sun has given up trying to shine and has slipped behind the clouds as the rain begins to thunder down from the sky once more.

# 14

Susan visits most days now and I like her. She just sits and chats away but doesn't expect me to talk back. She is a very pretty woman. Her vibrant blue eyes shine with pleasure when she talks about her family. She has one daughter called Edith who is around the same age as me and another called Iris who is seven. Her eyes cloud over when she explains that both her children have been evacuated to a farm in Cornwall where her in-laws live.

I love to listen to her. The expressions on her face bring everything she talks about alive and I pretend that I belong to her family. This helps me feel less alone. Sometimes the loneliness is like a constant dagger jabbing at my side. I'm frightened because I have no one in the world that cares about me, except Susan. The hospital has become my home and my sanctuary and I wonder where I will go when I have to leave. I remember that when the time comes, I won't need anywhere to go because I intend to join Bertie, wherever he may be.

Susan continues to chat away about anything and everything when, out of the corner of my eye, I spot a familiar figure walking into the room. I blink my eyes because I think I must be seeing things but as she draws closer, I can see that the person walking towards me is Mabel. I sit and wait. Susan turns and looks at Mabel as she approaches. When she reaches us Susan stands and introduces herself to her Mabel does the same then she turns to me.

'Oh Joyce, sweetheart, I'm so sorry, I didn't even know what had happened until a week ago; Mother decided against telling me, it was only when I visited home that I heard the terrible news, I'm a land girl now, it was difficult getting Mother to agree to give me permission to do the job when I turned sixteen but my dad talked her into it and told her it was my patriotic duty,' Mabel announced, proudly.

She leant down and squeezed me tightly. I put my arms around her and clung on. This was the first time I had been held by another human since Bertie died. It brought me comfort and made me feel less frightened. Mabel went and got a chair then sat opposite me and held my hands.

'I was really angry when Father told me what had happened, I couldn't believe that Mother had kept it to herself,' Mabel said as she shook her head angrily, ' I've been writing to you at Uncle Albert's address with no idea that he was dead,' she quickly swiped a tear off her cheek and carried on speaking.

'He was the loveliest man, I used to have such a crush on him when I was younger but as time went on I thought maybe it wasn't women he liked so he stayed single rather than break the law, now I realise he was just waiting for the right girl to come along. I'm so glad he found happiness with you Joyce and I wish he was still alive because I could have been your bridesmaid,' she chuckled.

For the first time since Bertie had died someone was talking to me as though I was a proper human being, not an invalid or some disgusting, dirty entity. Mabel was making me feel like a normal girl again, not like some sinner who deserved to rot in hell, I looked at her and smiled weakly. The action in itself felt alien to me, I couldn't remember when I last smiled at anything.

I leant down and pulled the cardboard box, which contained what was left of mine and Bertie's life, from under my chair. I kept it with me at all times. Shyly, I opened the lid and passed one of the poems Bertie had written for me to Mabel. She took it and read it with tears rolling down her cheeks.

'That's beautiful Joyce, it's clear he loved you very much, I'm sorry about Mother and furious with her, she claims to be a good Christian woman then abandons you at the very time you need her, it's going to take me a very long time to forgive her for that,'

I looked Mabel and whispered.

'Forgive her, you only get one mother and everyone makes mistakes, I should know,'

'Oh, I will,' Mabel answered, 'Just as soon as I've finished being angry with her; I work on a farm around ten miles from Bristol so we'll be able to see a lot of each other, I've just had a week's leave to see the family, I can't believe how quickly my little sisters are growing, so I'm not due leave for a while but you could come and visit, I sleep in a hostel with fifteen other girls and they're a great bunch, you could come and work there yourself if I knew how much you hated fresh air and countryside,' she laughed and she was right, I was a townie through and through.

'There's jobs going where I'm working,' Susan piped up, 'Would you like me to put in a word for you?'

I was at a loss. In my head, I had no future. I had everything planned. I was going to walk up to Clifton Downs and jump into the gorge below clutching my precious shoe box. It was simple. I looked at Susan and Mabel as they waited for my response. I was now confused and fighting the conflicting emotions I was feeling. I love Bertie and want to be with him but now I'm unsure if I want to die.

I now have two people who care for me, so I am no longer alone. I tell Susan and Mabel that I am not sure what I want and they nod. At the end of visiting they both promise that they will come back again tomorrow. I thank them then watch them walk away together; chatting amicably as though they had known each all their lives. I realise that my sixteenth birthday had passed by without me realising it.

I sat and pondered. Mabel was right; being a land girl wasn't for me. When we were little girls, I was always the dolly bird and she was the tomboy. I couldn't stand the thought of working outdoors in the wild winter weather or getting burned by the blistering sun in the summer. It definitely wasn't my cup of tea. Susan worked in a factory making parts for aeroplanes, I quite fancied that. Almost immediately, I felt as though I was betraying Bertie for planning a life without him.

That night, as I slept, I dreamed that Bertie had visited. He sat on my bed and held my hand. I could feel the softness of his palm touching mine and I could smell his wonderful Sandalwood aftershave. He was telling me that we would meet again but not for a long while and that I must live my life without him until then. He explained that he would always love and miss me but now was not my time to join him. I awoke the following morning with tears sliding down my cheeks and I knew he was right. I said a silent goodbye to the only man I would ever love and began to plan my future.

Susan and Mabel visited the following day as promised. For the first time since he had died I began talking about Bertie, I told them:

'It didn't seem to matter about the age gap, we just kind of fitted together like a pair of comfy shoes,' I knew I was crying as I spoke but I let the tears flow, for one last time.

'I've always felt a lot older than I actually am because of my mother, I can't find it in my heart to forgive her and I think it was Gods way of punishing me by taking Bertie away,' Susan leant forward and held my hand.

'God isn't vindictive Joyce love, I hate my father and will never ever forgive him for what he put me through and God hasn't seen fit to punish me, it was the Germans that killed your Bertie, not God,' she finished.

'Bertie was being sent away because of me, he felt ashamed, I could see it in his eyes and I hate myself for making him feel like that,'

'Bertie was a grown man who made his own choices,' Mabel piped up, 'as long as I've known him Uncle Bertie has done exactly what he wanted to so don't carry all the guilt and blame for a love affair that he chose to embark on,'

I sat and thought for a while. Mabel was right once more but I longed for Bertie to hold me in his arms one last time, Susan spoke,

'I got pregnant when I wasn't much older than you, I was terrified that my father would kill both Edward and I, I remember feeling ill with fear, thankfully we had a happy ending, Edward and I are married now and I can honestly say that I love him very much and am very proud of him,' Mabel joined in.

'I've been having a wonderful love affair with a Canadian soldier who's twice my age, luckily he knows how to prevent an unwanted pregnancy so we can enjoy as much of each other as we like,' she grinned.

I was shocked. In my mind, I was the only young girl silly enough to sleep with a man I wasn't married to. Now both Susan and Mabel were telling me that they did exactly the same thing. It made feel less isolated and I was grateful to them for confiding in me.

'Bertie and I never took any precautions against me getting pregnant, it just never happened,' I sighed

'Probably for the best,' Susan said, 'you'd have been left with a child to raise on your own and that would have been far from easy,'

'It would have been nice to have a part of him left though, but I know you're right,' I told Susan.

We stopped chatting while we drank a cup of tea then we began to sort the practicalities of my discharge. Nurse Mellor had told me that her elderly aunt, Miss Georgina Groves, let out rooms and had one vacant that I could move into. She explained that her aunt was little hard of hearing but a kindly soul who kept a clean house. Susan had secured a job for me at the factory where she worked so this would enable me to support myself financially.

A lady from the WVS had come to visit with a bundle of clothes for me as almost all my possessions had been lost when Bertie's house was bombed. I didn't even have a photo of the man I loved so dearly. On the day of my departure I felt inexplicably sad, as though I was leaving home but it wasn't my home. It was just a place that enabled me to repair myself mentally and physically. Nurse Mellor promised to visit as soon as I had settled in. She hugged me and handed me a little package.

I opened it and found a powder compact with its own little mirror and a lipstick in a stunning shade of scarlet. A lump formed in my throat which I quickly swallowed. I was humbled by the thought the kindly Nurse Mellor had gone out of her way to get me a present she knew I would love. Mabel had returned to the farm she worked on so Susan took the day off work to help me move in. I walked out from the sanctuary of the hospital carrying my few possessions.

It was a bitterly cold day at the beginning of May. The sky hung low and menacing and was dark grey. I shivered as I followed Susan to the bus stop. We arrived at my new home a short time later and I nervously mounted the steps and watched as Susan knocked on the door. It was opened by a small, dainty lady with the bluest eyes I had ever seen. They were vibrant and sharp and the colour of a field of iris's. She introduced herself as Miss Groves and hurriedly ushered Susan and I into the small passageway.

She then quickly closed the door behind us and the warmth of the little house wrapped itself around me like a comforting blanket. We followed my new landlady up the narrow stairs and to a small doorway on the right of landing. Mrs Groves pushed open the door and gestured for me to enter. I walked in and smiled. The room was small but cheerfully decorated. Bright flower patterns adorned the curtains and the bedspread.

The whole place smelt of detergent and polish. Along with the narrow single bed in the room, there was also a wardrobe and dressing table. On the opposite side there was a small table and chair and a paraffin heater. I loved the room and immediately thanked Mrs Groves. She smiled and said she'd leave me to unpack then Susan and I should come down and join her for a cup of tea. Meals were included in the rent which I had to pay at the end of the month so I gave Mrs Groves my ration book.

Later that evening, as I sat in my new home, I was worried that I would feel lonely. To my surprise, I actually felt liberated. I was independent for the first time in my life and was happy that I didn't have to rely on someone else to take care of me. I pushed the little shoebox that contained mine and Bertie's life under the bed and out of sight. I would always love Bertie but now was the time to move on and take charge of my life and my destiny. There were two choices, life or death and I felt a huge longing, not only to live, but to live life to the full and enjoy every moment I had left.

# 15

The first night in my new home was very eventful. No sooner had I snuggled down into my comfy bed and wrapped my knees around my hot water bottle, the dreaded air raid siren screeched into life. I quickly threw my blanket back and cursed myself for not finding out where the nearest air raid shelter was. Susan had told me that was one of the first things I should do. I grabbed my handbag then pulled my dressing gown on.

The door opposite to mine opened simultaneously and Mrs Groves rushed out. Her thin grey hair was contained in a hairnet and she was carrying a string bag full of bit and bobs. She beckoned me to follow her and I did. We rushed down the stairs as fast as the elderly lady's legs would allow. When I heard the burr of the approaching planes my heart began to beat so fast I thought it would pulsate its way out of my chest.

The dreadful noise took me right back to when Bertie had been killed. Mrs Groves wrenched open the door under the stairs. I stood trembling, unable to make my legs move because my terror was so great. Mrs Groves turned and literally manhandled me into the small space. She pulled the door close then switched on the light.

There was only a small bulb but that was all the confined space needed. The room was adequately illuminated. I was pleasantly surprised at how comfortable she had made the place but the noise of the enemy aircraft was sending violent shivers right through my body and I felt as though I couldn't breathe.

My landlady pushed me down onto a stool then sat down opposite me on a kitchen chair.

The noise of the enemy planes was deafening. I think they must have been directly above us. I was trembling violently and I couldn't stop my tears from falling. I felt Mrs Groves grasp my hands. I held tightly on to hers and looked into her eyes. It would have done no good if she had tried to talk to me as her voice would never have been heard above the racket coming from the skies.

Her bright blues eyes seemed to be urging me to keep calm. She stroked my shaking hands with her soft fingers. I could now hear the sounds of the bombs being dropped fairly close-by. All I could do was to wait and hope that one wouldn't land on us. Thankfully, the raid was a short one and the *'all clear'* sounded after a couple of hours. I helped my landlady up and thanked her for her kindness. We hugged each other and headed back to our bedrooms. It took a long while for sleep to come.

As I lay staring at the ceiling I realised that my entombment with Bertie had not just damaged me physically but it had affected me mentally. The noises and smells brought everything back. The feeling of hopelessness enveloped me whenever I heard the siren go off. I hoped that things would become easier as time went on. I fell into a fitful sleep where I dreamed I was trapped in a burning building and woke with a start.

I was bathed in sweat so I pushed the bedclothes aside and walked quietly over to the window. I pulled the blackout curtains back. The dawn was just beginning to creep over the horizon. The sky was a mixture of pink and purple hues. It was a glorious sight. The beauty of nature calmed my trembling body and mind and I felt ready to start living my life once more.

# 16

Mrs Groves had made us porridge for breakfast and although I enjoyed it at the time, it now felt like a lead weight in my stomach as I made my way to my new job. People, mainly women were making their way to their places of employment. I looked for Susan as I approached the factory gates. We had arranged to meet outside. I heard my name being called and spotted Susan darting around the crowd of workers trying to make her way to me.

It was near the end of the second week in May and the beginning of the rest of my life, at least that's what I thought. It was a little chilly but not too cold, in fact, quite warm for the time of the year. I didn't complain because I knew the icy winter would be upon us soon and I intended to make the most of the climate. Susan linked my arm. I liked it, it made me feel as though she cared about me and I smiled at her.

She led me through the factory gates. The place was enormous, a lot larger than it seemed from the outside. We walked the length of the long courtyard, passing several concrete buildings with tiny windows before eventually arriving at the largest structure. Susan pushed the door open and beckoned for me to go in. I did so and immediately the smell of engine oil and sweat hit me.

We left our bags and cardigans in a locker but kept our gas masks with us. I followed Susan into a side room. There stood an elderly gentleman holding a set of overalls and a turban which Susan told was to keep my hair out of the way of the machinery. I changed quickly and followed Susan into the main room. I didn't want to make her late for work. The noise that sounded from the room, when she pushed open the large double doors, was deafening.

Woman lined both sides of several benches and all were intent on doing their work. The clanking of metal and loud punching noises mingled with the sound of melodious music coming from several speakers hanging from the walls. All the women wore the same clothes as I now did and I began to feel hugely overwhelmed. The sheer size of the place took my breath away and every single person in the room seemed to know what they were doing.

Susan led me to a woman who then took me to a long table. Thankfully, Susan was standing opposite me and her presence made me feel a little less nervous. I was shown, very patiently, how to put various aircraft components together. The woman watched me for quite a while before she turned and walked away. I was terrified. What if I messed up and put the wrong parts in the wrong places. I felt Susan's hand on mine and looked across at her. She mouthed at me not to worry. I couldn't possibly work out how to not worry.

I felt a little better when we were in the canteen having our morning tea break. Susan explained that several people went over the work we had done before it was sent out to the hangars. I was glad. I didn't want to be responsible for causing a plane to crash. The day flew by and when the hooter sounded to indicate that my working day was over, I felt a lot more confident than I had done at the beginning of the day.

I was totally exhausted and happy to be heading home. I waited for Susan to catch up with me. She linked my arm and we walked out of the factory together.

'Well, how was your first day?' she asked with her lovely smiled spread across her face.

'I'm fine now, I think I've got the hang of it,' I replied.

'Do you want to meet for a drink later?' Susan asked.

I smiled and told her I was too tired to do anything other than eat my tea then go to bed. Susan nodded and told me which pub she would be in if I changed my mind. We said our goodbyes and headed for our respective lodgings. I unlocked the front door and was greeted by the delicious smell of rabbit stew.

I quickly went up to my room and put my things on the bed then headed back down the stairs and into the kitchen. Mrs Groves was standing at the stove stirring the contents of a huge black pot. She turned and smiled at me and we chatted to each other about how our days had been. I realised that Mrs Groves was an orderly lady and kept a strict routine in her life. After we had eaten, I retired to my room but not before thanking Mrs Groves for the wonderful meal.

Upstairs I sat on my bed. I was not exactly feeling happy but I was definitely a lot less sad these days. I found it a massive relief that my suicidal thoughts no longer plagued me and I could look forward to the days ahead with hope rather than dread. I know I had Susan to thank for that and I would be eternally grateful. After sitting for a while I began to feel restless and realised that a drink with Susan would be fun. I made my way to the Red Lion. Before I left I put a bit of make up on. I loved my bright red lipstick; it felt like I had painted on a smile.

It was only a short walk to the Red lion and when I arrived I quickly opened then shut the door and put the blackout curtain in place. Susan was sitting at a small table in the corner and she stood and beckoned to me when she saw me enter. I weaved my way through the throng of drinkers and sat at the only vacant chair at the table.

'I'm glad you changed your mind, the evenings can get pretty lonely with no company,' Susan explained, 'this is Dulcie and this is Myrtle,' she said as she pointed at her two companions, 'we all share a billet together,' she finished.

Myrtle and Dulcie were the polar opposites of each other. Dulcie was a little child-like woman who I guessed must be in her mid-twenties. She held a tiny glass of sherry and sipped at it daintily. Myrtle, however, was a gargantuan woman with hands like a navvy and shoulders wide enough for two people. She glugged down a pint of bitter and wiped her lips with the back of her hand.

Both the women said hello and smiled. Susan went to the bar and got a round of drinks for us all. The Red Lion was a pleasant establishment. It was filled with a mix of people. I could see servicemen and women on leave and other workers in protected occupations. I could tell this by the clothes they were wearing. In my mind, you could spot a dock worker a mile away. They smelt of oil and cigarette smoke and their faces were streaked with grime.

As I sat, enjoying my comfy surroundings, I noticed a uniformed man sitting at the far end of the bar. He was smoking a thick cigar and sipping at a glass of whiskey. He reminded me a little of Bertie which made me feel as though a sharp dart of sorrow was stabbing at my heart. He must have felt me looking at him because he turned in my direction. His eyes were not blue, like Bertie's; they were a deep almond colour that exuded warmth. He raised his glass to me and I smiled shyly. Susan nudged me.

'I saw that,' she giggled, 'I think you've got an admirer and a very handsome one at that.'

I told her not to be silly but inside I felt flattered. The man at the bar was very good-looking. He was smartly dressed in a military uniform and he had a thin moustache above his lip. The evening was a great success and I enjoyed Susan, Dulcie and Myrtles companionship. At around nine-thirty we decided to call it a night because we all had an early start the following day. As I walked past the gentleman at the bar he put his hand out.

'Geoffrey Floyd, at your service madam, may I compliment you on your exquisite beauty and may I buy you a drink?' he enquired as he smiled widely.

I giggled once more and nodded. I told Susan and the girls to go on. The Major pulled a bar stool close and I climbed up onto it. He handed me a drink. I was not familiar with the taste but didn't dislike it. Geoffrey Floyd informed it was a gin and it. We began to chat. Mainly about the war as that was all anyone seemed to talk about these days.

We got on very well and I was shocked when the 'last orders' bell rang at eleven o'clock; I'd no idea where the time had gone. Geoffrey offered me a ride home and I gratefully accepted. The blackout made walking outside at night very precarious. Geoffrey's car was an old Austin Seven that trundled along slowly as he tried navigating the roads with little help from the shuttered headlamps.

I directed him to my billet and we eventually arrived. He stopped the car, switched off the ignition and tugged the hand-brake up.

'Could I see you again, Joyce?' he asked through the darkness.

I said I would like that and felt his hand touching my knee then sliding up my dress until he reached the top of my stockings. It was a lovely feeling that made me quiver inside with joyous anticipation but I didn't want him to think that I was a tart so I pushed his hand off my leg. He leant over and kissed my cheek. He smelt delicious. I guessed he used Pears soap, his moustache tickled my face and I longed to have sex with the man.

I inwardly disciplined myself and arranged to meet him on his next day off which was the following Wednesday. I groped my way up the path and let myself into the house where I quickly pulled the blackout curtain across before feeling my way up the stairs. I undressed without putting any lights on as I didn't want to disturb Mrs Groves. I snuggled into my comfy bed and fell asleep almost immediately. I dreamed that I was making love to Bertie but when I actually looked at his face, it was Geoffrey and I didn't mind a bit.

# 17

Once I had learned my trade I began to enjoy my work at Strachan & Henshaw Munitions Factory, assembling parts for aeroplanes.

I was taught how to do several different jobs. It was difficult at first because it was a whole new world to me. I learned to make equipment for gun carriages, launching rigs and submarine-detecting apparatus. I became adept at assembling hydraulic pumps and pressure gauges.

It took me a while longer to perfect the art of assembling switch boxes for navigation lights but I persevered and triumphed in the end. The factory originally made paper bags until the war started and it was requisitioned for more important work.

I felt that I was helping hugely towards the war effort and this gave me an enormous feeling of pride. I was sure Bertie would be proud of me if he was alive. I'm quite certain that every single English family had been affected by the war in some way or another.

Anguished mothers were separated from their children and husbands. The constant worry for our loved ones was always at the fore front of our minds. Susan became like a big sister to me and I loved her very much. I also saw Mabel, my childhood neighbour, as often as I could. The war got in the way of many a reunion but I tried not to let it get me down. I had made several friends at the factory and I smiled as the lunch bell rang out.

I picked up my gas mask and hand bag and headed towards the canteen amongst the throng of the rest of the workers. I saw Susan beckon to me as soon as I entered the room and I waved back to let her know I'd seen her. I queued for my meal. I was feeling famished. The burly serving lady piled mashed potatoes, cabbage and lamb's liver on to my plate and my mouth began to water. I grabbed a mug of tea and wove my way over to where Susan was sitting.

I plonked myself down next to her and immediately began to tuck into my food. It was delicious and I didn't utter a word until I had cleared my plate. I turned to talk to Susan who introduced me to a new worker named Violet; I nodded then turned back to Susan.

'Geoffrey is taking me out tonight, we're going to the cinema then he's going to drive me to a country restaurant somewhere,' I gushed,

'I'd like to know where he gets the petrol coupons to take you out gallivanting, this is the third time this week, Susan replied then sipped her tea, 'and I thought you were going out with Herbie, the young sailor you met, this evening?'

'I was but his leave got cancelled right at the last minute so I called Geoffrey from the phone box on the corner of my street to see if he was free, I was looking forward to going out for the evening so that was the answer to my dilemma,' I smiled as I explained this to Susan then turned to see Violet gazing at me with an obvious scowl of disapproval. I didn't care. It no longer bothered me if people approved of my lifestyle or not.

Living in a country at war was terrifying and I knew every day might be my last. I had cheated death once when I was buried in the cellar with Bertie. I meant to live my life to the full as long as I was still alive. Olive, a small shy little girl who worked at the opposite end of the factory reached into her handbag.

'Do you want to borrow this for your date tonight?' she asked as she handed me a gold lipstick case. I took it and looked at the scarlet red coloured cosmetic and smiled widely.

'Yes please, there's hardly a stub left of my lipstick, God knows what I'll do when it's eventually gone,'

'Couldn't Geoffrey get you some? Susan asked, 'he obviously knows some important people otherwise he wouldn't be able to get away with using his petrol coupons to take you out,'

'You may be right, my dear Susan, I'll ask him later,' I told her and turned to look at Violet. Instead of the look of disapproval that I had been expecting she was smiling at me and said she hoped I enjoyed my date. I thanked her, feeling glad that she had changed her mind about me. I knew my lifestyle wasn't as chaste as it should have been, but I enjoyed it and it was my way of getting through the war and numbing my sorrow at losing Bertie.

The hooter rang and we quickly grabbed our belongings and headed back to our work- stations. Susan and I arranged to meet at the Red Lion the following evening to get the 'low down' on my date. She said I was all the social life she had. The afternoon flew by in a haze of business and concentration. Before I knew it I was shuffling along with the rest of the work-force heading towards the exits at the end of our working day.

It was now the middle of October and although it was just past five-thirty, it was pitch dark outside and freezing cold. Luckily it was only a short walk to my billet and I pulled my coat up around my neck to keep out the winter chill. I had only been walking for a few minutes when the dreaded air raid siren rang out, yet again, sending daggers of fear through my body. I looked around for the nearest shelter but the blackout made it almost impossible to see anything.

From somewhere in the dimness I heard a voice that was vaguely familiar.

'Are you all right, love?' he asked and I felt an arm around my waist,

'No, I'm not sure where the nearest Anderson shelter is,' I shouted above the constant wailing of the siren,

'You come with me, love, I'll take care of you,' the man's voice announced and he grasped my hand.

I was so terrified that I allowed the silhouetted figure to lead me quickly across the road. I only knew I had done this because of the dip and climb of the pavement. I felt my way along narrow alley way with my free hand. I began to wonder exactly which shelter the man was taking me to. I heard him jiggle some keys in his pocket then I heard a door open. I followed the man inside. I waited as he made sure the blackout curtains were in place then he turned on the light.

The place was gradually lit by a single bulb hanging from the centre of the ceiling. I could hear the drones of the incoming planes but they seemed to be a long way off. I could also hear the popping sounds of the *Ack Ack* guns as they tried to defend the city of Bristol. I silently wished them luck. My eyes eventually became accustomed to the dim light and I turned to see who my rescuer was.

It seemed like I was in some kind of allotment shed and I thought the flimsy structure would be little protection against a German bomb dropping on me. The man approached me and tried to pull me into his arms. His breath stunk of rotten teeth and rancid food. Now we were inside a compact space I could smell the man's body odour and it made me feel sick. He had obviously not washed in a long while and an acrid smell of stale sweat emanated from his wiry body.

As my eyes became more accustomed to my surroundings, I looked at the man. He was not much taller than me and there wasn't an ounce of spare flesh on him. I vaguely recognised him as someone from the factory where I worked but I couldn't put my finger on exactly where I had seen him. I pushed him away and looked into his face. What few teeth he did have left were rotten and blackened and I stepped even further back as he leered at me.

'Where is this place?' I asked sharply, all the while the noise of the bombers was getting closer.

'This is my little hidey hole,' he informed me, grinning like some kind of lunatic, 'I heard a rumour at Strachan & Henshaw Munitions that you like a bit of a good time so I thought I'd bring you here and show what a proper man is.' He moved towards me as he grunted involuntarily.

I wasn't sure what was more frightening, being in this space with this disgusting individual or listening to the bombs exploding around the city. The man was now standing directly in front of me. He was breathing heavily and he had his hand down the front of his trousers. I actually thought I would vomit if this person touched any part of me. He began to fumble with is trouser buttons. I lifted my knee and shoved it into his groin with such force I'm quite sure I heard something snap.

I watched as he dropped to the floor in agony, spitting out all types of obscenities. I stepped over the flailing form and walked towards the door. I put my hand on the latch and as I began to lift it up I felt his hand grab my ankle. With my other foot I kicked him squarely in the face and he fell backwards. I unlatched the door and raced outside before he had a chance to gather his senses. It was no longer pitch black as I ran away from the shed and back along the alley he had led me up.

Searchlights were focused up to the sky and their cone shaped illumination lit the blackness. I was mesmerised by the beauty of brightness. I then spotted the enemy planes. There seemed to be hundreds of them heading towards the city. I stood, rooted to the spot. I couldn't work out if I was safer outside or stuck in an air raid shelter shoulder to shoulder with strangers. I saw the barrage balloons in the distance. They were floating high above the clouds. They looked like giant silver orbs bouncing freely in the sky.

I watched as the bomb hatch of a plane began to open. It felt as though everything was happening in slow motion. I saw the bomb. Suddenly I could hear shouting. I looked to my left and saw an elderly ARP warden screaming at me and waving his torch towards the Anderson shelter he stood outside of. It was as though I had suddenly woken up. I heard the screech of the explosive as it was dropping towards the earth.

I turned and ran towards the shelter. I ran so fast I thought my lungs would burst. The warden dragged me inside and yanked the blackout curtain across the entrance. He then pushed me down on the end of one of the narrow benches that lined either side of the shelter and sat down next to me. My body began to tremble once more. The old man sat down next to me and I felt the quivering from his body. We both looked at each other; no words were needed, as we were united by a mutual terror.

A terrific explosion sounded and it was so loud it made my ears ring. The shelter seemed to lift a few inches off the ground. Women screamed and children cried. A series of thuds crashed onto the sides of corrugated iron structure that was our only shield against the onslaught of bombs dropped by a deadly enemy. I turned towards the ARP warden and saw that he was now praying. His hands were pushed together as he looked skywards and begged God to help.

It seemed like his prayers were answered when, a few hours later, the all clear sounded and all in the shelter had survived. We rose one by one and began to make our way outside. I was afraid that there would be no world left. The noise of the incendiaries had made it sound like the whole of Bristol was being smashed to smithereens. I followed a lady who was holding a small child. She looked around with her mouth agape.

'There won't be much city left if this keeps on,' she muttered to no one in particular. I silently agreed.

Everywhere I looked there was destruction and ruin. Flames flew out of the windows on nearby houses where the glass had shattered from the heat. Some buildings were only standing by the 'grace of God' and looked as though they would topple over at any second. Massive craters where homes once stood blighted the landscape and I wondered how I and my fellow shelterers had survived the attack.

The clanging bells from the ambulance and fire engines rang out. Some people stood looking hopelessly at the skeleton of their homes. The emergency services were doing a great job in taking care of the wounded and shocked. I couldn't help but think how lucky we were to have these people who would work for hours on end as long as they were needed. I watched as a van parked opposite me and two WRV workers got out and immediately began offering tea, from thermos flasks, to all who had been affected.

# 18

I made my way home. I still couldn't believe I had come out of the murderous attack unscathed. I shivered as I recalled the vile man who had tried to take advantage of me. I hoped my well-aimed kick had broken his jaw. That might deter him from taking advantage of other frightened young women. I assumed my date with Geoffrey was off. I should have met him over an hour ago but as I turned the corner I saw his car parked outside my billet. I rushed over as he climbed out of the car. I didn't realise I was still trembling.

I told him I just needed to pop in and let my landlady know I was safe. I also wanted to grab my overnight bag because most of my dates with Geoffrey now included an overnight stay. Once I had done this, I shut the front door behind me and climbed into the passenger seat of Geoffrey's car. Before long the city was behind us and we were hurtling through the countryside. We came to a stop outside a large country hotel-cum—guest-house called The Grange.

It was an old building with ivy covering the entire front wall. Six windows nestled amongst the foliage and looked like staring eyes scanning the landscape. Geoffrey climbed out of the vehicle and I followed suit. I waited until he had taken the baggage from the small trunk at the rear of the car then followed him up two granite steps and then through a pair of double doors. The black-out curtain was hastily pulled aside by a girl dressed as a porter and we walked into the foyer of the building.

I immediately felt the thickness of the red pile carpet beneath my feet. I was impressed with the opulence of the premises and wondered where they managed to get all the fixtures and furnishings from while the war raged about us. Geoffrey booked us into the onsite restaurant, in an hour's time, and we headed up to our room. The scowls of the mainly elderly staff did not bother me. They were cocooned in this luxurious building when less than an hour away bombs were dropping on a beleaguered city.

I was quite sure they couldn't begin to grasp the horrors of everyday life. The porter showed into our chamber. It was a lovely room with a large four poster bed in the middle and an en-suite bathroom. I had a quick bath in only two inches of water as the government had instructed. I immediately felt a little less shattered by the evening's events. Geoffrey handed me a glass of bubbly wine as soon as I entered the room. It was delicious; the bubbles went up my nose making me sneeze.

It wasn't long before Geoffrey had relieved me of the thick fluffy dressing gown, provided by the hotel and we made love on the bed. I sometimes wandered if I was abnormal. I adored having sex and the pleasure it gave me. I garnered from conversations with the other women at the factory that they regarded the marital act as a duty rather than a pleasure. A little later we walked down the staircase and into the restaurant. I was, again, amazed at the quality of cuisine they served. Food rationing had been brought in at the beginning of the year but this place didn't seem to suffer from any such problems.

I feasted on oysters and veal. The wine was citrusy and refreshing. The strawberry trifle for pudding was delightful. I felt really fortunate that I was able to escape the war, even if only for one night. Most people I knew weren't as lucky. When the meal was over we headed back up to our suite. This was my fifth date with Geoffrey and I enjoyed his company.

He poured me a drink then began to look for something in his case. I watched as he pulled out a long tube with a basin attached to the end. He then put a dark coloured substance into the receptacle and began to heat it. After a short time he put the tube in his mouth and inhaled deeply. He turned and gestured for me to join him. I was curious and did the same as him. When I first breathed in the odd smelling substance I coughed.

Then, without warning, an intense feeling of euphoria enveloped me. It was so penetrating I felt as though I had stepped out of my own body. I turned to Geoffrey and smiled. He grinned back at me then burst into laughter. I did the same. I lay down on the bed and felt like I was floating on a cloud of soft cotton wool. Geoffrey joined me. I don't know how much time had passed when the exhilarating feeling was replaced by nausea.

I pulled myself into a sitting position to try and still the waves of sickness passing through my body. Geoffrey smoked from the pipe once more then clambered back on the bed.

'We're going to get little Lizzie,' he said in a slurred voice.

I wondered if Lizzie was another one of his girlfriends but then why would he say 'we're going to get her?

He pushed himself up on one elbow and turned to face me.

'You know, Joyce, Hitler's not the bad chap he's painted to be,' he said, nodding his approval.

I was a bit shocked to hear what he was saying but I kept quiet.

'He's done wonders for Germany, dragged the whole country out of the doldrums, he made it a force to be reckoned with.' I smiled at him because I was unsure what to say. He lay back on the pillows and mumbled quietly.

'Yes we'll take Lizzie down, dent the morale…' he trailed off in mid-sentence and then he began to snore loudly.

I lay for a while and was glad when the feeling of sickness had subsided, although my head still felt a little muzzy. I took off Geoffrey's trousers and shirt and covered him with the blanket. He was sleeping peacefully. I undressed, washed and put my night wear on and slid in the bed beside him. I thought deeply about what he had said, something in his tone unnerved me a little. Everyone knew Hitler was a tyrant who had to be stopped and who was Lizzie?

I fell into a fitful slumber and dreamed that Geoffrey and Hitler were having dinner together with a glamorous girl called Lizzie. I awoke the next morning with a slight headache and vowed not to smoke, whatever I had the night before, again. It definitely didn't agree with me. I could hear Geoffrey whistling in the bathroom. I felt a bit uneasy but wasn't sure why. He came back into the room and lent down and kissed my cheek lightly. He smelt of shaving cream and toothpaste.

The laid-back man who breathed in the smoke from the receptacle the night before had disappeared and this was now the Geoffrey I knew. He was smartly dressed in his army uniform and urged me to get dressed so we could go down and get some breakfast. He informed me that he was, absolutely starving and I was feeling quite hungry too. The pipe and paraphernalia from the night before had been packed away with the rest of the Geoffrey's things in his brown leather suitcase.

I dressed quickly and walked down the plush staircase, following Geoffrey, into the dining hall. The kippers I ate melted in my mouth and I realised I hadn't felt so ravenous in a long while. Geoffrey also gulped his breakfast down. Once he had finished eating, he looked at me and said with a smile on his face.

'I didn't talk any nonsense last night did I, Joyce dear?' He was still smiling but I detected tenseness in his voice and demeanour, I leant forward and said in a whisper.

'You could have said anything you wanted, after I had smoked whatever was in the pipe, I have no recollection of anything until you woke me this morning with a kiss,' I told him.

I watched as he visibly relaxed and smiled. He told me to go back to the room to get my things while he paid the bill. For some unknown reason the hairs on the back of my neck prickled as I walked up the stairs. I was quite sure Geoffrey was watching me but I didn't turn back to check. We drove back to Bristol in relative silence. It was fairly early in the morning but there were still lots of people around heading for their various places of employment.

I had the day off. Geoffrey dropped me around the corner from my billet and promised to get in touch so we could meet up next week. This was usually a note through my door. I waved to Geoffrey and walked the short distance to my home. I unlocked the door and the delicious smell of frying bacon hit me and made my mouth water. I crept up the narrow stairs and put my things on the bed. I took off my outdoor things and put my slippers on.

I then walked noisily back down the stairs and into the small kitchen, my lovely landlady turned and smiled when she saw me enter the room.

'I thought the smell of bacon cooking would wake you up.' She said as she flipped the bacon rashers over in the iron frying pan.

I smiled back then devoured a bacon sandwich. As I sat drinking my tea I couldn't shake away the uneasy feeling that seemed to be hanging over me. I was glad I was meeting Susan tonight. She always seemed to be able to right the wrongs of the world and make me feel good again. Roll on this evening, I muttered to myself.

# 19

It was a fairly chilly and dark November evening when I walked the short distance to the pub to meet Susan. I felt my way along the narrow road by feeling my way past the familiar buildings. I knew I had arrived at the Red Lion because I could hear the sound of an out of tune piano being played. The music was accompanied by singing voices, mainly female with a few masculine ones sounding now and again.

I pushed the door open and slid around the blackout curtain. The warmth coming from the hearth of the large open fireplace was comforting and inviting. I spotted Susan sitting in the corner of the room at our usual table and I waved to her. I was glad to see that she was alone because I needed to talk to her about the events of the night before. She was sipping at a large glass of port as I approached her and she pointed to the gin and tonic she had bought for me.

I took off my coat, woolly scarf and gloves and put them on the back of my seat and took a long sip from the glass. The gin immediately warmed the back of my throat and stomach and I smiled at Susan and thanked her. We began to chat about our days. I told Susan how I wandered about the town gazing into the shop windows. Sadly, due to rationing, there was not much to be seen and it was quite a depressing sight.

Susan told me about her working day and I began to explain about what had happened to me during the air raid. Susan couldn't hide her disgust when I told about the revolting little man who had lured me to a shed. She asked why I didn't have my blackout torch on. I explained that the batteries were dead and I hadn't managed to get anymore. Susan told me she knew where to get some and would make sure I had a working torch as soon as possible.

I loved this part of Susan's personality. She obviously cared deeply about me and that made me feel less alone in this scary world. I couldn't put into words what I wanted to tell her about Geoffrey because I didn't know if I was making something out of nothing. I bought us another round of drinks and listened as Susan told me how her eldest daughter, Edith, wanted to be a land girl and her younger daughter, Iris, was only interested in was charging around the Cornish countryside like a tomboy with all of her friends, and finally about her baby son, Johnny who was eighteen months old. It was obvious that she missed them all. Susan suddenly stopped talking and said:

'Spit it out.' I asked her to spit what out.

'You've almost bitten your nails to the quick and that's not normally one of your bad habits, I know the dirty old bastard from last night must have upset you but you seemed to have dealt with him so what's on your mind?'

I found it hard to explain. Part of me was absolutely sure that I had nothing to worry about and the other half of me still felt very uneasy, but I didn't know why, I sighed.

'It's probably nothing but something is niggling at me,' I told Susan then took a sip of my drink. She nodded and told me to go on with what I was saying.

'My date with Geoffrey last night was at a lovely country hotel, I don't think the place knew there was a war on because there was certainly no shortage of food and drink, anyway, back in the room Geoffrey set up this contraption with a pipe leading from it and told me to inhale,' Susan's brow crinkled and she looked deep in thought so I continued with what I was saying.

'I've no idea what the stuff was but I'm not smoking it again, it made me feel queasy and unwell and I had the appetite of a bull this morning,' I watched as she lit up a cigarette and said;

'It sounds like opium, I think it's a kind of drug that the wealthy use to relax, Edward told me that a lot of people used the narcotic abroad, when he was home on his last leave,' she explained.

'Well they can keep it!' I pouted, 'Bloody disgusting stuff, anyway, there's more. Geoffrey smoked a lot more than me then began to say strange things, he said Hitler wasn't as bad as he was being painted and was actually a splendid chap, he then said they were going to 'get 'someone called Lizzy because of morale then he fell asleep.'

Susan looked as puzzled as I had been when I heard it. I waited to see if she could think of any explanation;

'Maybe the drug he smoked made him hallucinate or talk gobbledegook, either way I wouldn't touch the stuff again, didn't you ask Geoffrey what he meant? She asked me.

'No, there was something in the tone of his voice that made me lie and pretend I couldn't remember what he had said but I can't get rid of this uneasy feeling,' I told her as I gulped the last of my gin and tonic, Susan grimaced.

'If you think he's up to no good, you should go to the authorities, this country is struggling enough already with having traitors living among us,' she hissed.

I told her to keep her voice down. I didn't want to believe that Geoffrey was a traitor and I wished I hadn't told Susan.

I felt silly about what was obviously some mindless rambling from a drugged- up man. I made Susan promise to keep quiet about what I had told her and she swore she would. At that moment, a handsome young man walked over and put a couple of drinks on our table; he looked down at us and said.

'At your service, ladies, my name is Lieutenant Wilbur Hitchin, these are for you.' He then bowed dramatically.

I invited him to sit down and join us. He wasn't overly interesting but chatting with him and Susan took my mind off the constant nagging worry that kept jabbing at my stomach for no reason I could think of.

# 20

Christmas during wartime was an odd affair. We all wanted to celebrate and have fun but with bombs dropping on us and cities being reduced to rubble it wasn't an easy thing do. The government actively encouraged celebrating and gave us extra rations to ensure we enjoyed the festive season but I found it difficult.

The main thing that was different was the fact that, due to the blackout, no pretty coloured lights glistened out of the shop windows. When I was a child, I found the illumination magical and without them it didn't seem like Christmas. It was hard to find decent presents for friends and I wasn't much of a knitter so I found it a constant struggle to find gifts that Susan and my other mates would enjoy.

On December the eleventh, America joined the war and there were rumours that a lot of them would soon be posted over in England. That did give me cause to rejoice. I couldn't think of anything more romantic than meeting a Clarke Gable lookalike. On Christmas Eve I made my way to the pub to meet Susan and Violet. All three of us were working the morning shift on Christmas day so we were just stopping for an hour.

We all arrived around the same time and headed for our usual table. I loved the warmth and cosiness of the Red Lion. Sitting inside with blackout curtains drawn and the fire burning in the grate I could almost shut out the war and the coldness, if only for an hour or two, Violet began to talk.

'Have you heard what Hitler is doing to the Jews in Germany?'

Susan and I both shook our heads.

'They're being persecuted in the most awful way, they're no longer allowed to own property or to run a business, for God's sake, the poor devils are not even allowed to ride a bike!'

Susan and I watched Violet light a cigarette and her hands were visibly shaking, she continued with tears glistening in her eyes.

'They all have to wear yellow stars on their sleeves so everyone knows they're Jewish, their neighbours and friends are turning on them, I wish I could do something to help, at least a lot of the children managed to escape on the *Kindertransport* at the start of the war but the adults are being treated abominably, there's rumours that they're being herded into ghettos and forced to live in squalor, I really hope it isn't true but I think it is,' Violet finished.

'How do you know all this?' Susan asked as she put her arm around Violet's shoulder.

'Len, my husband, is Jewish and he still has family in Germany, information is filtering out bit by bit through letters and word of mouth, I think Adolf Hitler must be pure evil for what he is doing to innocent people,' she said as she slammed her empty glass on the table.

The sadness I felt when thinking what one person could do to his fellow man brought tears to my eyes. Why should one race be constantly persecuted? I picked up Violet and Susan's glasses and went to the bar to get more drinks. The conversation reminded me of what Geoffrey said and how Hitler wasn't a bad chap. I decided that when we went on our next date I would try and find out some more about his views on our enemies and who Lizzy was.

Christmas came and went and before I knew the Spring was upon us. The skies were cloudless and a graphite colour. It was unseasonably cold but I dressed warm and carried on making the best of life. Geoffrey and I had been on several dates but he hadn't smoked any opium or said anything weird so I wrote the whole episode off and put it out of my mind.

This particular evening was chillier than most. I groped my way through the blackout with my small torch shrouded and pointed to the ground. I was wearing a long mink coat that Geoffrey had bought me as a Christmas present but the temperature was so low that the cold seeped through the thick material and made me shiver. I was overly glad when I saw the metal sign of the Red Lion blowing in the bitter wind.

I quickly pushed the door and blackout curtain open then shut them behind me. I spotted Susan sitting at our usual table talking to a young man. He was thin and pale and my heart went out to him. He looked like a little lost puppy. I waved at Susan and made a gesture to see if she would like a drink, she nodded. I bought two large Sherries and wove my way over to her.

'My God, it's bloody freezing out,' I complained and Susan nodded in agreement.

'This is Ivan Powell,' she said pointing towards the young man who sat beside her sipping at a weak pint of beer, 'he's not been living in Bristol very long, he's an ambulance driver,' she explained.

I turned and smiled at Ivan and he did the same. His wide grin immediately transformed his sad face. He now looked handsome and his light blue eyes twinkled in the light from the bulb. At around ten o'clock I got up to leave as both Susan and I were on the early shift. Susan explained she wanted a quick word with one of our colleagues standing at the bar. I said goodbye and told her that I would see her in the morning.

Ivan then asked if he could walk me home and I said I would love him to. It was much easier negotiating the darkened streets hanging onto his arm. We chatted a bit about our lives and Ivan told me that he lived in Cornwall where his parents ran a grocer's shop. He described how difficult it was for his mother and father to get enough stock to feed the village even with the help of rationing.

He also explained that he had been invalided out of the army after fighting in France. I felt his body shiver a little when he told me so I squeezed him a little tighter. I had heard lots of horror stories about what had happened to the men who were evacuated from Dunkirk at the beginning of the war and I knew he must have suffered a terrible ordeal.

When we arrived at my door, I told him he could come in if he kept quiet. His face was a picture of happiness as we crept up the narrow, creaky stairs to my bedroom. At times like this I was glad that my lovely landlady was a little deaf. Once we were inside my bedroom I put my finger to my lips to warn Ivan not to speak and then I slowly began to take off my clothes.

I couldn't help but smile as Ivan stood, awestruck, gazing at my naked body. I moved closer and whispered in his ear.

'Aren't you going to join me?'

I laughed again as Ivan struggled out of his clothes in record time. I ignored his extreme thinness and the scars on his body. I felt sure that if he'd wanted to talk to me about what had happened to him he would when he was ready. I lead him over to my narrow single bed. Ivan's lovemaking was quickly over. He kept apologising but soon shut up when I told him that we had all night to be together. At some point we both fell asleep snuggled up closely together. I liked the comfort of another body next to mind and I hoped Ivan would want to see me again.

When I met Susan outside the factory gates the next day, she asked me and how Ivan and I had got on. I grinned at her and she giggled loudly.

'You be gentle with him, he's had a tough time,' she told me as she linked my arm and walked into the building.

'I'll be as gentle as he likes,' I replied and we both walked into the building sniggering like schoolgirls.

# 21

I was hurrying home at the end of a particularly gruelling shift at the end of April. The weather mirrored my mood. The sky was graphite grey and threatening to drench me at any moment. The clouds were low and dark and the few people that were out and about were huddled into themselves trying to keep warm. As I was putting my key into to the lock the first splodges of rain began to fall and I rushed indoors.

A rumble of thunder made me tremble; it reminded me of an air raid. My lovely landlady had left my plate of dinner warming in the oven as she had gone out to the bingo. I was late now more often than not. The urgent need for aeroplanes meant I spent a lot of my time working overtime with the rest of the girls. It was tiring but I was happy to be doing my bit and was looking forward to meeting Geoffrey for a drink later on.

I pulled my cottage pie out of the cooker with some old, overused oven gloves and sat down at the little kitchen table to eat. I enjoyed every morsel and it wasn't until my plate was almost clean that I spotted the letter addressed to me sitting on the mantel piece. I put the kettle on the hob then walked over and picked up the letter. The writing was familiar but I couldn't place whose it was. It definitely wasn't Mabel's very neat joined up writing. I picked up the small silver letter opener, slit the envelope and unfolded the paper inside and read.

*My dearest Joyce*
*I miss you so deeply I can hardly breathe. Being apart from*

*you is a nightmare that I can't seem to wake up from. Every day I see your face and imagine making love to you. I wait eagerly until we meet again.*
*Yours forever my love*
*Bertie xxxxxxxxx*

I groped my way back to my chair. I felt physically sick. Those few words brought back all the heartbreak and sorrow that I had fought so hard to contain. I couldn't stop tears falling down my cheeks. It was very difficult for me to comprehend the utter heartless cruelty of the letter writer. How could anyone be so sick as to pretend to me that my Bertie was still alive? In a robot-like fashion I put the letter back in the envelope and pushed it behind the wooden clock on the mantle shelf. I made myself a strong cup of tea and added half a teaspoon of sugar. I'd read somewhere that hot, sweet tea was good for shock and I was thoroughly blown away by the correspondence.

I took my tea up to my room and put it on my dressing table then sat at the little stool in front. I began to put foundation then rouge on my face. Geoffrey had been kind enough to supply me with a decent amount of make-up. As I sat, I tried to ponder as to what type of person would do such a despicable thing. I knew Bertie was dead and that the letter hadn't come from him but it brought the agony back.

I looked into the mirror in front of me. I styled my hair in a victory roll then put bright scarlet lipstick on my full lips. As I took the last sip of my tea, I heard the familiar sound of the horn beeping from Geoffrey's car. I took a deep breath and walked towards the door. I grabbed my coat and gloves and hurried out into the cold evening air. I made up my mind that

I would not let the person who had posted the correspondence upset me. This was obviously their intention so if I let that happen they'd have won.

Geoffrey stood by the car with the passenger door open and I clambered in. I loved his little acts of chivalry. It made me feel like a film star, for a short while at least. Geoffrey headed out of the city and told me we were going to the little hotel out in the country. I smiled, I loved the place, and it made me forget that there was a war on. For a little while, I could pretend that I didn't spend most of my life up to my eyes in grease and muck assembling parts for aeroplanes.

Also, the hotel was very luxurious so while in residence, I pretended it was my home. I was glad to have my rented bedroom but it was very small and a little pokey and a million miles away from the splendour of the suite Geoffrey rented. After a lovely meal we retired to our room. I went into the *en-suite* bathroom to powder my nose and when I emerged I saw that Geoffrey and set up the pipe and bits that he had done last time we had smoked, what I now know, was opium.

I smiled as he beckoned me towards him. This time I would not inhale the vile stuff, I'd just play along to keep Geoffrey happy. I put the pipe to my lips and pretended to inhale although I kept my tongue firmly over the hole. When the pretence was over I giggled to make Geoffrey think I had actually inhaled the noxious substance. I watched as he ingested a huge dose and saw his body visibly relax. His upright shoulders stooped forwards and he smiled widely.

After a few more puffs we both stood up and lay on the bed. Geoffrey's eyes seemed to be twirling around and he was having difficulty focussing, this seems to amuse him somewhat. He put his hands in front of his eyes and started to wave them around as though he was swatting away a bad smell. I lay down and closed my eyes. I wanted him to think that I was as stoned as he was. He began to speak, in a slurred, kind of nostalgic sounding voice.

'She's only gone and joined the Auxiliary Territorial Service,' he laughed loudly then continued, 'What utter nonsense, do they expect us to believe that she will be getting her hands dirty?' He sighed and shook his head.

'What's that?' I asked, making my voice sound slurred.

'ATS, it's a division of the woman's armed forces, everyone doing their bit and all that,' he finished

I didn't say anything else. I didn't want him to think that I was trying to get information although that was exactly what I was trying to do. The opium that Geoffrey smoked obviously lowered his boundaries regarding the secrecy of his war work and I was determined to find out more, especially after listening to what Violet had told me what was going on in Germany regarding the Jewish population. Geoffrey took another deep gulp of opium and I pretended to do the same and waited.

'Have you heard the chap, Lord *Haw Haw*, on the wireless? I'm never sure if the stuff he comes out with is accurate or not but I think it may be,'

'No, I haven't actually heard him but the women in the factory talk about him, they say he's a dirty spy, I prefer 'It's that Man Again', with Tommy Handley, he's really funny,' I giggled, trying to keep up the charade.

'Hmmm, did you know the Police in Rio de Janeiro have smashed a Nazi spy ring with the arrest of over two hundred operatives,' Geoffrey garbled, 'Don't believe it, myself, load of rotten propaganda.'

I lay on the bed thinking. Surely it was a good thing if a load of Nazis had been arrested. Geoffrey seemed to think the opposite and I was becoming very uneasy with the conversation. I snored quietly to make him think I had fallen asleep, that way I would not have to comment on what he said either way. I heard him speak once more.

'Honorary Second Subaltern, what poppycock,' he mumbled almost inaudibly, 'that little madam will get her comeuppance.'

'Lizzie?' I enquired.

'Yes Lizzie and anyone who else gets in our way,' Geoffrey spat then fell into a deep sleep.

I lay there and tried to work out what to do. My lover's views were disturbing but were they just a fantasy in his addled, drug infused mind, or were they his actual thoughts? In these perilous times it was important that we all pulled together to bring an end to the war. Geoffrey wore his British uniform with pride but was it all a big cover-up to shield his actual views? I had no idea and the question just kept rolling over and over in my mind.

In the distance I could hear the thud of bombs dropping on some innocent household. I shivered and thanked God that I was out of harm's way. I wanted to cuddle up to Geoffrey and hold him closely so he would diminish my fears a little and help me through the air raid but I couldn't. I was sure Geoffrey was not everything he appeared to be but I had to be absolutely sure. I needed to find out who Lizzie was and warn her that her life may be in danger. I really wish I knew who to talk to about it but I had no idea where to start.

# 22

As August approached, the weather became more clement. The bitter cold winds that seemed to have been around for months hardly blew anymore and the greyness of the skies brightened. Birds began to soar above once more and sing their melodies. My life passed by in a whirl of work and overtime and more work. A lot of the time I was exhausted but I made sure I went out as many evenings as I could.

Ivan and I began to spend more time together. I knew he wanted ours to be an exclusive relationship because he was forever asking me to be 'his girl'. I always told him no, I was very fond of him and didn't want to mislead him in anyway. I told him that 'life was too short' to be tied to one person and if he had any sense, he would find other girlfriends also. I don't think that was what he wanted but if he wanted to carry on seeing me that was how it was going to be.

As we sat on a park bench one warmish evening, I decided to broach the subject of Geoffrey with Ivan. I trusted him not to pass on what I said and to, maybe, point me in the right direction about what exactly I should do with my knowledge. Ivan listened thoughtfully as I told him about my other lover's strange ramblings when he was drug induced and of his hatred of someone called Lizzie. I watched as Ivan thought for a while.

'Maybe you should go to the police?' Ivan suggested.

I told him that I had thought of that but Geoffrey seemed to be above the law. He was unaffected by the shortages that every other Bristolian had to endure. I voiced how he always had a full tank of petrol and could get his hands on almost anything I asked him for. I also explained that I felt utterly out of my depths. Ivan thought for a while once more than told me to 'leave it with him'. I was grateful for his help. I didn't want to be harbouring an enemy but neither did I want to make a fool of myself.

Ivan and I continued our relationship as the months passed by. He reminded me of a comfortable old jumper that I didn't want to throw away. He was caring and kind but I knew he was not the man for me, in the long term any way. I couldn't imagine myself settling down and becoming his wife after the war. That idea didn't appeal to me one bit. I received another letter in the post, apparently from Bertie but this one just made me angry.

I couldn't work out what went through someone's tiny mind. Why would anyone want to inflict hurt on another person? When Mabel next visited, I showed the letters to her. She read them with an odd expression on her face. I couldn't quite work out what it was. She grabbed both my hands and told me to burn the letters. I asked her if she thought I should go to the police. She quickly told me that she thought they had enough to do and to hang on and see if I got anymore letters. I told her I would.

It was chilly December day and the grey sky was cloudless as Mable and I walked into town. We were hoping to find a few Christmas bargains in the shops. Something stopped in our tracks as we rounded the corner. In front of us stood half a dozen men, they wore pristine uniforms with small wings on the shoulders. The clothing was a marked contrast to the British soldier. After four years of war, their clothes were old and faded.

The American soldiers wore a four pocket coat and trousers that were light olive in colour. Their wool shirts had two patch pockets and were a light tan shade. They also wore a mohair woollen necktie. They looked like someone who had just walked out of a Hollywood film set. They must have felt us gawping at them because they all turned around at the same time. Mabel and I flushed bright red and giggled awkwardly.

'Well, good afternoon ladies, Corporal Max Cavendish from the United States Airforce, how do you do?'

I stood, almost transfixed, by these handsome young men. They seemed full of optimism and confidence. Most of the population, myself included, had been ground down by the war. The constant air raids and loss of fighting men made most of us subdued and thoughtful. These men were like a breath of fresh air, I held my hand out.

'I'm Joyce and this is my friend, Mabel,' I gushed

Instead of shaking my hand he lifted it to his mouth and gently brushed the back of it with his soft lips. I was immediately captivated. That small gesture made me feel like a princess.

'Very pleased to meet you mam,' he said as he smiled widely, showing a straight set of white teeth,' you too mam, he said to Mabel as he kissed her hand also. 'Do you ladies happen to know any places to go around here, we only arrived a few days ago and are still finding our feet,'

'There's always the pub but they sometimes run out of drinks,' I answered, trying to think of somewhere a little better, I thought for a while then remembered a club that Ivan had told me about. It was in some underground tunnels that made it one of the safest places to be.

'The Warren is a good place to go,' I said confidently, even though I'd never actually been there.

'In that case, would you like to accompany me there?' Max Cavendish asked me.

I didn't hesitate. The thought of walking out with an American was beyond exciting. We arranged to meet on New Year's Eve outside a nearby cafe. When another of the chaps asked Mabel for a date, she had to decline as she was leaving the following day for the farm to continue her duty as a land girl. As we walked back to my room, I chatted enthusiastically about my date. Mabel moaned that she, also, could have been going out with an American if only she didn't have to get back.

The Americans had joined the war in the previous in December when the Japanese had bombed Pearl Harbour. We had not seen any in this country until now. I told Mabel that I thought there would be plenty more Americans coming to this country in the future to help us win the war. The farm where she worked was close to an, as yet, unused naval base. I pointed this out to Mabel and said maybe the Americans would be billeted at the place. If so, this meant that she would have more than her fair share of foreign partners. She happily agreed.

Meeting the American airmen had quickly taken my mind away from the nasty letters. I decided to take Mabel's advice and let the matter lie as long as I didn't receive any more of the wicked correspondence. I couldn't wait to meet Susan and tell her about my day. The arrival of a new batch of fresh and ambitious military men had lifted my spirits no end. Hopefully this was the beginning of the end of Hitler's ruthless and violent attempt to take over the world.

I was counting the days until my date with max Cavendish. I was so looking forward to my date with my dashing airman that

I could scarcely contain my excitement. It was lunchtime and Ivan and I were in the red Lion having a drink. Ivan scowled when I told him about my evening plans. I didn't tell him who I was going with but he guessed it was another man. He did concede though that the venue, The Warren, was one of the safest places to go. Ivan was working on the ambulance shift that New Year's Eve. He was none too happy to be working on that evening but I told him he wasn't alone. I kissed him good-bye then headed home with big grin plastered across my face.

As I gently pushed my way through the throng of shoppers heading home I was sure I saw Mabel's mum, my old next door neighbour but I must have been mistaken. She would be at home in Plymouth preparing the home for the festive season. I felt a momentary stab of sadness that I was no longer part of that precious family.

I quickly pulled myself out of the doldrums when I spotted a pair of pearl earrings on a second-hand stall I had wanted some for ages and managed to get them at a knock-down price. All was good in my world once more.

# 23

I sat and ate an early tea with my lovely landlady. I was constantly surprised at how she managed to make such delicious meals with all the rationing that was now in place everywhere. I'd told her about my date with the American air man and she seemed as excited as I was. Her faded blue eyes shone as she told me she wanted to know every detail of my evening out the following morning at breakfast.

Upstairs I put on a chiffon 'swing' style dress. The main body of it was dark purple with little lilac cuffs and collar. I wore high heeled ivory court shoes with a matching and handbag. My new earrings finished off my outfit well. I applied some dark purple lipstick to finish off my make-up and was pleased with the reflection that stared back out from the mirror. I needed to get the bus to the nightclub and allowed myself plenty of time to walk to my stop. My dangerously high heels were a little difficult to walk in.

Finally, the bus trundled to a stop opposite the Warren Nightclub. Butterflies danced eagerly around my stomach as I began to daydream about a new life in America with a handsome pilot. I was a little early but so, to my surprise was my date, Max Cavendish. He wolf whistled appreciatively as I stepped down from the bus. As we were both early we decided to go for a cup of tea in a teashop a short distance away.

We sat at a window table and chatted comfortably to each other. Max told me that he had four younger sisters waiting at home for him. His father worked at a car show room, he explained as he pulled a photo out of his wallet. I looked at it and immediately thought that he took after his mother's side of the family. They both had strawberry blonde hair and piercing blue eyes. His sisters and father had darker hair but the same coloured eyes.

I loved listening to his American accent. He had a genuine and warm smile. When he asked me about my family I made up a story about my parents and younger brother who lived in Plymouth and I explained that we were a really happy family and I missed them all tremendously but had moved to Bristol to do my bit for the war effort.

When we got up to leave, he paid the bill and pulled my small hand into his large paw. I was shocked that his hand was not rough and work-worn like most men's hands were. His palms were as soft a silk and fingers had a far better manicure than I had seen on any woman. I happily led the way into the Warren. The bulb must have been broken because it was practically dark as we felt our way down the three flights of stairs. There was a marked contrast when we finally came to the big double doors, that opened out into the bar area.

The place was not only well lit but bright and prettily decorated with Christmas lights and colourful ribbons. The room was enormous and this was a good thing because there were a lot of people in the place. A band played at the far end of the room on a makeshift stage. Alongside one wall was a bar that seemed amazingly well stocked. I wondered where on earth they could have found that amount of alcohol. On closer inspection I realised that a lot of the bottles were empty and just put in place for 'show'.

Max guided me to a table and wove his way over to the bar

to get some drinks. He returned with a glass of port for me and a pint of beer for himself. The atmosphere in the place was electric. A lot of couples were dancing on the floor in front of the band. Most were simply doing the waltz or foxtrot, but some were actually doing a dance called the jive that the factory girls had told me about. The men were actually hurling the girls around the room.

I looked on and longed to be able to jive. I turned to see Max looking at me then he smiled and said he could teach me the dance. I immediately stood up, nodding at the same time. He began to show me the moves and I picked them up pretty quickly. My high heels were starting to hamper my movements, so I kicked them off. For the next joyous half hour I was thrown up and down and from side to side like a rag doll. It was exhilarating. I felt free and full of happiness and hope.

For that wonderful time I could forget about the war and everything. Tonight I was just going to dance the night away and worry about tomorrow when it arrived. We walked back to the table and reclaimed our drinks. I was breathless and grinned widely at Max. I decided that I liked him in a casual way, not as the potential husband I dreamed about on the bus journey. I got the impression he wasn't after anything too serious either and that suited me just fine.

My wonderful evening was destroyed in a millisecond when a tremendous explosion rocked the building. I actually felt the concrete floor shake beneath my feet. The band became quiet. Everyone stopped what they were doing; it was as though time had frozen. After what seemed like an age but could have only been seconds, someone shouted that we were 'as safe as houses' down in The Cavern. The next minute I felt my arm being tugged frantically. I turned to see that Max had stood up. He was trying to pull me out of my seat but I was dazed and frightened.

I could hear a noise that started off like a curtain swishing shut then it began to escalate in volume. I turned to Max; he bodily hoisted me from my seat and hurled me towards the dancefloor. I felt myself flying through the air; I was winded when I hit the floor. Then a sound like a massive thunderclap reverberated around the room. It was so loud I put my hands over my ears and closed my eyes. I was afraid of what was to come.

The silence that followed was, in my mind, worse than the noise. It was eerie and terrifying. I slowly lifted my head up. I watched as some of the people who had obviously dived to the ground for cover begin gingerly lifting themselves up and then began checking their bodies for injuries. I did the same. I realised that I was absolutely covered in a fine, grey dusting of concrete powder. I shook my head and sneezed when the powder went up my nose.

I pulled myself up with the help of a nearby chair and found myself uninjured. I shouted to Max. There was no answer so I turned to where I had last seen him. He was lying on the floor. Only the top half of his body was visible, the bottom half was hidden under the remains of the wall. I raced over and bent down.

'Max, are you ok?' I asked as I gently shook his warm body.

His head lulled to one side and I saw his non-seeing eyes staring into nothingness. I screamed and began to sob. How many more were going to be killed before this horrific war came to an end? I felt myself being helped to my feet and was then guided to a chair. I sat down and clasped my hands in my lap. I let my tears fall; Max had died saving my life. The poor man would never again go home to be with his family. I felt like some kind of jinx.

I became aware that a group of men were hammering at the wall that was still standing. I looked around and what I saw almost paralysed me. There were about twenty of us and we were all entombed in a tiny space which was all that was left of The Cavern. I felt as though I couldn't breathe. Dust cloyed up the air and the heat of several bodies in one little area made me sweat. I could see the remains of the dead and dying and felt agonisingly helpless.

# 24

It felt like I had been sitting on the chair listening to indistinct chatter for hours but it could only have been minutes. Such was the stifling atmosphere we would all have suffocated if we had been trapped for that long. I couldn't make out what the male voices were saying; I just hoped they would be able to get us out of here. I couldn't stop looking at Max. He seemed to be staring back at me, silently asking me why he was dead.

Then, like something wonderful I had conjured up out of my imagination, I looked up to see Ivan standing over me. I blinked twice to make sure it was not some figment of my mind's eye but he was still there. His kind and concerned eyes stared into mine and he put his hand out as if to pull me up off the chair.

'I can't leave,' I told him. 'Max is dead because of me,' I turned to the body that was trapped under the collapsed wall.

'Max is dead because of Hitler, it was nothing that you did Joyce,' Ivan said soothingly.

'He saved my life,' I stuttered as fresh tears dropped down my face.

'If you don't leave, Joyce, his sacrifice will have been for nothing,' Ivan lent closer and lowered his voice, 'I can smell gas Joyce, we have to leave and quickly.'

I knew that he was right and stood slowly up while holding Ivan's hand. Just as I did this a fountain of flames shot out of a gap in the wall and I screamed as my flimsy dress was engulfed by them. Ivan immediately ripped of his jacket and smothered them in seconds. I did not feel any pain and stood, like a small child in need of attention, as Ivan then tied his jacket around my waist to contain my modesty.

Ivan then bent down and gently closed Max's eyes. I heard him thank him then he grabbed my hand and headed for the opening they had made in the wall. Ivan yelled at everyone to follow him as quickly as possible. I held onto Ivan as tightly as I could, at this moment it was only him that stood between me and death. He led us through a range of long, dark tunnels. At one point he seemed confused then suddenly, it was as though he remembered the way out and hurried onwards.

We finally came to the end of the final tunnel and above us was a small window. This was our escape route. Wasting no time at all, Ivan yelled for help and the other men joined him. A face appeared at the window and ordered us to climb out as quickly as we could. I felt myself being lifted into the air and I put my hands up and grasped the ones that were reaching down to me. The cold air hit me in the face like a welcome blanket.

I staggered away from the window as quickly as I could to let the rescuers pull the remaining survivors out. I sat down on the cool grass to wait for Ivan. I counted twenty-one people being pulled out of the stifling tomb. Finally I saw Ivan's head appear. Suddenly, there was an almighty explosion and Ivan was tossed in the air like an old rag doll. I screamed but could not make myself go over to where he landed. I was frightened what I would find.

I watched as a portly ambulance man raced over to the prostrate figure of my rescuer. I was flooded with an avalanche of relief as I saw Ivan begin to flail his arms around and try and lift himself off the ground. Once he had calmed down he was loaded onto a stretcher and carried to one of the many waiting ambulances. The man that had gone to Ivan's aid now came to mine and led me towards the vehicle they had just loaded him into.

I sat on the bench opposite the stretcher as the door was closed behind me. I could not contain my trembling body. I was embarrassed at the ferocity of my quivering but there was nothing I could do to stop it. Then I felt a warm, comforting hand cover mine and I turned to see Ivan smiling up at me. Finally my body stilled and I clung onto his hand like a limpet stuck onto a rock. I had come through another nightmare.

# 25

I spent a few days in hospital as my wounds had become infected, probably from the grass I sat on as I waited for Ivan. It was not until we'd almost reached the hospital that the pain of my burns began to hit me. When I was in danger, it was as though I was numb but now I was safe, it felt like my body needed to remind me that I had been injured. I squirmed on the uncomfortable bench and shrieked every time the ambulance hit a pot hole.

I was very relieved to be lying face down on a hospital bed with ointment and bandages covering my injuries. The pain had become so unbearable it had actually made me vomit but I was comfortable now and alive. Although my dreams were peppered with dead bodies and explosions I was still happy to be alive, the following morning. I was discharged as quickly as was medically safe to do so. I felt that the doctors would have kept me in longer, had the hospital not been full to capacity after the air raid.

My kindly landlady, Mrs Groves, caught the bus and met me outside the hospital. This small act of kindness humbled me to the point of tears and I bent down and hugged the little old lady. I was genuinely happy to see her and over joyed that she had survived the raid. She explained that she had managed to knit a cardigan sleeve as she took refuge under the stairs as the bombs dropped around her.

When we arrived home, we feasted on cottage pie and carrots, followed by apple crumble and watery custard. The food tasted delicious and even the weak tea tasted like nectar. I was giddily happy that I was alive and hoped all my workmates and friends were also. I knew that Susan and Violet were fine as they had visited me in hospital. I hoped that Mabel, my childhood friend and neighbour was all right. Working on a farm some way out of the city meant that she was more than likely safe.

I was allowed the following two days off of work to let my injuries to heal. I woke the following morning and felt rested. Sleeping in my own bed was comforting and warm. The New Year had begun while I was in hospital. My landlady told me that dreadful night most of the city had been under attack and many lives had been lost. I again, had been spared and uttered a prayer of thanks before I went to bed that night.

The following morning, I had an unaccustomed lie-in and then I padded down the stairs in my slippers. I found some porridge warming on the stove. I ladled some into a bowl then poured myself a cup of from the large, brown earthenware teapot that stood on the warming plate. I told myself that I could get used to doing nothing as I ate and drank without the usual bolting down of food and drink. I usually stayed in bed too long then I would have to rush everything to make sure I got to the factory in time to start my shift.

Just as I had finished my meal I heard the jangle of the letter box as the post was pushed through. I got up gently so as not to cause any more damage to my injured legs and retrieved the post from the mat. There was an airmail letter addressed to Mrs Groves and a few bills, obvious by their brown envelopes. The last letter sent shivers down my spine. I tore it open and unfolded the single piece of paper inside and read,

*My dearest Joyce*
*I smell your sweet perfume*
*And call out your name*
*My life will be empty*
*Until I see you again*
*Love Bertie x*

I shivered but I was far from cold. I was wearing a winceyette night dress and a thick dressing gown over the top. The thing the chilled me the most was the writing. It was very similar to Bertie's and whoever wrote it must know that he penned poetry for me. I decided that I would take the letters and go to the police. I was beginning to feel like someone wanted me to go mad. I knew Bertie was dead and this was some kind of sick game someone was playing.

I put the rest of the post on the hall stand then padded back up the stairs to get dressed. My leisurely day had been ruined by the sender of the correspondence and I was annoyed with myself for allowing it to do so. I put on a long pencil skirt to cover my bandages and some low- heeled court shoes. I then put on a blue silk blouse that Geoffrey had given me as an early Christmas present. I then pulled on a warm cardigan that had been knitted by Mrs Groves and headed back downstairs.

I picked up my gas mask and handbag then walked down the hallway towards the coat stand. I almost jumped out of my skin when someone knocked loudly on the door, dropping my gas mask at the same time. I pulled open the door and was over joyed to see Mabel standing there smiling widely.

'You going somewhere?' she asked, as she looked at the coat I was about to put on.

I quickly pulled her indoors. It was a freezing cold day and I didn't want the chill to seep into the warmth of the house. I hung my coat back up onto the hall stand, Mabel did the same with her outer garments, and I then gestured for her to follow me into the kitchen. Once we were sat in front of the warm range I handed her the letter I had received. Mabel went a little pale as she read it.

'I was going down to the police station, there's some sick person out there intent on making me miserable and I'm going to put a stop to it,' I declared

Mabel looked at me.

'Why don't you just throw it away?' She asked but her eyes would not meet mine. I instinctively knew that Mabel knew something about the letters. I thought back to the times I had shown her the previous letters. I realised that she seemed very reluctant for me to contact the police then.

'I think you had better tell me what's going on,' I told Mabel as she sat with her head down gazing at the letter, she sighed.

'It's mother,' she said barely above a whisper.

I gasped, I knew Mabel's mother hated me but I didn't think she would do something as downright nasty as sending poison pen letters. All the letters had been delivered by hand because there was no stamp on the envelope. I thought back to a few weeks before when I thought I'd seen Mrs Johnson in the marketplace.

'Why?' I asked Mabel, feeling totally bewildered and terribly upset. I knew I had hurt Mrs Johnson by being with Bertie but why would she want to wage such a terrible vendetta against me, what could she possibly gain from it? I felt a tear drop down my face and quickly swiped it away.

I'm still going to the police, I can't believe that she could turn so nasty, She's been a like a mother to me but to do this'…. I trailed of and let my tears fall.

Mabel pulled her chair closer to mine then leant forward and hugged me. I sobbed on her shoulder; I liked the feeling of warmth and comfort her embrace was giving me. When my tears subsided she got up and poured us both a cup of tea. I sipped at my drink and it soothed me a little, but I was still at a loss to understand Mrs Johnson's motives. Mabel began to speak.

'Two years ago, the bombing around the docks became so dangerous that my father decided that my sisters needed to be evacuated to a place of safety, my mother didn't argue because she wanted them to be safe but I knew she was heartbroken. All she ever wanted was to be a mother and we all meant the world to her, now our home seemed to her like an empty, echoing shell.'

She paused for a moment then continued;

'Every time I saw her she seemed more and more distraught, the straw that broke the camel's back was when the call up came for my dad, she couldn't hide her distress and begged him not to go but he had no choice, I promised him I would visit her as often as I could and told him to take care of himself and not to worry, I thought he would have enough to contend with without fretting about Mum,'

'Are your dad and sisters are alright?' I asked Mabel.

'The girls are absolutely fine,' she said and smiled brightly, 'they love life in the countryside, they write all the time and tell me about what's going on in their lives and how happy they are to be away from the bombing. I don't know exactly where dad is but I got a letter from him the day before yesterday and he said he'd made lots of friends and was proud to be serving his country,' she continued as she pulled a photo of her father out of her handbag. He looked very smart in his army uniform, I handed it back to her.

'What about your mother?'

Mabel looked down and sighed. I visited her as often as I could, like I promised, but she began to act strange. On one visit I found her ironing my sisters school dresses, she said they were starting a new term and no child of hers would walk through the school gates looking anything but tidy, I told her that the girls had been in the countryside for the last eighteen odd months. She got angry and started telling me off for lying then said that she would get dad to have a word with me when he got home from work. When I told her that dad was in the army she slapped my face,' Mabel looked so full of sadness that I felt it was my turn to give her a hug which she gladly accepted.

'To cut a long story short, I went to see the doctor and he advised that she shouldn't be left on her own. My dad has a sister living in Bristol so it was arranged that she would go and live with her until we all come home when the war is over,' Mabel explained.

'What about your house?' I enquired.

'I've rented it out to a young family that had been bombed out,' she told me.

I sat and thought a while. All this had been going on in Mabel's life and I knew nothing about it. I was quite sure she had been trying to shield me from any heart ache because of what happened to Bertie. I was angry with myself for being selfish and not taking the care to ask how Mabel was getting on. I looked up.

'I've not been a very good friend to you Mabel and you've been marvellous to me and I'm very ashamed of myself, I'll give the letters to you and you can burn them, what unnerved me most was how similar the handwriting was and the fact that someone knew he wrote poetry for me, now I know your mother looked in the box before bringing it up to the hospital to me, at least that mystery is solved.'

We both remained where we were, lost for a little while in our own thoughts. So much had happened over the past two years it was difficult to take everything in. We decided that we would treat ourselves to lunch at the Lyons tea shop. As we walked arm in arm, snuggling together to keep the cold out, I felt closer to Mabel than I had in a long time. I was still angry with myself for not being a kinder friend to her but I resolved to do better in the future.

I could not keep blaming the war and Bertie's death for my behaviour. Every person in Britain was suffering while Hitler continued his assault on us. I was not the only one who had lost people I loved. I had come to terms with Bertie dying but had become a little selfish and self-absorbed along the way and only thought about myself and my own happiness. I told Mabel, as we tucked into our spam sandwiches what I thought about myself and she assured me that I was one of the best friends a girl could want.

After lunch I walked her to the train station and waved until it had steamed out of sight. I walked back home and felt a good deal lighter, mentally. I hadn't realised how much the letters had been upsetting me. I felt sorry for Mrs Johnson but also angry that she had felt the need to hurt me in some way. I hoped that when the family were back together again, her broken mind would mend. I intended to visit Ivan in the hospital later in the day, so I wandered around the shops while I waited for visiting time to commence.

Luckily there was nothing much I needed. The shop windows looked to be in short supply of just about everything. It must have been hard for the shop keepers to make a living with all the rationing and shortages. I tried not to be despondent but I couldn't help but wonder when the war would end so everyone could return to their families and continue with their lives without fear.

# 26

The flowers that Geoffrey had sent me were now beginning to wilt. They were a beautiful cacophony of colours and smells; I couldn't imagine where he could have found such a beautiful bouquet. I also didn't know how he knew that I'd been injured but he must have found out some way. It was now Thursday morning and I was very much looking forward to spending the weekend with Geoffrey but this afternoon I was going up to the hospital to visit Ivan Powell, the wonderful man who had rescued us from The Cavern nightclub.

The sky was now a dirty grey colour as I made my way to the bus stop. I pushed my gloved hands into my coat pockets to try and warm them up. It looked to me like rain was in the air and that was good thing in times of war. The enemy never flew in bad weather so that would ensure our safety. There was nothing quite so terrifying, in my mind, as a bright moon glistening in a star-studded night sky. It turned us all into sitting ducks with very few places to hide from Hitler's bombers.

I believed that, even if I lived to be a hundred, I would never understand how one small man could wreak such havoc on the world and his fellow man. I could not comprehend what could be going through the warped mind of a German pilot when he unleashed his deadly load on innocents down below. They truly must be the devil reincarnated and we had to do everything in our power to ensure they didn't win the war.

I had been speaking to Violet a couple of evenings ago and she explained that her husband, Len and his brother Michael had been trying to find news of their parents for many years. Both men had fled Germany in 1932 when they were just young boys. Their parents had given them the means to do this and both boys owed them their lives. Now, they were increasingly worried. Len's parents were German Jews and Hitler was intent on wiping the Jewish race off the planet.

Violet explained that both boys now actually hoped that their parents were dead and not living in the horrendous conditions that had been forced upon them by the Nazis. There were rumours about them being herded together into ghettos and even worse, gassed to death at camps specifically designed to snuff out anyone Hitler decided was not fit to be part of his frightening master race. I knew I could never live under the command of such a monster and prayed to God that it would not happen.

The bus finally ground to a halt outside the hospital and as I stepped the vehicle, the first few drops of rain began to dance down from the sky. I quickly mounted the steps and pushed open the two double doors. The warmth inside the building was a thankful contrast to the cold outside and I quickly shed my outdoor clothing. The hospital was painted pristine white and was very brightly lit. All the uniformed personnel were going about their business in a very orderly manner.

I arrived at the door of the men's ward just as the bell sounded out to indicate that 'visiting time' was about to commence. I made my way down the ward and walked pass the rows of beds to where I knew Ivan would be. I had visited him when I was in hospital. Once he spotted me, he waved a bandaged hand and smiled widely. I reached his bedside and leant down to give him a peck on the cheek. This made his smile wider and his eyes sparkled.

Both Ivan's hands had been badly damaged in the explosion. His left wrist was plastered and also in a sling and his right hand was heavily bandaged. His face was dotted with small cuts and bruises and a metal cage at the foot of his bed kept the blankets off his burned feet. The nurse wheeled a trolley down the ward carrying cups of tea and I grabbed one each for me and Ivan. We chatted about mundane things like the weather and rationing as I held his tea to his lips so he could drink it.

I laughed as I noticed him wink at a petite nurse as she tidied his bed.

'I saw that Ivan Powell,' I said grinning at him with mock sternness on my face, Ivan grinned back.

'Aren't you the one who is always saying that we should live for today and have fun?' he teased.

'Indeed, I am Ivan and now you know I'm right,' we both laughed, Ivan was such a lovely man, I knew he'd meet someone who was right for him some day.

I then I spotted that his water jug was empty and picked it up and made my way to the nurse's station to get it filled.

When I returned a few minutes later Ivan had another visitor at his bedside. She turned as she heard my heels clicking along the floor. I could see that she was a young girl with a heart-shaped face and strawberry blonde hair. I leant over her and put the now filled water jug on the bed side table and asked Ivan if he would like some water. He shook his head and introduced me to his visitor.

'This is Cissy, she lives in Treruth in Cornwall,' he turned to Cissy.

'Cissy, this is Joyce,' Ivan finished.

Cissy looked me up and down and I could tell that she

had taken an instant dislike to me. I looked back at her and smiled, I was quite used to the disapproving looks of people who didn't know me and it was now *'water off a duck's back'*. I wondered exactly what part of me she didn't like, was it my yellow blonde hair or my blood-red lipstick? It could well be my heavy mascara that made my eyelashes resemble curved spider's legs or my tightly fitted pencil-style dress. I guess I would never know which it was, neither did I care.

I sat on the edge of the bed and we all indulged in a little small talk about the weather and the war. These were the subjects that dominated the minds of the British people at present, the war in particular. When I glanced at Cissy I noticed that she was looking at Ivan with undisguised adoration and was hanging onto his every word. The penny dropped. It didn't matter what I was wearing or what I looked like. She was obviously in love with Ivan and assumed that I was his girlfriend and I guess I was, in a way.

After around ten minutes, Cissy stood and said she had to leave to catch her bus. I knew she was lying. The town's buses had a regular route to the hospital and could be caught at fifteen-minute intervals and there was another twenty minutes before visiting time was over. Cissy leant over and patted Ivan's bandaged hand and told him to write to her regularly. Ivan promised he would.

Once Cissy was out of sight I told Ivan that I too must be making a move. Ivan lowered his voice to a whisper and said that he had news regarding my predicament with Geoffrey. I told him that I would be back the following day and that we would talk about it then. I knew that it was important to report my suspicions about Geoffrey to the authorities but I desperately wanted to catch up with the sad-faced girl before she headed back to Cornwall. I had suffered heartbreak and I could see it etched on every feature of her tiny face.

I pulled my winter coat around me when I had exited the hospital. The wind was buffeting around me and I had to dodge flying rubbish and people hurrying around with their heads down to keep out of the weather. I spotted Cissy at the bus stop just as the vehicle was approaching. I sprinted towards it as quickly as my high heels would allow.

As it came to a stop, I heaved myself onto the vehicle. Tottering up the narrow aisle I saw where Cissy was sitting and plonked down next down next to her. To say that she wasn't pleased to see me was an understatement. She looked as though she wanted to scratch my eyes out, but she smiled sweetly instead. She then turned to face me.

'How long have you and Ivan been stepping out?' she asked, as her smile tightened involuntarily, I smiled down at her.

'Well, we're not really stepping out,' I explained, 'I have lots of boyfriends,' I told her.

First, her face had a puzzled expression as if she was trying to digest the news, then she smiled.

'I see,' she said, 'the way things are at the moment, it doesn't really do to get serious with a bloke,' she agreed in her cockney accent.

'Precisely,' I replied, 'I know you're in love with Ivan, I was in love once too, men are a little slow and I'm quite sure he doesn't have a clue about how you feel, give him time and it'll suddenly come to him, like a lightbulb in his head and he'll realise that he's in love with you too.' I concluded. Cissy giggled.

'I doubt that,' she said as a deep crimson blush spread from her forehead to her neck. We then carried on a pleasant conversation as the bus trundled back towards the centre of Bristol.

Susan was waiting at the bus stop for Cissy, like the young girl had said she would be. I watched as Susan rushed forward and pulled Cissy into her arms. The bus pulled away and Susan was obviously surprised to see me standing there. I quickly explained how Cissy and I had met while visiting Ivan at the hospital. Susan asked how he was and I told her that he was well on the mend and enjoying the attention from all the pretty young nurses.

Susan smiled as she linked one of her arms in Cissy's and the other in mine. The three of us then strolled purposefully onwards taking up the width of the unevenly tiled pavement as we chatted animatedly about life in general. We arrived at Susan's billet after a short walk. Once inside the warmth of her room, we drank hot, warming tea and ate broken biscuits in companionable silence while our bodies thawed out.

When we were a little warmer I listened as Susan asked Cissy about her children, Cissy's brother Alan and life at Carmarthen Farm. Cissy painted a joyful picture for Susan to cling onto but also explained that Susan was missed sorely by all the family. A bit later on Susan heated up a large tin of broth and we all tucked into delicious bowls of oxtail soup with chunks of the 'national loaf' of bread. The loaf was not very tasty but quite filling and the meal thawed us all out nicely, as well as the little paraffin heater in the corner of the room. With our meal over we began to discuss what we would do this evening.

There was nothing much we all fancied at the cinema, so we decided on drinks at the Red Lion pub. Susan, playfully, began to tease me about who I would be meeting after we had had our drinks; she reeled off a list of various men's names. We both laughed, amicably, and Cissy joined in. Cissy then told us that she was looking forward to an evening out and was glad that she had packed her smart dress and Edith's high heels. It was very rare for her to enjoy an evening with friends.

She explained that as much as she loved Johnny and Alan, having a little time to herself was something new and exciting. The room darkened as we chatted. I looked out of the window and saw that the sky was cobalt grey and getting darker by the second. I told Susan that I would make my way home before the heavens opened and left to begin the short walk home.

As I walked, I wondered what Ivan had to tell me regarding Geoffrey. I was meeting him at the weekend, and we were going to our favourite hotel. I was very much looking forward to getting away from the war-torn city and indulging in a spot of luxury even if it was only for a short time. I hoped Ivan had come up with an answer to my dilemma and I really wanted to be wrong about Geoffrey. However, I decided, time would tell, and I began to concentrate on the here and now and what I would wear that evening.

## 27

Cissy, Susan and I chatting animatedly as we walked, arm in arm, to the pub to meet Violet. I had decided to wear a lilac pencil skirt with a yellow blouse. The two colours complimented each other, and I was glad I had chosen the outfit. My high heels hindered my walking a little, but Cissy was also struggling with her footwear, so we all held each other up and helped one another along the way. The icy wind swirled around us and we all glad to arrive at our destination.

I was greatly relieved once I was ensconced inside the cosy pub and out of the bitter cold weather. I brought two gin and tonics and a glass of lemonade for Cissy and carried them over to our usual table where Cissy and Susan were already sitting, Violet had yet to arrive. Susan told us that she had not heard a thing from Edward for several months and was worried was for his safety.

She could only surmise that he had been posted a long way away and was unable to write. She also hoped that no news was good news. Both Cissy and I assured her that this was the case but in reality, we had no clue, all we could do was be there for Susan if anything terrible had happened to her husband.

Out of the corner of my eye I spotted the familiar face of two American airmen as they gently pushed their way through the throng of people to where we were all sitting. Both Susan and I were obviously pleased to see the men as both of us grinned widely as they asked if they could join us.

Susan introduced one of the men to Cissy as Jimmy Fairly

while the other headed for the bar to get some drinks. He quickly returned and I began to introduce him to Cissy as Donny Costello. I had been on a couple of dates with him and found his American accent quite charming. The uniformed man sighed heavily then pointed out that his name was actually Danny and implored me to try and remember this while uttering *jeez* under his breath.

There was muted giggling and I apologised to Danny for getting his name wrong, then we all sat down to enjoy our drinks. The pub was a very old building with walls at least three feet thick and wooden beams criss-crossed along a once white painted ceiling that was now tinged yellow with cigarette smoke. It was a cosy place that was alive with the hum of laughter and friendly chatter.

I looked across at Cissy, she was staring at the couple next her and I could see by the expression on her face that she was surprised at how close Jimmy and Susan sat next to each other. She later whispered to me that if she didn't know Susan was married, she would have jumped to the conclusion that she and Jimmy were boyfriend and girlfriend. She then decided that it was none of her business and proceeded to enjoy the evening, conversing with people of a similar age to her and also enjoying the break from childcare.

Without warning the screeching cat-like sound of the air raid siren screamed loudly to warn of us all of the approaching attack. With minimal fuss or panic we all began to make our way down the narrow, uneven concrete steps into the basement. Violet arrived just at that time and joined the crowd making its careful way down the uneven steps.

Cissy clutched her drink and told me what a pleasant surprise she had when she reached the room underneath the pub. When we arrived at the foot of the stairs she grinned when she realised the basement had been turned into a make shift inn. There was a barrel of beer in the left hand corner, and in the centre of the room was an old piece of green and red patterned carpet. This added a little comfort and hid the dull, concrete floor.

A sturdy table acted as a make-shift bar that served gin and sherry and there was also a tea urn for non- drinkers. A wind-up gramophone stood in the other corner opposite the beer barrel and various sofas and chairs were dotted around the room covered in old blankets and assorted cushions.

Susan led Cissy to a settee against the far wall while Danny proceeded to steer me in the same direction. My body began to tremble, as it always did during an air raid, and there was nothing I could do to still it. The feel of Danny's strong arms on my shoulders helped to quell my panic a little and I was grateful for his thoughtfulness.

The memories of the previous attacks returned with full force causing me to endure a terrible, suffocating anxiety which I did my best to ease with deep breaths and glugs of gin. Dear Susan clung tightly onto my hand and Cissy placed a comforting arm around my shaking shoulders. I could also see the terror etched deeply into the features of Cissy's face and immediately began to wonder what horrors she had had to endure during this long and exhausting war.

Susan asked if I had seen Jimmy, but I shook my head. A few minutes later the man himself hurried through the door carrying an elderly man over his shoulders. Danny rushed over to help him and they both lowered the ageing gent down onto the nearest available seat. They both then pushed the heavy cellar door shut and looked around the room.

Just minutes after the alert sounded the droning sound of enemy planes could be heard approaching menacingly. Jimmy and Danny explained that they had to leave and head back to base to see if there was anything they could do to help.

They were about to do this when an enormous explosion shook the building and knocked the people still standing, including Danny and Jimmy, to their knees. It blew the wooden doors open and a torrent of dust raced into the room. Both airmen quickly stood and hastily shoved shut the thick wooden cellar door once more then began to drag one of the large sofas towards it to block it shut.

Grey grime now covered most of the people in the room and we all began to brush ourselves down while coughing and sput-tering at the same time. I couldn't stop myself from weeping quietly; the terror I felt was like an ever tightening strait-jacket wrapped around my body. Susan leant over and pulled me into her soothing embrace. She also began to talk to me and the gentleness of her voice began to calm me a little.

When I finally found a semblance of composure, I turned to look around the room. Most of the facial expressions showed some nervousness or apprehension. I noticed Cissy looking in the direction of old Ernie, the man Jimmy had carried down the steps. He had slumped forward in his seat. Cissy rose and walked towards him. It seemed to me as if she was walking in slow motion but I don't really think she was. I guessed she was going over to offer the poor old gentleman some comfort.

I watched as she touched his shoulder and shook him gently. He didn't respond so she put her hand under his chin and care-fully lifted his head up. I couldn't stop another tear trickling down my face as we both found ourselves peering into Ernie's lifeless grey eyes.

With overwhelming sadness, etched into her face, Cissy lovingly closed the unseeing eyes. She then picked up an old candle wick bed spread, which was folded onto the back of one of the equally old armchairs, and covered his body with it. As the noise of the planes reverberated around the room, I wondered if the cellar was to become our tomb and hoped that someone would take care of my loved ones if that should happen.

Another deafening blast shook the building once more. I watched as Cissy clutched her lemonade. It now had a film of murky grime floating on the top. When the noise subsided a little she returned to her seat. The landlady, of the pub began to wind up the gramophone and quite quickly the notes of some delightfully cheerful dance music began to fill the room. Some couples got up to dance, others just sat close to each other. Cissy and I began to hum along as we waited patiently for the dreadfulness to end.

The raid was a long one and when the all clear finally rang out I was stiff and tired and longed to be in my cosy bed. It was now almost three o'clock in the morning. As we all trudged to our respective billets we all hugged as we parted, thankful that, once more, we had survived another night of German onslaught. It was colder still now, and I shivered as I walked the last bit of my journey home. My winter coat was thick and lined but the cold still seemed to find a way of creeping underneath and chilling me to the bone.

I quietly let myself into the house and took my shoes off. I didn't want to wake my landlady. Luckily, she was a very heavy sleeper and I had not done it since I moved in. I removed my clothing and pulled my winceyette night gown over my head. I then quickly snuggled underneath the blankets covering my narrow bed. The quietness was a sharp contrast to the last couple of hours and I soon fell asleep. I only had a few hours before I had to go to work, but I intended to get the best sleep I could until my alarm rang.

# 28

My shift finished at five o'clock so I knew I wouldn't have time to change out of my grubby overalls before I visited Ivan in the hospital, but I was eager to find out what he had to say regarding my situation with Geoffrey. Today had been particularly gruelling. I had managed to sleep for a solid four hours before my alarm clock began clanging away, pulling me from my glorious slumber. However, on arrival at work we were informed that we all had to pull our weight, even more so than usual.

Some of the aeroplane parts we were compiling were needed urgently and we were asked in a very persuasive manner if we could work through our breaks to ensure the order was completed on time. We all agreed and were rewarded with a hefty bonus but that didn't do anything to ease the utter exhaustion that seemed to drag my body down.

Thankfully, I didn't have to wait too long for the bus and very soon I was heading towards the outskirts of Bristol to the general hospital. Again, rain threatened and I hoped it would wait until I was in the warmth of my home. I hurried up the concrete steps and through the double doors of the hospital. The wall of warmth hit me immediately and I quickly took off my outdoor clothes.

Ivan was propped up in his bed attempting to read the local newspaper. Someone had laid it out on the table over his bed. He was struggling to turn the pages. There weren't that many to turn as the government had decided that all broadsheets contained only two or three pages to save paper. I clumped over to his bed, wearing my heavy work boots, and gave him a peck on the cheek. I then turned the page for him. He smiled and asked me how my day had been.

'Well,' I replied, 'we were stuck down in the cellar of the Red Lion until bloody gone two this morning, and then we had to work through our breaks to get an urgent order out, so I'm pretty exhausted,' I explained.

'You look in need of a good soak and some uninterrupted sleep but there's little chance of you getting either these days.' Ivan said.

The government had also instructed its people that they should have no more than two inches of water in the bath to save water, so Ivan was right; a good soak was out of the question. A good night's sleep was a bonus with Germany's nightly raids, so I wasn't holding my breath for either. I leant forward and lowered my voice.

'So, what have you found out about my problem with Geoffrey?' I whispered.

Ivan looked around the room suspiciously then leaned further towards me.

'Douglas, my pal from the ambulances, used to be a policeman before he retired, he has friend in uniform who would be happy to advise you on what to do,' Ivan told me, still looking around the room to ensure no one was listening, these were dangerous times, I sighed.

'But what if I'm wrong and the police think I'm some stupid airhead?' I asked, 'I mean I'm not exactly the brightest person, what if they laugh at me?'

'They won't laugh, they'll be pleased that that you're looking out for your country and if you are wrong then nothing is lost, Geoffrey won't know either way.'

I thought for a moment, and the conversation I'd had with Violet in the pub came into my mind. What Hitler was doing to the Jewish population was terrible. I knew that if Geoffrey did actually admire the man, then that would make him a very dangerous individual. That meant I had no choice and had to tell those in authority about my suspicions. I nodded and asked Ivan what I should do.

Ivan explained that there was a narrow alley way at the back of the police station. I needed to walk up this alley and then turn into an even narrower lane about half way along. There I would find a green painted door and I had to knock on it four times, with a pause in between, and someone would let me in. If I wasn't so worried, I would have laughed at the 'cloak and dagger' operation, it sounded like it had come from one of my childhood story books.

I listened as Ivan continued to explain that if a person didn't know that the doorway was actually there, they would be hard-pushed to find it. The location was a secret, specifically for information like mine. The end of visiting bell rang out. I stood and kissed Ivan once more and told him I wouldn't be able to visit for a few days as I was working the late shift.

Ivan made a mock sad face and I told him he wouldn't miss me at all with all the pretty little nurses attending to his every need. He smiled and told me that Cissy had popped in before she headed back to Cornwall. I told him that she was a pretty little girl and Ivan nodded as though the idea had just occurred to him.

The bus journey home seemed to take forever, but in reality, it was no longer than usual. I was tired, hungry and cold. I wanted to throw off my overalls and eat a hot meal. Finally, I made it home. Sadly, the house was in darkness. I was hoping my landlady would be home. I enjoyed our little chats but remembered that she was out with the WVS. The dear old soul had left me a cottage pie warming in the oven.

I wolfed it down without changing out of my overalls. After a quick cup of tea, I dragged myself up the stairs and got ready for bed. It really was a case of my head hitting the pillow and me being out for the count. I had a gloriously uninterrupted night's sleep and woke the next morning feeling much better and more confident about the task ahead. I decided to visit the police station as soon as I had eaten my breakfast, and before my afternoon shift at the factory began.

It was bitterly cold, but at least it was dry. I knew where the police station was as I had passed it many times since I moved to Bristol, but I was unaware that there was an entrance around the back. As I got closer, tiny butterflies began to flutter in my stomach and my mouth felt dry. I walked past the police station, trying not to look in that direction, before I reached the end of the row of buildings.

I turned around past the last building and spotted the alleyway. It was a little overgrown. Ivy hung down and its tendrils grasped at my hair. I pushed my way through and was surprised to see the small pathway open up into an alleyway as Ivan had told me it would. I walked past the back of the grey, concrete buildings until I found the narrow lane. Nervously, I looked to the front and behind me to check that I wasn't being followed. When I was certain I was not, I ducked into the narrow passage way.

I searched around for a door way but couldn't see one. I squeezed myself forward and suddenly the green door was there, almost hidden from sight. I knocked four times as instructed and suppressed a nervous giggle. I really did feel like some kind of spy. After a few seconds the door was pulled open and a hand beckoned me inside. I slipped in and the door was closed quickly behind me.

The difference between the outside and inside was astounding. I walked into a bright, airy room. Immediately I could feel the warmth from a large iron radiator that almost covered an entire wall. A man wearing an expensive looking suit entered the room and held out his hand, he looked to be in his mid -forties and he wore round spectacles, his hair was thinning at his brow but he had a friendly face and he put me at ease a little.

'Hello Miss Dean, my name is Harry and I understand you may have some information for us,' I swallowed and nodded.

'Please call me Joyce,' I answered, 'I'm not sure if I'm being silly, I just got a feeling that he's not all he says he is.'

'First things first,' Harry answered, 'please give me your outdoor things and can I get you a cup of tea?' I nodded and handed him my coat, gloves and scarf.

He left the room with my outdoor garments and asked me to sit and wait while he sorted out the tea. I sat down on a comfortable chair behind a very large desk. The room was huge and every wall but one, had tall filing cabinets placed along them. There were no windows, but I didn't think it was necessary because the lighting was so bright. Also, the walls were white and this added space and illumination to the room. Harry walked back in and closed the door behind him. I had no idea where it led to; I could only assume it was into the main police station.

'Tea is on the way my dear, now can we start by taking the gentleman's name,'

'His name is Geoffrey Floyd, I haven't known him for long, maybe six months,' I explained.

'What is your relationship to Geoffrey Floyd?' Harry leant forward and asked.

'Um, I guess you could call him my boyfriend,' I said, as I looked down into my lap, 'but I do go out with other men as well,' I finished, and felt myself blush.

'We're not here to judge you Miss Dean… Joyce, we're here to protect our country, wherever necessary. Now how old is Mr Floyd and what exactly are your suspicions?'

At that moment, there was a knock at the interior door and, Harry put his hand up, indicating that I should not speak.

'Enter!' he ordered.

The door was pushed open by a young man, also wearing a suit. He was carrying a tray with the two cups of tea on it and two slices of fruit cake.

My mouth watered when I saw the cake. I had not seen anything like it since the early days of the war. It was a rich brown colour and was laden with fruit. Once the young man had put the food and drink on the desk, he left the room. Harry told me to eat and drink then we would continue with our conversation. The cake was absolutely delicious and far too big a slice for one person. I asked Harry if I could take what I couldn't eat home with me. I wanted to share it with Susan. Harry smiled and nodded, then asked me to proceed.

'Well, we meet up whenever we can, I don't know if he's

married but I assume he's in the army because of his uniform,'

'Any idea what rank or position he holds,' Harry enquired.

'I don't know, he has three stripes on his shoulder,' I replied, pointing to my own shoulder. 'I think he must be pretty high up because he doesn't seem to have to worry about petrol rationing and isn't short of money. We go to a little hotel about five miles away from the outskirts of Bristol, it's very posh and that place too, doesn't seem to know that there is a war going on.'

Harry asked me the name of the place and wrote it in his little notepad when I told him, as well as everything else I had said. He then asked me what exactly Geoffrey had said that made me suspicious. I thought for a moment. I didn't want to tell Harry about the opium. For some silly reason I thought that it would be disloyal to Geoffrey, yet here I was, telling a complete stranger about him.

'Um, he talks in his sleep and some of the things he says worry me,'

'Go on Joyce, take your time. Harry's voice was both cajoling and soothing at the same time.

'He once said that Hitler's not a bad old chap and that he's doing a lot of good in Germany, but I know that's not true. I have a friend, whose husband is Jewish, what the Germans are doing to their fellow man is definitely not good. He also mentioned someone called Lizzy, and said she should get her comeuppance, and that it would be good for morale,' I stopped and sipped at my tea, I noticed Harry's eyes widen as he listened to the last part of my sentence.

'Did he mention a surname or why she should get her comeuppance, could she be his wife and he simply doesn't like her?' he asked.

'I did think of that, but he mentioned a rank and said its bloody ridiculous'.

'Is there anything else you can tell me, it's vitally important, so please try and think?' Harry pleaded.

I wracked my brains, but I couldn't remember anything else and I told Harry this.

'No matter you've done the right thing in coming to us, you say you are going out with him this weekend, please listen carefully to anything else you hear and don't be afraid to come here at any time, just be on your guard and make sure you're not followed, now, I'll get this cake wrapped up and let you get on with your day,' Harry said, smiling as he turned and walked from the room.

My nervousness came back and I began to wonder if I'd made a mistake coming here. What if I was doing Geoffrey a terrible disservice? I thought not. Something was nagging at me and I needed to get to the bottom of it. Harry returned with the cake wrapped in brown paper and tied with string. He also had my coat with him. He helped me into it then handed me my scarf and gloves. He thanked me, and shook my hand, before opening the door and ushering me out.

I made way back up the constricted lane and out into the alleyway. Again, I checked both ways and was confident that the coast was clear. I made my way back into the street and found that I was trembling a little. I breathed deeply then made my way to my billet to get changed for my shift. I was relieved that it was over but wondered exactly what can of worms I had opened.

The words *honorary second subaltern* came into my head and I made myself write them down as soon as I was home. I would tell Harry that that was another of the things Geoffrey had said. Right now, I needed to concentrate on getting ready for work and doing my bit for my country.

# 29

The first sprinkling of snow began to dance down from the skies when I heard the familiar toot of Geoffrey's car horn. I was momentarily mesmerised by the wonderful sight of a million tiny snowflakes falling from the heavens. Their delicate shapes were dimly illuminated by the hooded lights of Geoffrey's car. The magical vision took me right back to my childhood when I had peered out of my bedroom window. In my innocent mind, it looked like there was a myriad of tiny angels floating from the sky.

'Are you going to stand out there all evening old girl, or would you like to climb into the car?'

Geoffrey was grinning widely, as he shouted the words through his open car window. I giggled and walked around to the passenger side of the car. I put my overnight bag in the back of the vehicle then climbed into the passenger seat. Each time I travelled in the car my nostrils inhaled the scent of the leather from the car's plush interiors and the smell of Geoffrey's aftershave. I couldn't work out quite what manly scent Geoffrey wore and when I asked him, he told me to guess, I couldn't.

I was filled with conflicting emotions. One was of joy. I loved this hotel and its comfortable surroundings. Also, the food and drink were out of this world. This time, however, a semblance of nervousness crept into my body and wrapped itself around my soul. I, again, questioned myself over why I should be doing this to Geoffrey when he treated me so well. The answer came silently and quickly when a vision of Violet's haunted face sprung into my mind. It was when she was talking about what was happening to the Jewish population in Germany.

My resolve strengthened at that very moment. If Geoffrey was innocent, then he had nothing to worry about. I knew that if he was guilty and was actually some kind of spy for Germany, than he deserved everything coming to him. I really hoped that I just had a very vivid imagination. Only time would tell. After a half hour journey Geoffrey drove the car into the car park of The Grange hotel.

As usual, the place was well-lit and welcoming. The lights seemed to be beckoning us in and the smoke that swirled from the many chimneys made me feel warm even though I was outside. The place itself looked like something on the front of a Christmas card. The falling snow added to the authenticity of the festive looking scene. Geoffrey pulled open the car door for me and helped me out.

He then retrieved my luggage from the back seat. I loved his gentlemanly ways. Since the beginning of the war the female population had been asked to perform more and more masculine jobs. I thought it robbed me of my femininity, so I appreciated these tiny, old-fashioned, gestures. We held hands as we walked up the few steps and in through the double doors. The heat from the huge fireplace in the foyer was absolutely wonderful after the cold and draughty journey.

I waited while Geoffrey went to talk to the man at the counter and paid for our room. My mind wandered back to Susan. There was something troubling my dear friend, yet I didn't know what. She was very grateful when I had given her the slice of cake that the detective had given me, but she didn't unwrap it and eat immediately, like she would normally have done.

Also, there were dark rings under her eyes, and she seemed to have lost a lot of weight in a small amount of time. I made up my mind to talk to Violet about it when I next saw her.

I was shaken from my thoughts by Geoffrey putting his hand on my back and steering me towards the lavish, carpeted stair case. I always felt like a film star when I walked back down them. I would usually be wearing a long, glamorous evening gown with high heels. Geoffrey would walk beside me, with my arm in his, wearing his smart uniform. His shoes were always highly polished and he always wore a smile on his face.

Later on, I enjoyed a sumptuous dinner and felt a little giggly after three glasses of champagne. I ordered some coffee afterwards, to make sure my head was clear for what I had to do in the evening ahead. As I expected he would, Geoffrey got out his opium-smoking contraption and began to inhale deeply out of the pipe that was attached to it. I pretended to draw in the ghastly stuff then lay on the bed in a pretend stupor. It was not long before Geoffrey plonked himself down next to me then said with slurring speech.

'Apparently, she likes to get her hands dirty, likes to feel grease under her finger nails…what bloody tosh, trying to ingratiate herself with the British public, she'll get what's coming to her and no one deserves it more, bloody stupid girl…'

He carried on mumbling, but I couldn't catch what he was saying because he was falling asleep. I wished that I could write it down so that I would remember every word, but I wouldn't know how to explain to Geoffrey what I was doing, if he caught me. It sounded to me like he was talking about some ex-girl-friend who was getting on his nerves. I hoped so, I really wanted to be 'barking up the wrong tree' I decided that I would report to Harry what I had heard and tell him I thought I'd made a mistake. I hoped he would agree.

Thinking of Harry made me smile a little. His eyes were such a vibrant blue that they reminded me of a tropical ocean, ones that I'd seen pictures of in my *Woman's* magazines. His smile was so friendly and his voice was reassuring and kind. I got ready for bed and climbed in as Geoffrey snored fully dressed next to me. I had a wonderful dream about me and Harry making love on a warm beach while lying on the silky golden sand. I woke up with an even bigger smile.

# 30

Ivan was being released from the hospital the following day and I had arranged a little welcome home party for him. Mrs John, his landlady was in on the secret and was hoping to be able to bake a few bits for Ivan and his friends. I had invited Susan, Jimmy, Violet and William. William was riding on his motorcycle up from Cornwall especially for the occasion. I wanted it to be a complete surprise for Ivan. I wanted to thank him for saving my life.

Mrs John let us all in an hour before Ivan was due home. Violet, Susan and I set about decorating his room with a few colourful banners. Susan looked even worse than she had when I'd seen her previously and I asked her if she was feeling all right. She nodded a little too vigorously and with an overly bright smile that didn't fool me one bit. I didn't want to upset her, so I let it go but I was very worried about my dear friend.

Susan pulled a chair into a corner and climbed up on it to pin a few streamers onto the wall. Although she was virtually skin and bone, I couldn't help noticing a slight bulge around her stomach and I was a little shocked. I was quite sure that Susan was pregnant and that would explain the haunted expression on her face. Edward had been away fighting for more than eighteen months so there was no chance that the baby could be his.

My heart went out to Susan's predicament but there was little I could do in the way of help or, comfort so I said nothing and continued to decorate Ivan's room for the little party.

Susan had managed to buy a cake with mine, hers and Violets shared rations. Violet and also made some meat pies and I had provided hard boiled eggs and pickled onions. As we all fussed about I couldn't help looking over at Susan with a pitying look.

I was lucky to have never found myself *in the family way*. I was now quite sure that I was incapable of carrying a child. I had slept with too many men to be that fortunate. I wasn't sure if it was a blessing or a curse. At this moment it felt like the former but I'm quite sure that if I ever met a man I'd like to marry, I would definitely feel it was a curse.

I had called in at the police station after arriving back from my weekend with Geoffrey and I had told Harry exactly what Geoffrey had said. I added that I didn't think it was much information at all, but Harry informed me that I was very wrong and that it was very significant information. He told me that I was doing a sterling job and to keep up the good work but also to be careful. I looked into his eyes as he said it and was sure I detected a fondness in his voice.

I quickly dismissed the idea as I saw him twist his gold wedding ring around his finger. We finished our tea, and as I left, I could have sworn that he held onto my hand for a little longer than necessary. I decided that it was probably in my head or what I actually wanted to think. I did feel attracted to him. I headed off to work humming happily to myself.

I was startled from my thoughts by a quiet knock on Ivan's door, it was then pushed open and William and Jimmy, Susan's friend, entered. William had a large bottle of scotch in his hand which he passed to Susan and Jimmy was struggling to carry several bottles of beer. I rushed forward to relieve him of the drinks. We all chatted away for a while. Ten minutes after he had arrived, William, Ivan's friend and confidante from his home village, pulled a brown envelope from his pocket and put it on the mantelpiece.

I asked him if he knew what was in it and he explained that Ivan had been nominated for a bravery award. Neither Susan nor I could hide our joy. This was the very tonic Ivan needed. It would show him what a hero he was and diminish his thoughts of cowardice for ever. I was so very happy for him. I had also managed to get a bottle of sherry from Geoffrey. I opened it and filled three teacups for Susan, Violet and I while the men drank beer from the bottles.

A few minutes before four o'clock, we switched off the lights and became silent. Ivan's landlady had banged on the ceiling a few moments earlier. This was her sign to tell us that Ivan was putting his key in the lock to alert us to his home coming. We had devised the little plan when we arrived. As I heard Ivan climbing the stairs, I had to suppress a little giggle of excitement. I couldn't wait to see his face.

As the door was pushed open, I jumped forward and switched the light on. Everyone in the room shouted 'surprise' in unison and poor old Ivan nearly jumped out of his skin. When he realised what was going on, his shock turned to happiness and he grinned broadly. He hugged Susan, Violet and I warmly then he shook hands with William and Jimmy. I handed him a beer and we all sat down on any seat available or the narrow, single bed.

Soon after Ivan arrived, there was another quiet knock on the door. I pulled it open to find Mrs John, Ivan's landlady standing on the landing. She was holding a plate of sandwiches in one hand and some sausages rolls in the other. I invited her in and she added the food to the modest feast that was laid out on Ivan's dressing table. I asked her if she would like a glass of sherry, but she refused and said she would 'leave us youngsters to enjoy ourselves.' She then bustled out of the room.

For the next hour the five of us had a wonderful time, chatting and laughing. I was happy that Hitler had decided against bringing the little party to an end before we'd had time to enjoy ourselves. Jimmy was the first to leave as he was on duty that evening. We all said our goodbyes and Susan walked him out to the landing. I couldn't help hearing Susan tell Jimmy that she needed to talk to him but would tell him what about next time she saw him. I tactfully closed the door to allow them to say goodbye in private.

After another half hour or so of merriment, Susan, Violet and I had to leave. We were on the early shift the next morning so needed to get an early night. William asked Ivan if it was ok to sleep on his bedroom floor that night so they could spend the morning riding their motor cycles. Ivan's eyes brightened like stars twinkling in the night sky and I knew that this was the proverbial icing on the cake for him and I was really glad. I gave him a small peck on the cheek before I left and told him to drive carefully the next day. He promised he would.

The three of us, Susan, Violet and I, made our precarious way home in the blackout and said our goodbyes as we reached our prospective billets. Once inside my cosy room I got ready for bed. As I sat looking into my dressing table mirror while rolling rags into my hair, I became deep in thought. I was really fond of Ivan; he called me 'his Juicy Joyce' and longed for me to be his girl, he never seemed to tire of asking.

Sadly, I didn't love him and having been lucky enough to

have been in love once I didn't want to settle for anything less. Out of nowhere, a picture of Harry, the plain clothes policeman, who I informed about Geoffrey, came into my head and made me feel warm all over. As I snuggled into my bed, I tried to push his image away from my thoughts, but it stayed in my mind and dominated my sleep.

# 31

In the dark days of war my mind often wandered back to my mother. The more I thought about her the more I came to realise what a selfish cow she was. I knew it was unhealthy to store bitter thoughts. Susan had warned me about doing it, but I couldn't stop myself. I thought about how my fellow men and women had all come together to try and win a war against domination and greed. All my mother ever did was wallow in her own self-pity and ignore the sadness of others. I knew, in the deepest chasm of my heart, I would never forgive her for the loss of my childhood.

I thought of my dear friend Mabel toiling in the field, no matter what the weather, to ensure the country was fed. Susan, Violet, me and countless other women slogged away doing heavy manual labour. No one turned down a request for extra hours if that was what was needed to get the job done even if we were virtually dead on our feet.

Then I thought of the brave fighting men and women. Wrenched from the hearts of their families and homes to fight in as war they didn't want. I knew that each every one of them would fight to protect their families and many had paid the cost with their lives. I longed for the war to end and felt very miserable sometimes because of it but I never let it show.

My mother never harboured any such ideas. She wore her sorrow like a badge; she wanted everyone to know of her so-called deep suffering but cared, not one jot, for anyone else's pain. I was glad she was dead. I hoped that wherever she was, she was suffering as she had made many others suffer over the years.

A few days after Ivan's party I arrived at work to see Susan looking even more wretched than usual. She had obviously been crying because her eyes were red and swollen. She told me she was suffering from hay fever. I nodded but didn't point out that no-one suffered from that condition in the cold weeks of February. Violet confided that Jimmy had been suddenly called away and Susan had no idea where he was. This and her unwanted pregnancy was obviously the cause of her distress.

Again, I really wished I could help Susan the way she had helped me. I'm quite sure that if she had not visited me in the hospital I would have stayed in my depression and ended my life. When I ate the apple pie she bought in it was the first time I had actually enjoyed the taste of something for months. I found out, sometime later, that Susan didn't actually make the food; she bought it from a nearby bakery with the sole intention of helping people like me. All her room contained was a single ring, on her cooker, so baking of any type was out of the question. I laughed when she told me.

A few days later Susan didn't come to work. As soon as I could I sought out Violet to find out why. She told me that Susan had gone to visit a sick aunt in Ireland for a few months. I knew, for a fact, that Susan had no relatives in Ireland. We often talked about our families, so I was absolutely sure that this was the case.

I looked quizzically at Violet. She touched my arm and said everything was going to be ok. Looking into her eyes, I could see what she was trying to tell me, without saying it out loud, that Susan had found a solution to her problem. I thanked her and smiled. I guessed that Susan had gone to Ireland to have her illegitimate child and would probably get him, or her, adopted. I was happy that, in a few short months, her torment would be over. I would never breathe a word to anyone. It wasn't the ideal solution, but it was the only one for Susan. It was a shame I would never meet her new born son or daughter but then, who knew what the future held?

I often found myself thinking of my mother whenever I thought about children. I couldn't hide the bitterness I felt towards her. Susan continuously told me that harbouring dark thoughts would only harm me. I didn't agree. I tried to find the good points in my mother, but she simply had none. She was so tightly enveloped in her own all-consuming misery that she had no time for anyone else. I knew, in the depths of my heart, that she never spent a moment caring about anyone else other than herself.

Images of the courageous fighting men jumped into my head once more. They had been forced away from the heart of their families and made to fight in a war that was not of their making. Yet, they went, and they fought without complaint or blame. They didn't feel sorry for themselves and scream about their woes, they just faced the challenges that lay before them and hoped that, at some point, they would get home to their families and regain a semblance of their normal lives once more.

I swelled with pride when I thought about all us women who were now working in labour intensive jobs originally intended to be done by men with the much-needed muscly physique. Of course, we all fussed and groaned when we asked to work overtime to ensure a certain part was delivered on time, but never once did we think about not doing the job in hand. I was proud to be doing my bit for my country.

I was absolutely sure that if my mother had not chosen to take her own life she would still be wrapped up in her own misery. She would not have given a jot about the war and the death. Her own sorrow was paramount, and she sapped the energy out of anyone who loved her or tried to help her. I believed that the world was a better place without her in it and I wished that, wherever she was now, she would be repentant about the selfishness of her actions and, maybe, paying the price. I could only hope.

Violet and I met up regularly in the Red Lion. We both missed Susan, but we didn't talk about her. Her secret was too great to be overheard by flapping ears. Violet did tell me about the terrible things happening in Poland. She explained how the Nazi's were closing down the Jewish ghettos and sending the inhabitants to camps. Poor Violet had to fight back the tears when she explained that these places were notorious and known as 'death camps'. The thought that one human being could treat their fellow man in such a way made me sick to my stomach. I would never, ever be to be able to comprehend such evil.

We also spoke about the rumours regarding a horrific incident in London. There was nothing written about in the papers and nothing was heard on the radio. It was all passed down by word of mouth. Apparently nearly two hundred people had been killed when someone tripped up racing down the stairs to the underground tube station. Such was the panic, when the air raid siren screeched, the crowds of people poured down the steps into the underground shelter.

Some poor, unfortunate soul tripped and fell. This resulted in a massive crush as body after body fell on top of one another and the people underneath suffocated as a result. I sometimes wandered if there was a God. These terrified human beings were already running from one evil when they were caught up in another and it cost them their lives. I really hoped there was a God, but I felt that if He did exist, He was not coping well at the moment.

The government was also trying to prevent able-bodied men from using the tube station for protection from the raids. They advised that they must be used to shelter women and children only. I couldn't understand why the government thought the life of a woman or child was any-more important than that of a man. In my mind their top priority should have been the preservation of life, all life, regardless of their gender or age.

As the spring arrived and the darkness of winter retreated once more, I felt my spirits begin to rise. A clear, sunny day was a great tonic. I realised that the short, shady days of winter could be suffocating in a city already dimmed by the blackout. The noise of birdsong filled my heart with joy. I hummed as I walked to work one morning in early May. I had styled my blonde hair into rolls at the side of my head. This style was all the rage, and the government called them victory rolls, I really liked the sound of that.

As I approached the factory, I grinned widely at the sight of a familiar figure standing outside the gates. I called Susan's name and ran over to meet her. We hugged tightly and I was glad to see that she looked so much better than she did the last time I had seen her. I looked into her face and although she had some colour in her cheeks, I could still see worry lines etched into her face. I couldn't think what might be troubling her.

I assumed her 'problem' was now sorted. I asked her if she

was all right. She nodded and asked if I would come to hers for tea later that day. She had brought home some butter and cheese from Ireland and I gladly accepted the invitation. Maybe then, she would tell me what was obviously now troubling her.

That evening, we had feasted on the delicious cheese sandwiches she had made. The dry 'national loaf' we ate was brought to life by the lashings of butter and thick chunks of cheese. Susan explained that Lucy, Violets sister-in-law, had also given her some eggs and cream and she said that Violet and I were invited over, for omelettes, the following evening. My mouth watered at the prospect.

Once we had eaten our fill and cleared away the dishes. I asked Susan if anything was troubling her. She looked at me and I saw that her blue eyes were awash with sadness. I listened as Susan told me what was troubling her,

'I'm a grandmother, 'She told me with a faltering smile,

'That's wonderful, isn't it?' I asked her, I knew Susan was thirty- five which I considered quite young to become a grandmother.

'Oh, it is,' She smiled a wide, genuine smile then continued, 'Edith, my eldest has recently given birth to healthy twins, they're called Verity and Charlie and are the most beautiful babies I've ever seen,' Susan explained then paused for a minute. I waited to hear what she had to say. She continued,

'Edith is only seventeen and she's not really coping with motherhood, I know it early days but I can't stop worrying about her, I've employed a lovely lady from the village, called Ethel Haversham, to come to the farm every day to help out but I'm not sure if Edith might even need more help than that,' Susan sighed then sipped at her tea.

'Well, there's a telephone at Carmarthen Farm so they can get in touch with you in the daytime if there's an emergency,' I replied, 'and you could call them a couple of evenings a week from the telephone box on the corner to check everything is going well, also, I'm quite sure Mrs Haversham wouldn't hesitate to contact you if she was worried?' I said soothingly, Susan sighed once more.

'I know you're right,' she replied, 'I just wish I could do more, Edith seems so young and unprepared for motherhood, her fiancé, Chuck is missing, presumed dead, so she's also grieving over him and the stigma of having children out of wedlock upsets her and I wish it didn't. The war is making young people rush into things they wouldn't normally do, I'm not ashamed of her and I wish everyone else would mind their own business, the bloody nurses at the hospital where she gave birth treated her appallingly!' Susan finished her tea and marched over to the sink to swill her cup out, I walked over and hugged her.

'I think you're doing all you can, in the circumstances and I'm sure Edith will be fine, given time, it's not easy for anyone who's looking after two tiny babies, my old neighbour struggled to cope with just one new born in the early days so just give Edith time and write often, if she's anything like you, she'll do the job splendidly.' I told her and I meant it, I thought she was a wonderful mother.

Susan smiled but I could tell she was still worried. Once the war ended, she would be able to move to Cornwall where she would be of some practical help for her daughter. Until that time, like everyone else in the country, we just had to pull our weight and get on with things.

# 32

I'd been out with Geoffrey on several occasions since the last time I went to the police station. On all of these occasions he had not smoked Opium; therefore, he had not mumbled anything that bothered me. He did, however, shout out in his sleep about Hitler ruling the world. I passed this onto Harry, the undercover police man and he told me to 'keep at it' and I promised I would. Secretly I hoped that I was wrong about Geoffrey, but a little voice inside me argued with that hope.

It was near the end of July 1943 when Hamburg, in Germany was attacked by Britain over and over again. This city had a sizeable port so destroying it would affect the German stronghold and any strategic plans they had. I couldn't celebrate this small victory when I read that up to forty thousand people had been killed in what was named the first '*Firestorm*'. I knew that these people were our enemy but I was also aware that they were just ordinary people, caught up in a war they didn't ask to be in.

I shed a few tears for the massive loss of life and the nonsensicality of a war that killed thousands of innocents on both sides. I prayed for it to be over. Edward, Susan's husband came home on leave in August and this really put some colour into Susan's cheeks. She told me how talking to Edward about her daughter Edith helped immensely.

She thoroughly believed in the old adage, 'a problem shared was a problem halved'. I was glad that some of her burden had been lifted. She told me that Edward was going to Cornwall to spend some of his leave with his mother and daughters at the farm and he would let Susan know about Edith's progress.

Walking home from Strachan & Henshaw Munitions Factory one balmy evening, I come across a chance encounter that would change my whole life although I didn't know it at the time. I was still wearing my overalls and had my hair was pulled back by a colourful scarf. It was late in the afternoon as I made my way towards my billet. I was totally lost in my own thoughts and literally barrelled into Harry when I rounded the corner to turn into my street.

Harry grabbed me before I fell backwards and I giggled and apologised, explaining that I had not been concentrating on where I was going. Harry assured me that it was fine. At the same moment we both gazed into each other's eyes and I shivered involuntarily. It felt to me as though we were the only two people in the world. In reality the street was teeming with people going about their daily business. To me, it was as though time had stopped turning and nothing mattered but the here and now, this definitive moment could not end.

Suddenly the sight of a silver barrage balloon bobbing in the corner of my eye caught my attention. At the same time the air raid warning siren shrieked into life. As always, I was shrouded with a heavy cloak of terror and beads of sweat formed on my forehead. Harry grabbed my hand and we raced towards the galvanised air raid shelter on the edge of the park. It was no longer a playing area; it was now a massive allotment that grew a variety of vegetables, fruit and herbs.

I'm not sure if it would have been closer for me to go home. Either way, there was no room for three of us under the stairs, so the shelter was probably a better choice. A lot of other people were also heading for the same place. Harry squeezed through the small door way and we sat down on one of the narrow wooden benches that ran down either side. As more and more people entered, we found ourselves being squished together tightly. It felt like I had been given a mini electric shock when Harry's thigh touched mine.

I turned to look at him and he was gazing down at me. He had bright blue eyes flecked with grey specks. His lips were full, and he was smiling. I smiled back and he caught hold of my hand. I knew there and then that something had happened that would change my life. I felt as though I had always known Harry. I was sure I could guess his favourite colour and would know what food he liked to eat. His hand was rough and warm. I felt safe just sitting next to him.

I heard the familiar drone of planes and then the bombs began to fall. They fell some distance away. Oddly, fear did not visit me when I was sitting with Harry. I knew that this was ridiculous because there was nothing he could do if one of Hitler's bombs had our names on it. It was just a strange feeling I had. It was as though Harry had put a protective bubble around me. I also felt that if I died there and then, it wouldn't matter because I was with the man I loved.

The thought shocked me. How could I be in love with a man I hardly knew? I had no idea, but I knew that I loved Harry. Simultaneously, we both gazed at the gold wedding band on his third finger. I didn't care. My heart now belonged to this lovely man and I felt as though I could sing with joy. Thankfully, the raid was a short one and a few hours later we emerged into the bright sunlight. I could see no obvious damage, so I could only assume the attack had been unsuccessful.

My body was stiff from being in one position for such a long time and the bright glare of the sun almost blinded me. None of this mattered. Harry asked me if I would like to come to a small café he knew for a cup of tea. I nodded without hesitation. I would have followed him to the ends of the earth if he asked me to. We walked for around ten minutes then we turned into a narrow alleyway that I hadn't seen before.

It eventually opened up into a small square that housed three businesses. One was a sweet shop, the other was and second-hand clothes shop and the third was a café simply called 'Rita's. Harry pushed the door open and I followed him inside. He pointed to a table for two in the corner and I walked over to it while he went to the counter and ordered two cups of tea.

The café was tiny but very clean. It was brightly decorated. Red, check table clothes covered the few tables in the place and red curtains were pulled back at the windows. The salt and pepper pots matched the colour of the curtains and there were a few pictures dotted on the wall of seaside scenes. Harry returned with two mugs of tea and sat down opposite me.

'I'll get a divorce,' he said and sipped at his drink. I nodded. I still felt a little dazed at the speed of our union.

'I've really only stayed with Brenda, my wife, out of habit,' Harry went onto explain, 'Since the girls, we've got two daughters, were evacuated I realised that we have very little in common and even less to say to each other,' he finished.

'What are their names, your daughters?' I asked.

'Evelyn and Shirley,' he replied as a big smile spread across his face. He obviously adored his two children. Reaching into his wallet, he pulled out a black and white photograph. He handed it to me. I guessed that the two little girls in the picture were around five and six years old. They both wore their long blonde hair in plaits and had grins that were a mirror image of Harry. I handed back the photo and told him how pretty they were. He smiled once more.

'I think I fell in love with you the minute you walked into my office,' Harry confessed, 'I didn't think for a minute that you might feel the same way, a beautiful young lady like you must have her pick of gentlemen suitors.'

I smiled and my face reddened a little; he knew that I had at least one, in the shape of Geoffrey Floyd.

'I guess you're wondering why I'm not in one of the armed forces,' he looked at me and sighed, 'I have, what the medical profession call, an irregular heartbeat but it's absolute nonsense, I'm fit as a fiddle, I tried to enlist in 1914 and again when this war started but they wouldn't take me either time. It wasn't through want of trying, I can tell you that,' he told me and sighed once more.

'Not everyone can be in combat, fighting on the front for England, Harry, there are other ways of 'doing our bit' for our country and both of us are doing just that,' I replied.

'I don't want you to go anywhere near Geoffrey Floyd,' Harry said loudly then he quickly looked around and lowered his voice, 'we've reason to believe he is a traitor to the country and a nasty piece of work,' he whispered conspiratorially.

'Then I'd better make sure we find out exactly what his plans are,' I replied, leaning towards Harry so only he could hear what I was saying.

I wasn't angry with Harry, at first, he was obviously warning me because he cared about me and because he was concerned for my safety but I felt it my duty to help capture Geoffrey if he was, indeed, a threat to the country.

'Joyce,' Harry hissed quietly, 'I repeat, he's a dangerous individual and I forbid you from seeing him again.'

I looked into Harry's eyes. They were staring directly at me, as if he was challenging me to disobey him.

'You don't get to tell me what to.' I informed him coldly then scraped my chair back, stood up, and walked out of the café without a backward glance.

I almost ran the short distance home and quickly let myself in the door. My mind was whirl of emotions. I knew, deep within my heart that I already loved Harry but that did not mean he could rule my life. If he wanted us to be together, he needed to know that. I could hear Mrs Groves, my landlady humming away in the kitchen. I walked in and she smiled. She was a lovely woman and I was becoming very fond of her. Referring to the air raid, I asked her,

'Did you go under the stairs?'

'Yes,' she sang, 'with my knitting and my '*Woman's Own*' magazine, the time flew by,' I laughed; only Mrs Groves could be happy about being cooped up in a cupboard in the middle of an air raid. I told her that I would go up and change my clothes before tea.

I padded up the stairs and had a quick wash in the upstairs bathroom. Harry was never far from my mind the whole time and I felt a little sad at the way things had turned out. My heart told me he was the one, but my head over- ruled it and I found that quite depressing.

I changed into a mauve pencil skirt and a cream coloured silk blouse. Both were presents from Geoffrey. I was meeting Susan in the Red Lion later on and thought my outfit looked rather nice. As usual, my meal was delicious and after I helped

Mrs Groves with washing and drying up we parted company.

It was still warm outside, but I carried a knitted cardigan with me anyway in case it cooled down later on in the evening. I was wearing sensible white leather sandals so the walk to the pub was quite pleasant. I was just a few minutes away when I heard my name being called. I turned around to see Harry chasing after me.

'Joyce, I'm sorry, I don't know what came over me, spouting orders at you like that, can you forgive me?' He pleaded, I told him I needed to think, and he nodded. He then leant forward and gave me a light kiss on the cheek. This was the closest I had ever been to Harry and his masculine smell mixed with the odour of *Brylcream* filled my senses. I had to fight to make sure I didn't pull him into my arms and kiss him passionately. He then nodded and walked away.

I longed to run after him and to tell him that I loved him with my body, heart and soul but I knew I had to be sensible. I needed to be sure that he meant what he said. I then turned and walked into the Red Lion. Susan and Violet were sitting at our usual table and I could see that they had already bought a drink for me. I squeezed through the crowd and sat down with them.

It was a good evening as I always enjoyed the company of my best friends. We chatted about work and the war. When Violet nipped to the loo, Susan asked about Geoffrey. I told her that I'd been mistaken. Harry had told me not to tell a soul about Geoffrey. Susan nodded but I don't think she was convinced. Violet returned and we finished our drinks. Immediately, some American servicemen sauntered over to our table and offered to buy us refills.

For the first time ever, I politely refused and told them that we were all spoken for. I turned around to see Susan and Violet staring at me with incredulous expressions across their faces.

'Well,' said Susan, as Violet nodded in agreement, 'I've never seen you turn down the offer of drink or a date with a handsome American serviceman, that must mean you're feeling ill, or you're in love, there is no other explanation,' she leant forward and dramatically put her hand on my brow, 'Hmm, definitely no sign of a fever,' she said grinning.

I grinned back but said nothing. My relationship with Harry was only just budding into life. I was still a little unsure but I did know that Susan was right. I loved the man and I ached to see him again.

## 33

Daytime raids were, thankfully, very rare so when the air raid siren screeched into life on a warm August afternoon we were all taken unawares. Such was my surprise that I initially mistook it for the hooter announcing our tea break. When I finally realised what it was, I quickly gathered up my bag, gas mask and sandwiches and joined the throng of my fellow workers heading quickly to the large cellar below the workshop at Strachan and Henshaw.

The ominous droning sound of the enemy planes made the procession simultaneously move a little faster. Once we were in the safety of the cellar, Susan, Violet and I found ourselves somewhere to sit on the benches that stretched the whole length of the building. Colourful cushions were dotted along them which made them a lot more comfortable to sit on.

Once we had secured our place, Susan and I joined the queue that led to the large tea urn in the corner of the room. Susan poured a cup for herself and Violet and I followed behind with mine. Sometimes, during an air raid, we could hear very little, sitting in the bowels of this very old building but this time it was different.

It sounded, to me, like the planes were directly above us. I sat in between Violet and Susan. We held each other's hands tightly and trembled in unison when the sound of a bomb, dropping precariously near-by, almost blew our ear drums out.

I could also hear the noise of our own planes as a terrifying cat fight was played out in the skies above us. It sounded like a clap of thunder intensified a hundred times. We couldn't even chat to each other to try and calm our nerves because the noise was too great.

I looked around the cellar and the rest of the workforce looked as frightened as I felt. They all sat tightly together as though the warmth from another person's body would bring them comfort or protection. I felt sorry for the older supervisors who were men too old to be fighting in the armed forces.

The terror on their faces matched mine but their masculinity forbade them from snuggling up with their fellow shelterers. After a while, it seemed that the British Airforce was succeeding in driving the enemy away from the centre of the city. The noise began to abate a little and the sounds became more distant. I heard the screech of a plane's dying tailspin and I hoped it belonged to the enemy. Above the din I began to hear the sound of an upbeat tune. I looked up and saw that several of my comrades in arms had begun to sing. The uplifting words of 'The White Cliffs of Dover' rang around the room and I joined in.

The song took everyone's mind of what was going on outside. Even when we were all liberally sprinkled with a coating of dust, from the creaking building, we sang on. It was our only defence against a ruthless enemy. The raid seemed to go on forever and I was grateful for the makeshift toilet at the far end of the building. It was really just a large bucket with a curtain pulled around it to hide the user's modesty, but it was better than no facility at all.

When the all clear sounded there was a communal sigh of relief. I rubbed the dust from my face and gathered up my few possessions then followed the rest of the workforce up the stairs and along the length of the factory until we reached the external door. Outside, the sun was still bright in the sky and almost blinded me. It was such a stark contrast to the dark, dull cellar that my eyes took a while to get accustomed to the brightness of the early evening.

There were several of the emergency services on the site. I looked around me and saw that there was destruction in every direction and the factory had not escaped totally unscathed. The supervisors told us all to wait where we were while they made a quick check of the factory. As we were waiting Susan looked to her left then opened her mouth with surprise. I turned to see what she was looking at and saw a lady walking towards her pushing a large carriage-built pram. Susan told me it was her mother.

The woman approached Susan and explained that she was worried when news had spread that the factory had been hit so she had come up to make sure her daughter was all right. Susan smiled and reached into the pram. She lifted out a tiny little being swaddled in blankets and walked back over to where we were all standing.

I peered at the little child. Her tiny hand had managed to claw its way out of the blanket. It was screwed up into a fist, making it seem like the little child was angry. Her eyes fluttered open and were the brightest blue I had ever seen on a baby so young. She had blonde downy hair that I leant down and touched. It felt like the finest silk. The sight of the infant made me long to have a child of my own but I had come to realise that it probably wasn't going for happen to me.

Suddenly I heard a loud scream. I turned around and saw, as if it was happening in slow motion, the wall of the factory beginning to fall towards us. Susan stood terrified and pulled the baby close to her. Violet raced forward and pushed us all backwards towards the interior wall. I heard a tremendous whooshing sound as the wall hurtled towards us then it stopped as quickly as it began as it became lodged on the structure behind us. We were now in total darkness, such was my terror it felt like it had grasped me in a strangle hold and I found it hard to breathe.

After what was probably less than a minute but seemed like hours, a small prism of light filtered through and marginally illuminated the area. I swallowed deeply as I looked around. The dust fluttered around the confined space and immediately caught in my throat, making me cough and splutter. It looked like the wall had partially fallen and was now resting against another wall.

Around twelve or thirteen of us were now trapped in a tiny, triangular space. I could see bodies lying underneath the rubble to the left of me. Lifeless eyes stared out of dust covered faces. Many of their mouths were open showing the terror that they felt when the wall toppled on top of them. I couldn't hide my horror.

Seconds ago, I was standing in the sunshine talking to these people. We were so thankful to survive the raid and the long hours in the factory cellar. Now, we were in an even more precarious position. It looked to me like the wall was going to come down, on the lot of us, at any second to finish the survivors off.

I made out the figure of Susan in the dim light. She was wiping the dust off the face of the child she was holding. She then opened the child's mouth and used her finger to clear out any debris. The poor little girl was coughing and snuffling. Violet walked over and helped clear the child airways. Both had the maternal protective instincts of a mother. These were natures that I did not possess.

All I could feel was an over whelming emotion of compelling doom. I struggled to breathe and was absolutely positive that I could see the wall getting closer and closer to me. I was deadly sure that very soon we would be joining the corpses at the far side of the space. Most of the trapped were obviously in a state of extreme shock. They just stood and stared into nothingness with their lips slightly apart, resembling the expressions of the dead.

All I could do was stand and weep. I wept with terror and injustice. Why had God let us survive one attack only to let us die in another incident? It seemed like a very sick way to treat us. It was less than half an hour later when I heard the voice of our rescuers, but it seemed to me like it had been hours and hours. The whole time I stood in my would-be tomb I felt like a coil of wire was wrapping itself around me and getting tighter every second. As the hole, made by the rescuers, appeared and began to get bigger, the light from the evening sun filtered in. Every inch of my body shook.

I watched as the survivors pushed Susan out first. I had to fight an almost unstoppable urge to shove everyone out of the way and race out of this mind numbingly terrifying place. My eyes and body began to twitch at the same time as I waited for repatriation. Then I felt a gentle push from behind and I was propelled towards the opening. I was seconds away from escape but I seemed to be moving further away.

Then I was out. The sunlight was caressing my face and a

warm gentle breeze ruffled my grimy hair. I looked around and could see about thirty or forty bodies covered with anything at hand. I stumbled towards a low wall and sat on it before my legs broke from under me. I started to sob. I tried to supress it by putting both of my hands over the front of my face. It didn't seem right for me to be crying when I had survived but the thought didn't seem to be getting through to my brain.

I felt as though I was balancing on the edge of insanity and was about to topple into an abyss of madness. I heard my name being called but I didn't look up. The effort of trying to control the intensity of my desire to quell my rising waves of panic engulfed me. Then I felt comforting arms around my shoulders and heard Harry's voice. He was saying over and over again that I was all right, and he would never let anything bad happen to me.

Harry was rocking me gently as if I was a tiny baby. The motion and the calmness of his voice were penetrating through the subconscious of my brain. I looked up through the mist of my tears. There was no need for any more words. Here in Harry's embrace I felt safe and protected. I don't know how long he held me but at some point I became aware of where I was and of the people around me.

Harry helped me to my feet. I realised he had wrapped a blanket around my shoulders. He led me slowly to his car and helped me into the passenger seat. As he started the vehicle up, he turned and smiled at me. To me it felt as though a thousand stars were twinkling down at me, lighting up a black, moonless night.

Harry drove me to my lodgings and walked me up the steps. I was feeling better now. Earlier, I had felt as though I was in another world where no one could see or hear me. Now, I knew where I was and who I was. Mrs Groves answered the door and put her hands to her face in alarm. She quickly pulled herself together;

'Oh, my little love, am I glad to see you, I've been out of my mind with worry since I heard that Strachan & Henshaw had been hit, come on in, let's get you cleaned up, thank you Mr….?' she finished as she looked at Harry.

'Shawcross, Harry,' he replied, 'there's been a lot of fatalities at the factory and every spare hand is needed so I thought I better drop Miss Dean off myself, now I'd better get back to the factory to see if I can be of any help,' He then raised his trilby hat, smiled at me, and left.

Mrs Groves helped me into the house. I realised that I hadn't a clue that Harry's surname was Shawcross. It struck me that I knew very little about him. It didn't matter though. I knew I loved him and wanted to be with him forever. When this horrible war was over, we would get married. We would live in a little cottage with roses around the door and I would be a step-mother to Harry's two daughters.

The very thought filled me with warmth and hope for the future. I longed for the day when we could be together as man and wife. That night as I lay in my comfy bed, I thanked God for saving my life and asked for his forgiveness when I doubted Him. Being trapped had frightened the living daylights out of me but I had to be thankful. I was one of the lucky ones while so many weren't. God must think that my life had some meaning as he had saved me once more. I promised Him I would do my very best to make my survival worthwhile.

# 34

I met up with Harry a few days after the factory had been bombed. We had arranged to meet at Rita's café. Harry was already waiting for me when I arrived. He stood up as I approached the table and pulled a chair out for me to sit on. He gazed lovingly at me then asked the ageing waitress to bring us two cups of tea. She nodded and this made the ash from her cigarette drop onto the floor.

'How are you, Joyce?' Harry asked, sitting so close to him and not being able to touch him was torture, I saw the same look in his eyes.

'I'm very well thank you Harry, I get the occasional flashback from being trapped but I just breathe in deeply and get on with my work, it's all I can do,' I replied, the waitress brought our drinks over and put them on the table.

'Over forty people were killed over at Strachan & Henshaw,' Harry told me, I nodded, I already knew, it was all Susan, Violet and the other factory workers had talked about over the last few days, Harry continued.

'I've got some leave owing and I've been reliably informed that Strachan & Henshaw will be closed for the next four or five days...will you come away with me Joyce?' Harry asked as he gazed at me intently. I was stunned, this was the last thing I expected Harry to ask me. I assumed that he would talk to his wife before we began a full-blown affair but I knew he couldn't have done because she was visiting their daughters in the countryside, I didn't hesitate though, there was nothing I wanted more than to be with Harry.

'I'd love to,' I replied, 'have you got anywhere in mind?'

'Cornwall,' Harry replied, 'it's wonderful at this time of the year, I have a friend who owns a small holiday home on the edge of the beach,'

'When will we go?' I squealed, excitedly, I'd never been to the seaside before.

'Will about an hour be all right?' Harry asked with a big grin spread over his beautiful face.

I nodded happily and finished my tea. Harry told me to go home and pack a few things and he would pick me up on the corner of my street. I said goodbye and quickly headed for my lodgings. I was beyond excited and not just at the prospect of a holiday by the sea. I couldn't wait to be with Harry properly. We could pretend, for a few short days that we were a married couple.

It would give us the time we needed to get to know each other intimately. I shouted out to Mrs Groves as I had pushed open the front door but found the house empty. I was glad. This would save me having to lie to her about where I was going. I packed a few things in the overnight case that Geoffrey had bought me. I wished that I owned a swimming costume, but I had never needed one in the past.

I put my two favourite summer dresses in and a pair of leather sandals. I also packed a cardigan in case the British weather changed as it was apt to without warning. I left a note for Mrs Groves telling her that I was going to go and visit my old friend, Mabel Johnson, for a few days while the factory was being repaired. I asked her to let Susan know if she happened to call around then I hurried out of the door and up the street.

I spotted Harry's car at the same time as he saw me. He got out and loaded my small suitcase into the boot of the vehicle then went around and opened the passenger door for me. I quickly climbed in. I couldn't remember the last time I had felt so deliciously excited. I waited until we were quite a way outside of Bristol before I leaned over and kissed Harrys cheek. He winked at me and put his hand on my leg. It made me feel tingly all over and I couldn't wait to arrive at our destination.

Harry drove quickly along the roads. The outskirts of Bristol disappeared and then we were travelling along narrow, winding country lanes. Four or five hours later Harry parked outside a small bungalow that was actually right on the edge of a beach. I jumped out of the car, whipped off my shoes and walked on the sand.

It was warm and soft and snuggled between my toes. I laughed loudly. Harry grabbed our luggage and unlocked the door. I followed him inside and looked around. The place was very compact but had everything we needed. One room was a kitchen-cum-dining-room-cum-living room. There was one small bedroom and tiny bathroom. I loved the place the minute I stepped inside.

Harry went into the bedroom and pushed the window open. He explained that the place needed airing as it had not been used for a few months. I watched as he pulled back the bed clothes then I looked around the little room that was the kitchen. I found the kettle, filled it with water, then I put it on the electric hob to boil.

I didn't know Harry was behind me until I felt him slip his hands around my waist. I turned to look at him. His blue-grey eyes were staring directly at mine. He kissed me gently on the lips. I kissed him back and then it became more frenzied. Clinging onto him, I felt him slide his tongue into my mouth and the sensation drove me wild with passion.

I grabbed Harry's hand and led him to the bedroom. He shut the windows. I turned towards him and he began to unbutton my blouse. It seemed to me that time had stood still. I swore I could hear the buzz of electricity fizzing through my body. I let Harry, undo my skirt, and remove my under-garments. Harry told me how beautiful I was. Our love-making was intense and mind-shattering.

We spent the next few hours locked in a magical, ecstatic world of our own. I exploded with rapture at Harry's delicate touch and never wanted the moment to end. We finally fell asleep, wrapped in each other's arms. It felt to me as though Harry and I were one person in two halves, we were two people that fitted together to make a whole being. When we woke it was late afternoon and the sun was still shining.

I asked Harry if we could swim in the ocean. He nodded and I quickly pulled my clothes on. I then remembered that I didn't own a swimming costume. Harry remedied that by pulling open the bottom drawer in the large chest on the far wall. He then held up a blue, woollen bathing suit. He explained that it belonged to his friend's wife.

It briefly came into mind that Harry may have visited this place with his own wife but I quickly put it out of my mind. I didn't want anything to spoil the short time we had together. The costume was a little on the large side, but I didn't care; I couldn't wait for my first ever swim in the sea.

Harry put his swim wear on and, hand in hand, we walked along the silky sand to the water's edge. It felt so natural doing this small act, like any other couple, and I longed for the time when we could hold hands freely in our home city. The water was icy cold. I waded in gently, toes first. I laughed as Harry raced past me and, when he was waist deep, dived straight under the glassy water. He emerged seconds later grinning and sweeping his blonde-grey hair off his face.

I walked out to him then took the leap and hurled myself into the briny sea. The coldness took my breath away, but it also made me feel refreshed and alive. After our dip, we lay on a towel on the beach until the heat from the sun began to fade. After a while, we walked back up the beach to the bungalow where we bathed together in the four-legged bath then we strolled, leisurely, into the nearby village.

We bought enough food and provisions for our stay. In the evening we sat and ate a meal we had cooked together. This entire scenario that, before the war, most couples did every day was a new and exciting adventure for me. Being with the man I love and acting like husband and wife made me feel content and happy to be alive. Pictures of Bertie danced in my mind and I couldn't work out if he would be happy about Harry and me. I chose to believe that he would give me his blessing until we met again.

I knew that Harry and I would be here for a just short while but none of that mattered. Living our lives through a war meant everyday was precious because we could never be sure we would have a tomorrow. It was wonderful not being terrified by the wail of the air raid siren. Cornwall felt like another world that was untouched by the horrors of war. Instead of cat fights, birds filled the skies. I loved watching the seagulls soar lazily above.

Harry hated their squawking, but I told him it was much preferable to the sound of bombs dropping and gas mains exploding, he had to agree. On our last day, I asked Harry what he meant about Geoffrey being a 'nasty individual'. Harry replied that he had said far too much out of concern for my welfare and that I must not repeat anything he had said.

I promised I wouldn't tell a soul but that made me more determined than ever to bring Geoffrey to justice. The journey back seemed to be much quicker than the drive to get there but I knew it wasn't. My heart felt very heavy as I climbed out of Harry's car at the end of my street. I had become used to kissing him and holding his hand in public, but now we had to revert back to our original relationship, and it brought me to the verge of tears.

I think Harry felt the same, judging by the expression on his face, and his sadness hurt me even more. He had said that he was going to leave his wife. I didn't push him. It had to be in his own time, which was the penalty I must pay for falling in love with a married man. She would be home tomorrow and I secretly hoped that he would tell her about me and his plans for the future. I would have to wait and see.

# 35

The war rumbled on and the citizens of Great Britain continued to do what they could to help their country through one of the hardest times in its history. I dreamed about moving to Cornwall with Harry where we could be safe and happy together but I knew this would not happen while our country was at war. I realised that if everyone moved into the countryside, there would be no protection for our cities.

There would be no one to build the bombs, make the aeroplanes or float the ships that carried our brave men overseas to fight a doggedly determined enemy. We all had to pull together and continue working to defend our country. It was hard on everyone. Most families had been wrenched apart, and some mothers had only seen their children a handful of times in the last four years.

Many of my workmates had not seen their husbands since the war began but they muddled through. Waiting for every letter and reading them, time then time again, helped them feel closer to their men. Hearts were broken when the dreaded telegraph arrived in the menacing brown envelope to tell a loved one that spouse was either dead or 'missing in action' It was an horrendous time to live through.

At the same time, we all ensured we had our fun when we could and just prayed that we and all those we loved would survive. Friendships were an important life line for many of us. They were a sorry substitute for family lives and missing relatives, but it was better than nothing at all. For a while, friends became the family we missed and filled the gaping hole left by all who were not with us.

I broke off my relationship with Ivan, due to my love for Harry. I felt as though I was betraying him. I refused to think about Harry's wife and waited patiently for him to tell her about us. Ivan was not overly concerned. He was seeing a young lady called Odette. She was a nurse who he had met while he was in hospital and he was also stepping out with a posh lady called Felicity Chambers who seemed very fond of him.

He was no longer the nervous, unsure man who I first met. His bravery award told him that he was not the coward that he once thought he was. I always knew that. As well as driving an ambulance he would ride his motor cycle to pivotal points in the middle of an air raid to relay messages to the people that needed them. I couldn't imagine how terrifying it would be to be out in the open and hopelessly exposed when bombs were falling all around.

The wonderful warm and bright summer soon slid into autumn bringing with it the dark evenings and chilly winds. In late October Ivan was hospitalised once more. Whilst digging trapped victims out of bombed- out buildings, he had cut his hand on some jagged masonry. This had developed into a serious infection. He was lucky to be treated with a new type of drug called anti-biotics. He was now on the mend and convalescing in Cornwall.

I hated the long dark evenings and longed for the scent of summer and the noise of birdsong. After one particularly gruelling shift, I arrived home to find Geoffrey sitting in his car outside. He asked if I would like to come out for dinner. I told him I would love to but I needed to wash and change.

He told me to take my time. I blew him a kiss and headed up the short pathway to my home.

I don't know if it was because of the cold weather but I struggled to get my key to turn in the lock. I was just about give up trying and knock on my landlady's door when I heard a strange, crackling noise coming from inside Geoffrey's car. The window was wound down ever so slightly. I assumed this was to stop the car windows misting up as Geoffrey waited for me. I quietly edged back towards the vehicle, hidden by a large leafy hedge, I strained to listen. Geoffrey was speaking to someone which I found strange because I knew there was no one else around.

I peered around the hedge. Geoffrey had a metal band over his head with two, what appeared to be, mufflers over both ears and he was holding something close to his mouth and talking into it.

'Yes, she's learning to drive an ambulance, I have someone working out her daily route.' He paused, and I guessed someone was talking to him. I peered closer and realised that what were actually covering his ears were earphones.

I tried to see what else was in the car. In the back was what looked like, a leather suitcase. I'd seen it before but assumed it was what Geoffrey used to pack his clothes in when we went away. It was now open on the back seat and I could see that it didn't hold any clothes. It actually contained a plastic unit. It was lit up by a green light. I could see two small plastic knobs and, some brown wire. On closer examination, I could also make out the word 'waveband' on a raised square button and two words on the actual case that said '*Datnow* product'. Geoffrey started talking again.

'Don't worry, old chap, it's all in hand, but we must tread carefully,'

What he said next chilled me to the bone.

*'Es lebe Deutschland*, over and out.' He signed off.

I hastily staggered back up the pathway and tried my key once more, desperately hoping it would work. If I knocked on the door, Geoffrey would hear me through his open car window and would know I had been listening. I breathed a sigh of relief as, this time, the key turned effortlessly in the lock. I was totally stunned by what I had heard. I didn't know exactly what he had said but I knew it was German.

I let myself into the house and shouted 'hello' but was met by silence, so I assumed Mrs Groves was out. I raced upstairs to wash and change as quickly as I could. My hands trembled when I applied my lipstick as the enormity of what I'd heard sunk in. Geoffrey was either a German or was spying for Germany and I was at a loss about what to do.

For now, I would go out to dinner with him so not to rouse any suspicion. I walked out of the front door and pulled it closed behind me. It was a chilly evening and I was glad of my warm coat. I pulled open the car door and climbed in. I apologised for keeping him waiting and he said I was worth it. I flashed him a smile and hoped that he couldn't see the fear behind it.

Geoffrey cranked the car into gear and began to drive towards the centre of Bristol. I glanced round and the suitcase was on the back seat but it was now closed. I found it difficult to try and relax as we enjoyed a wonderful meal in a sumptuous restaurant in a very smart part of Clifton, which was on the outskirts of Bristol.

The restaurant was lavishly decorated, and the cutlery sparkled. Thick, white linen napkins were placed on our laps after our chairs had been pulled out for us to sit on. Normally, I would have been in my element and would be throughly enjoying my opulent surroundings, but I was too disturbed by my discovery to take much notice.

Geoffrey must have noticed that something wasn't quite right because asked me if everything was satisfactory. I assured him it was but told him that I had a headache coming on and that I was tired after a long day at the factory. This seemed to satisfy him, and we continued our meal in silence. I couldn't wait for the evening to end. I felt like my whole body was on tenterhooks and that Geoffrey could actually read my mind and knew what I was thinking.

Finally, the food was eaten, and the wine was drunk. Geoffrey helped me into my coat, and I followed him to the car. I had no idea if he wanted to have sex with me, but I sincerely hoped not. I wasn't sure how much longer I could continue with this charade. I needed time to accustom myself to who the man I had been spending so much time with actually was. I was, thankfully, given a reprieve. The car ground to a halt outside Mrs Groves front door. I thanked Geoffrey for a lovely evening then lent over and kissed him softly on the mouth.

I had done this many times before and enjoyed the tickle of his moustache and the warmth of his lips. This time I actually felt I would be physically sick. I hoped I hid what I was feeling like inside and asked him when I would see him again. He told me that he had to go away for a few weeks but would contact me on his return. I told him to hurry back because I would miss him. He smiled and promised he would.

He got out of the vehicle and opened the door for me. We kissed once more then I walked up the path and to my front door. I heard the car start then the noise of the engine driving away into the distance. I let myself in and kicked off my high heeled shoes. It was now too late, to contact Harry, I was quite sure the office would be closed. I was on the early shift tomorrow so I would have to go to the police station straight after work. What I had discovered was something Harry needed to know as soon as possible.

I found it difficult to concentrate on what I was doing at Strachan and Henshaw the following morning. I couldn't get the sound of Geoffrey speaking German out of my mind. It frightened me when I realised what a dangerous person I had been spending my time with. My shift seemed to drag and I was mightily relieved to hear the hooter sound that marked the end of it. Susan and Violet were on the late shift, so I didn't even have them to talk to during my breaks to take my mind off Geoffrey.

Still wearing my work overalls and boots I made my way along the crowded pavement, as quickly as the slow-moving throng of people would allow. When I was free of the crowd of workers I began to walk more quickly, almost breaking into a run. I arrived at the narrow street that led to the back door of the police station. As I always did, before I turned into it I checked in both directions. The coast was clear.

I hurried up the road then dashed into the narrow alleyway. Arriving at the doorway, I glanced around once more before knocking. It was pulled open almost immediately and there stood Harry gazing at me. Seeing him brought back all the wonderful memories of our trip to Cornwall and I longed to throw myself into his arms. I didn't, however, this was business and I needed to conduct the meeting appropriately.

As we drank tea and ate cake, I told Harry exactly what I'd heard and saw. He asked me if I could remember the words that Geoffrey had used. I thought hard but I couldn't, I just knew that he was speaking German.

'I don't want to tell you what to do Joyce, but I really think you should stop seeing him,' Harry pleaded.

'There is nothing I would like more,' I replied then sipped at my tea, 'but if I do that, how are we going to catch him?' I asked.

'Don't worry; we have measures in place that will ensure he doesn't get away. With the information you have given us, we have come to the conclusion that he is either a German spy or a double agent, now he is on our radar and it's all thanks to you,' Harry replied and smiled his beautiful smile that made my stomach turn over in somersaults.

I heaved a sigh of relief. I was perfectly willing to carry on seeing Geoffrey if it meant I was helping my country, but it was the last thing I wanted to do.

'That is good,' I replied, smiling back. 'I wasn't sure if I could keep up the pretence any longer and Geoffrey has the kind of eyes that look as though they can see right inside a person's head,' I finished.

Harry smiled and leaned across the desk and held both my hands in his. I instantly felt safe and protected, I leaned closer to him.

'I don't have any other boyfriends anymore, there's only you,' I told him shyly; he smiled widely and squeezed my hands a little tighter.

'I'll tell Brenda, my wife, soon I promise,' he replied, and I nodded.

The sound of the door being pushed open made us both spring apart as though the touch of each other was burning our skins. The young constable who entered didn't seem to notice. He apologised for not knocking and Harry gave him a stern reprimand before asking him to wrap up the remains of my cake. My demeanour reverted back to its business-like self. I stood up and pulled on my coat, gloves and scarf. With my cake tucked in my pocket I said goodbye and walked out of the door.

I was vigilant, as always, making my way home precariously in the blackout. I had forgotten the torch that Susan had bought me. I knew she would be angry that I was out, in the pitch dark, with nothing to help me along the way, but such was my urgency to get the information to Harry that everything else went out of the window. I literally felt my way home. The blackness of the evening made me feel like I was walking through dense smog. It felt suffocating. I could hear the coughing and footsteps of others but had no idea how far or near they were to me. I was relieved when I finally reached home.

Entering my tiny hallway was like walking into another world. I quickly closed the door and black-out curtains behind me and found myself standing in an oasis of light and warmth. Mrs Groves called a greeting from the kitchen and I shouted back. Once I had relieved myself of my outdoor clothing I walked into the small room.

My wonderful landlady was just turning away from the hob and putting two plates on the table. My mouth watered as I smelt the onions and mince beef. She placed a large bowl of mash potatoes and carrots, to go with it, in the centre of the small table. We both sat. I bowed my head and clasped my hands as Mrs Groves said a prayer then we began to devour our food. After the meal we both shared my leftover cake and talked over a cup of tea.

As Susan and Violet were both working that evening, I didn't go to the Red Lion pub. Mrs Groves was also in for the evening. Once we had cleared away the dishes, we sat either side of the AGA cooker on small but comfy armchairs. My landlady then continued to teach me the unenviable task of knitting. I concentrated furiously on what I was doing. It was important to me that I supported our men on the frontline by supplying them with socks and gloves.

After a few hours, both my landlady I and were happily surprised when I finished knitting a half-decent pair of socks. Mrs Groves repaired a couple of dropped stitches and then handed them back to me. The evening we spent was a pleasant one and a world away from my other life.

In my head, I turned over a new leaf there and then. I decided that there would be no other men; I was done with that life. I would wait for the time when Harry and I could be together as a proper couple. The prospect made me smile. In bed that night I dreamt that I was Harry's wife and I couldn't wait for my dream to come true.

# 36

Ivan returned to Bristol at the end of October. I sat in the audience at the Town Hall and watched as he received his bravery medal from the mayor. I couldn't have been more proud, if we had been related by blood. Ivan looked delighted and I waved at him as he walked off the stage. He winked at me and I laughed. He was definitely no longer the shy, uncertain young man I had first met, and I was glad.

After the ceremony I walked out into the cold, afternoon air and watched as the young nurse who I recognised from the hospital, climbed onto the back of Ivan's DKW 5B 500A motorbike. She clung onto him tightly as he sped out of the carpark. I was glad that he seemed happy and had found a new girlfriend. Now that I had found happiness that was all I wanted for everyone else.

I had no further plans for the day so decided to go into the city and look around the shops. It was quite a disappointing excursion as there was not a lot to be seen in most of the shops that lined the roads. War rationing had seen to that and I wondered how he shopkeepers could possibly make a living. I decided to head home. The light was just beginning to dim as I turned into Boscarne Avenue, where I lived. I stopped and looked in my bag. I needed my torch for the last bit of my journey.

As I did this, I noticed a movement in the corner of my eye. I spun round and was quite sure I saw the silhouette of someone dive into the garden of a nearby house. I kept looking for a minute then shrugged my shoulders. I couldn't, however, shake off the feeling of unease the enveloped my body and made me shiver all over. I walked quickly into my home and was only happy once I had locked the door behind me.

Christmas duly arrived and it was almost impossible to find any decent presents in the shops. Luckily my knitting prowess had come on in leaps and bounds. I unpicked an old cardigan and made three very lovely pairs of gloves for Susan, Violet and Mrs Groves. I also made a warm scarf for Ivan. I found some embroidered handkerchiefs in a second- hand shop which I thought would be perfect for Mabel. Working outside, as a land girl, in all weathers made it seem to me that she constantly had a sniffle or a cold. They were still in their box.

Mabel had already written and told me that she would have to work over Christmas, and I didn't envy her one bit. Working on a remote farm out in all the elements certainly didn't appeal to me and I wondered how she could stand it working in December. She wrote and told me that sometimes the ground was so hard with frost they had to use pick axes to break the earth open and pick the turnips out of the ground. She said that by the end of the day she could no longer feel her fingers or toes. I much preferred working in the confines of the factory even with the threat of air raids.

I sent the present to her and told her to visit as soon as she could. Mrs Groves was going to spend Christmas with her sister in Brighton. She very kindly asked me to join them, but I declined. As fond as I was of my landlady, I didn't fancy spending Christmas in a strange place with someone I had never met. As luck would have it, for me at least, both Susan and Violet would also be alone for Christmas so we decided we would all spend it together.

Violet was the only one that lived in a house with a kitchen so we decided we would all spend the day there. Susan had had to rush back to Cornwall on two separate occasions in the last month. Once when Carmarthen farmhouse had been hit by a bomb and her mother-in-law had been hurt and again when her Grandson, Charlie had been injured. She had been given compassionate leave on both these occasions so she thought it only fair that she was granted no more time off.

For the first time since I had started working at Strachan and Henshaw, it was closed for Christmas, much to the delight of all the staff. We didn't really know why but didn't bother to question it either. Most of us were just glad to have the day off to spend with what family and friends we had. Susan, Violet and I put our rations together and managed to buy a good sized chicken. Violet had just returned from a visit to Ireland to see her sister- in law, Lucy.

Susan's illegitimate daughter had now been adopted by Lucy. Violet had returned home to Bristol with a Christmas pudding made by her husband's cousin, Gerta, who lived next door to Lucy in Ireland. She had also bought home some cheese butter and cream. We feasted like kings and drank a little too much sherry. It was a lovely day. We all loved the presents we had given each other. Susan had bought me a lipstick in a dark mauve shade, which was quite beautiful, and Violet had bought me a pair of fake- pearl clip -on earrings.

The day flew by and, sooner than I would have liked, it was time for me to head home. We all had to be at work at five o'clock in the morning, on the following day. I knew I needed a good night's sleep beforehand, as did Violet and Susan, but it was still with a great reluctance that we said our goodbyes. It was only just after four o'clock in the afternoon when Susan and I left for home but it was already dark and the coldness crept under my coat and gloves. We parted at our usual place and I switched on my torch for the final leg of my journey. I couldn't wait to get home and make myself a hot cup of cocoa and read my 'Woman's Own' magazine in bed.

I could almost feel the warmth of my hot water bottle on my toes. My huge Christmas lunch had made me feel far too full to want any dinner. I turned the corner into my street and gasped with pleasure. Parked a little way up the road from my house was Harry's car. I waved my torch and watched as he opened the door and climbed out.

'I thought you were never coming home,' he said as rubbed his gloved hands together in an effort to warm them up.

'What are you doing here?' I asked unable to disguise my obvious pleasure.

'Let's get into the house and out of the cold before I freeze to death and I'll let you know,' Harry said as he gently guided me up the short garden path.

I unlocked the door and gestured for Harry to go in. I looked around though I was not sure what I was actually looking for. We then stepped inside the door I pulled the bolt across behind us. There wasn't really any reason for this because I knew my landlady would not be coming home until the New Year. Harry followed me into the kitchen which was the warmest room in the house due to the *AGA* being constantly used for heat and cooking.

I took Harry's outdoor garments and hung them, with mine, on the end of the bannister. I then returned to the warmth of the cosy kitchen. Harry was holding his hands over the cooker and he turned and looked at me. He smiled as he told me,

'Brenda is gone to visit the girls, she was particularly tearful because they weren't here for Christmas, as soon as we'd had lunch, I drove her to the station and told her what a happy surprise it would be for the girls if she made an impromptu visit. I felt a bit guilty because she was so grateful. I then drove straight here, I know you told me Mrs Groves was away and that you were spending Christmas with Susan and Violet but I thought you'd be home a bit earlier, I've been sitting in the car for over an hour,' he said.

'If I had known you were here my feet would have grown wings and I would have flown to you,' I told him as I filled the kettle then put it on the hob to boil. I thought a nice cup of tea would thaw us both out.

I felt Harry's arms slide around my waist as I turned my back on him to spoon tea into the teapot. I turned to face him, and he kissed me softly on the lips. I felt the passion in me rise and I knew it was not a cup of tea I wanted.

I grabbed Harry's hand and led him up the narrow stairway to my bedroom. It was freezing cold. Both are breaths became visible clouds of air. The chilliness of the room wasn't what made me tremble as Harry unzipped my dress and let it fall to the floor. We both tumbled onto my single bed. It turned out to be one of the loveliest Christmases I had ever had. I certainly intended to make the most of Harry's wife being out of the picture for a few days.

We woke up on Boxing Day wrapped around each other. I couldn't wait until we could be together, as a couple, and every morning would be like this one. I slipped out of the bed and drew my dressing gown around me then I pulled the curtains aside and looked out. Snow had fallen overnight, and the outside world looked like a magical scene straight from a picture book. The snow glistened in the trees as a low winter sun illuminated its beauty.

I heard Harry climb out of the bed and walk towards me. He too gasped at the enchanting view before us.

'As soon a Brenda gets home, I'm going to tell her,' Harry whispered.

I looked into his eyes and I knew he meant it. Even though the world was at war I began to feel like nineteen forty four was going to be a good year. We ate breakfast and remained in my home, happy to be in one another's company and enjoy what most couples took for granted. I left for work, that morning, with a heavy heart.

I arrived home after my shift and instantly smelt the delicious aroma of a rabbit stew cooking on the hob. Harry came out to the hallway and helped me out of my outdoor things. Later that evening he gave me a beautiful silver necklace for Christmas. It had a thin, delicate chain with a small charm which was the shape of two hands clutching each other. It was beautiful and I loved it. To me, it seemed like a symbol of our future. I wanted the war to be over and to marry Harry. I decided that we would move to Cornwall and I would take care of us both. That was my dream and I longed for it to come true.

## 37

Mine and Harry's mini honeymoon, as I called it, was cut short when Harry received news that Brenda had arrived home sooner than expected. He rushed away after he told me that a colleague at work had answered the telephone and it was Brenda saying she needed a ride home from the station. Harry's workmate happily obliged. Waiting on the platform was not only Brenda but Harry's two daughters also.

When Harry arrived home, he told me that Brenda was distraught. Her surprise visit to see their children had been a dreadful shock to her. He explained how she had been to see them before for a pre-arranged stay and had been shown their lovely shared bedroom and indoor family bathroom. However, when she had turned up unexpectedly it was a very different story.

The children, Evelyn and Shirley were actually sleeping on the cold, hard kitchen floor. Thankfully the heat from the oven kept them warm but that was the only comfort they had. Harry told me how they had both lost weight through lack of food because the people who were supposed to be taking care of them were stealing their rations.

Harry was almost in tears of intense anger as he told me that both girls' hair was matted, filthy and rife with head lice. They obviously hadn't had a bath or even a decent wash in months. The jolly letters they had sent home were lies that they had been forced to write. I was horrified, but Harry's disgust turned to fury, and he told me that he had reported the dreadful people to the authorities, and both had been arrested.

My heart almost broke when tears formed in Harry's eyes as he explained what had happened to his beloved girls. This made me love him even more, if that was possible. My parents had showed very little love for me but Harry was obviously a very caring father. It was clear that he loved his daughters very much and explained that they were staying right here in Bristol and he was never sending them away again. I thought that very wise. We hadn't had a bombing raid for a while and Harry could take care of his children and help them through what they had suffered.

However, I still couldn't shake off the feeling that someone was watching me. I had no evidence to substantiate my worry. No one had been spotted lurking in corners or darting up alleyways so I couldn't really explain why I felt the way I did. Maybe, I thought, I could be feeling guilty about seeing a married man and my guilt was making me suspicious for no reason, who knew? I wondered if it could be Harry's wife but I hadn't actually seen anyone so there was little I could do apart from get on with my life and wait until Harry and I could be together. I hoped this would be soon.

I discussed my suspicions with Harry one day, in mid-January, when he popped in for a quick cup of tea, he told me he was sure I was worrying over nothing. Sadly and shockingly, my little bubble of happiness burst at the end of that very month. The previous few times Harry and I had met up, he had been quiet and subdued. I assumed he had things on his mind regarding the secrecy of his work but when I asked if he was all right, he just stared down at his feet. One day, I decided that I needed to get to the bottom of whatever was niggling away at him,

'Harry, you can talk to me, I won't tell a soul anything, what is bothering you, maybe it would help to talk about it?' I caught hold of his hand as I finished the sentence, but he whipped it away.

'I can't do it Joyce,' Harry said, barely, above a whisper.

'Do what?' I asked, but I think I already knew, he was silent for a minute or two then he said.

I can't leave Brenda, it's not fair for me to lead you on, you're young enough to find someone else,' It felt as though someone had punched a hole in my chest and twisted my heart out. I sat down and tried to stop my tears falling.

'Are you still in love with Brenda? I asked, but I didn't really want to know.

'No, no, of course not,' Harry said, 'It's not Brenda, I can't leave my girls, Evelyn's only four years old, they're so young and they need a stable family home after what they've been through, I can't just walk away from them,' he replied.

I sat still, feeling totally shell shocked by what Harry had said. In a few short moments he had ripped my entire future away from me. I felt broken and adrift and in desperate need of someone to hold me and reassure me that this was a nightmare and that Harry was not leaving me. I heard the door open.

'Bye Joyce, take care of yourself,' Harry muttered as he pulled the door closed behind him.

I have no idea how long I sat there. At some point I heard the key turning in the lock of the front door. I bolted up to my room. I couldn't face seeing my landlady feeling the way I was. I knew that she was fond of me, as I was of her, but she would not allow me to stay in her home if she knew I had been stepping out with a married man. Mrs Groves was a very principled and religious woman and the fact the she liked me wouldn't change that. I didn't make a sound; I just lay on my bed staring at the ceiling.

For the second time in my life my future and been taken from me. Everything about my existence felt unfair. I decided I would walk up to the Red Lion to see if Susan and Violet were there. Anything had to be better than being here, alone with my thoughts and drowning in heartache. I got changed and painted on a happy face. No one wanted to be with anyone miserable.

I went down the stairs and said hello to Mrs Groves. She was surprised to see me, so I told her I had been having a little nap after a busy day and was off to the pub to meet friends. She told me to enjoy my evening then went back to her knitting. She had the wireless on and was humming to a tune. I listened to it and almost became angry; the song playing was *I'm just wild about Harry*. The song was written at least twenty years ago. I wondered why it was being aired now, was it just to rub salt into my festering wound?

## 38

I put my warmest coat on and pulled the belt tightly around my waist. I also put on a woollen hat, scarf and pair of gloves. I hoped this would keep the chilly, damp weather at bay. I pulled the door closed behind me and began my short journey. I heard the sound of a car approaching and it stopped beside me. I recognised it as Geoffrey's car. He wound the window down.

'Good evening, Joyce, I've just arrived back and hoped I'd find you, fancy a night on the town?' he asked, smiling as he looked up at me.

I thought for a minute then nodded. Geoffrey climbed out of his car and went around to the passenger seat and opened the door. I slid in and Geoffrey got back into the driving seat. Before he started the car, he reached into the back seat and put a blanket around my legs. I thanked him and noticed that suitcase containing the radio set was no longer there.

Harry had told me to stay away from Geoffrey and I had done. Now, I didn't really care what happened to me. The man I loved had left me. I knew what Geoffrey was, but I no longer cared. I made the decision to toughen up and to never give my heart to another man ever again. I would focus on having fun. As the car headed out of the town and into the outskirts of Bristol, I felt a momentary stab of panic, but I pushed it to the back of my mind.

We pulled into the carpark of a small hotel called The Windsor. I had never been to the place before. As usual,

Geoffrey was a complete gentleman. He opened doors for me and made sure I was warm. We feasted on roast duck, which was so succulent and delicious, it melted in my mouth. I realised that I had missed being treated to evenings like this. The only place Harry and I ever went was Rita's café and that was so no one would see us together. I began to feel bitter about Harry's treatment of me.

After the meal, Geoffrey escorted me up the stairs to a small double room that he had obviously booked in advance. I neither liked nor disliked the sex; it was just part and parcel of our relationship. We didn't stay the night because Geoffrey needed to be somewhere later on that evening. On the way home Geoffrey asked what I had been up to as he hadn't seen me lately. I lied to him and told him I'd been doing a lot of overtime at the factory. He seemed satisfied with this.

I could hardly tell him that my 'policeman boyfriend' had forbidden me from seeing him. I kissed him goodbye and told him I looked forward to seeing him again soon, now that my work load was a little lighter. He told me he would pick me up on Friday and we could spend the weekend at 'our hotel'. I liked it when he called it that, it made it seem less seedy and more romantic.

I was deep in thought as I made my way back up the path to my home. I had no idea what I would do if Geoffrey started talking in his opium-induced sleep again. I certainly wasn't going to see Harry about it. He might think that it was some type of ploy on my part to get close to him and I couldn't give him that satisfaction. The hurt he had made me feel was turning my love for him into a strong, unleashed hatred.

At work there was talk of plans to drop hundreds of thousands of troops into France to free it from German Rule. This was good news. Violet, Susan and I talked about it and decided that Hitler had spread his army far too thinly in an effort to conquer Europe and that he was fighting for his survival. No one talked about this outside the confines of the factory. It was difficult to trust anyone these days.

At work, the day after Harry had told me his shattering news Susan asked me if I was all right. While we took a tea break, I told her that Harry was staying with his wife. Susan held me as I sobbed on her shoulder.

'It's all I deserve,' I told her when my tears had dried, 'he was never mine in the first place, it serves my right for taking up with a married man,' I also thanked her for not judging me.

Susan told me that she was hardly an authority on extra marital affairs, and I smiled at her sadly. Both of us had had our hearts broken and maybe this was Gods revenge for us for committing the deadly sin of falling in love with someone else's husband. I was glad that Susan could understand how I felt. It helped lessen the loneliness that had enveloped me. I couldn't, however, explain to her about how I felt about the future.

I wanted to tell her that I was scared and that all that stretched before me was emptiness and fear. I couldn't put it in to words though in case that made it more real. Friday arrived and I packed my suitcase ready for my weekend with Geoffrey. Arriving at the hotel felt a little bit like arriving home. All the staff knew us by our Christian names and were very attentive to our needs. This was probably due to Geoffrey's generous tips, but I didn't care what their motives for their kindness were, I was just grateful for it.

We were shown to our usual bedroom. The staff had

thoughtfully lit the fire. I walked over to the grate and held my hands towards the flickering flames. Geoffrey walked over and helped me out of my coat. He explained that he had a small amount of work to do and asked me to change into my dinner dress and go down for a drink in the bar and he would join me shortly. I did as he asked.

As I walked down the plush staircase of the hotel, I felt like Greta Garbo. My light blue, long, silk evening dress showed off my hour-glass figure. The hem brushed my high heeled suede shoes. I was wearing a pair of sapphire earrings that Geoffrey had given me as a late Christmas present and my hair was pulled into a chignon at the back of my head.

As I rounded the corner of the staircase that led into the hotel bar, I was almost sure I saw the back of Harry's head hurrying out of the side door. I knew it was wishful thinking though. I didn't like myself for the pitiful yearning I felt for the need to get a fleeting glimpse of him. I sat at the bar and ordered a gin and tonic. As I slowly sipped at it a man dressed in a naval uniform approached me. He was a lot older than me and his hair was slicked back with *Brylcream*.

He offered to refill my drink. I accepted and told him that I was waiting form my escort and he nodded. I didn't really know what to call Geoffrey. He was too old to be a boyfriend and I certainly wasn't going to pretend he was my husband. Besides, I'd long ago given up caring what people thought of me. We had a conversation about the weather and the war which was what most people talked about nowadays.

Ten minutes later I spotted Geoffrey walking down the stairs and I put my hand up and waved. He approached the bar and I introduced him to the person whom had bought my drink.

The two of them exchanged pleasantries then Geoffrey took my arm and escorted me to the dining room.

The smells coming from the room made my mouth water and were not dissimilar to the smells that used come out from my neighbour's home when I was a child. This immediately sent my mind swirling down into a trip through memory lane and I made a mental note to write to Mabel the following day. I hoped her mother was feeling better.

Dinner was, as always, delicious. The wine was also, enjoyable, and I had to stop myself from drinking too much. I needed to be awake if Geoffrey started talking in his sleep. The man himself was as complimentary as he usually was and constantly told me how wonderful I was and how beautiful I looked. His words made me feel better. They were a salve on the gaping wound left by Harry leaving me.

When we had finished our meal, Geoffrey ordered two brandies and we carried them up to our room. It was so cosy and warm. The brandy slid down my throat like warm liquid gold. Geoffrey was studying a notebook on one side of the room while I sat in an armchair close to the fireplace. I made a mental note to try and take a look at what was in the notebook, while Geoffrey was in the bathroom, later that evening.

I gazed into the amber flames as they flickered in the hearth. Those and the brandy started to make me feel a little sleepy. I pulled myself up and walked into the en-suite bathroom. Once inside, I locked the door and took off my make- up. I then splashed my face with cold water in an effort to wake myself up a little. I had to keep reminding myself what my purpose was in coming here. I realised I had started enjoying the luxury of the place a little too much and had forgotten what I was supposed to be doing.

I walked back into the main suite and began to rummage around my bag until I found my night dress. It was cream coloured silk with lace sewn around the low neckline. Just the feel of the soft material on my skin made me feel as though I was in some enchanted place where there was no war and no heartbreak.

I smiled when Geoffrey wolf-whistled at me as I swirled around in the beautiful garment. It was not long before we were making love on the large double bed. The garment, quickly discarded, was lying in a heap on the floor. The whole time Geoffrey and I had sex I couldn't take my eyes of the silken night gown. It was exactly how I felt. Harry had discarded me in exactly the same way, and I knew the pain of our parting would never leave me,

I was glad when the act was over, and I could put my night wear on once more. Geoffrey went into the bathroom to prepare for bed. I took the note book out of his bedside drawer and quickly scanned through the pages. I had no idea what was written in it though. Obviously, it was some kind of code that my brain simply couldn't decipher. I quickly put it back in the drawer just as Geoffrey re-entered. He made sure the curtains were pulled tightly then damped down the fire.

Geoffrey then brought out his contraption and began inhaling large amounts of opium through the long rubber tube. I did the same but did not breathe the substance in. He then climbed into the bed next to me then switched out the lights. I was now feeling wide-awake. I stared into the darkness waiting and then Geoffrey began to mumble. I strained to listen to what he was talking about.

I could just make out what he was saying, it was something about a Wednesday then I caught something about 'her driving an ambulance, regular route' then he was quiet once more. I decided I would write down what I had heard on my return to Bristol. I would then post it through the secret door. That way I would not have to see Harry, but I would still be assisting the authorities in to bringing Geoffrey to justice. I would also tell them about the note book.

The rest of the weekend passed without incident, so I made the most of my little holiday. I wrapped up warm and went for long, invigorating walks in the chilly, breath-taking weather. Geoffrey was unable to accompany me as he had to work in the hotel room. This didn't concern me. I was happy to be alone while I thought about what life held for me. I could not shake of the unease I felt when I tried to think what my existence would be like after the war.

I concluded that I would be out of work as the men would want their jobs back when they came home from war. I was now sure that we would eventually win, through talking to my workmates and listening to the news bulletins. The tide was definitely on the turn in our favour. Hitler's Germany was fighting for its very survival. There were rumours that the country's people were starving and cold. I wasn't sure what to think about them. They were, after all, the aggressors but they were still human beings.

I walked back into the hotel grounds. It housed a long, expansive garden surrounded on one side by a large wooded area. The rest of the boundary was surrounded by a high privet hedge hiding the hotel from the road that ran along one side of it. The light was now beginning to fade, and the hotel could barely be seen now that the blackout curtains had been drawn. Suddenly, out of the corner of my eye I saw a movement. I spun around and was sure I could make out the shape of a person ducking into the wooded area.

I stood staring for a moment then shook my head, was I going mad? Had Harry broken my mind as well as my heart? I sighed as a shiver ran through my body and I didn't think it was just the cold weather that caused it. Looking at the spot, where I had seen the movement, I strained my eyes to see what could have startled me. Shaking my head, I hurried back to the hotel and decided it must have been the movement of an animal that had frightened me.

The following day Geoffrey drove me back home. We left the hotel early in the morning and the countryside, once again, looked like a magical mystery land. A covering of frost dusted the hedgerows and tiny icicles hung from the tree branches. It was a truly breath-taking scene that made me feel lucky to be alive.

We arrived at my billet and I thanked Geoffrey for a wonderful weekend. I snuck quietly into the house. Even though it was early Mrs Groves, my landlady was up. I knew this because I could hear music coming from the wireless in the kitchen and my landlady singing along to '*Don't go under the apple tree with anyone else but me*', I took off my shoes and crept up the stairs. Ten minutes later I entered the kitchen as though I had just got out of my bed.

Mrs Groves smiled at me and spooned some porridge into a bowl and put it down in front of me. It was delicious and warmed me inside and out. I was doing the afternoon shift so decided I would write down what Geoffrey had said and post it through Harry's secret door. I would also mention the coded note book. This way I could pass on my information without having to see Harry.

Once I had helped clear away the breakfast things, I went up to my room to write my down what I had heard Geoffrey saying. I longed to see Harry again and had the ideal excuse right here, but I knew it would be silly. If I actually saw him I was afraid that I would beg him to come back to me; I didn't want to do that though, I needed to hold onto a small iota of self-respect otherwise I had nothing at all.

I wrapped up warm. The sky was the colour of dark-grey granite and threatened to spill its load at any minute. I decided to pop in a see Susan first as I had a couple of hours to spare. Before the war, I would have spent some of the time browsing around the town but now there was not much to look at. Britain was struggling to keep its shops supplied and it would get worse before it got better. I stamped my feet to keep out the cold and also with frustration. This bloody war was bringing our country to its knees. I would just have to be patient and wait for it to be over.

I arrived at Susan's feeling chilled to the bone. She smiled when she opened the door and saw me standing there and quickly ushered me inside. I stepped inside Susan's cosy little room. Sitting on one of the two kitchen chairs was Cissy. She was the young girl I'd met when we both visited Ivan at the hospital earlier in the year. In November of last year, she had moved from Cornwall to Bristol

Susan was a little angry about this. She told me that she felt that Cissy was abandoning her family when they'd taken her in when she had nowhere to go. Cissy had been evacuated to

Treruth with her baby brother, Alan and had been taken in by Susan's mother-in-law. The situation worked well both ways because Cissy helped out with the house work and the childcare.

Susan explained that Alan, Cissy's brother, now lived with Edith Haversham, who was once Susan's housekeeper. Her son, Johnny and her two grandchildren all attended the local crèche in the village and Edith, her eldest daughter now worked as a clippie on the local buses. It seemed to me that Cissy had every right to move, as long as she knew her brother was taken care of, but I didn't question Susan as to why she was upset with Cissy as it was none of my business.

Cissy looked up and smiled as I walked into the room. She had a smattering of freckles across the bridge of her nose that made her look younger than her sixteen years. She worked as a bus driver and was wearing her uniform. She got up to leave. I told her not to leave on my account, but she assured me that she'd just popped in for a quick cuppa on the way to work and if she didn't get a move on, she'd be late.

I told her that I hoped to see her in the pub some time and to wrap up warm. She promised she would, and then she left for the bus depot. Susan poured us both a cup of tea and we sat down on the two kitchen chairs and put our cups on the small Formica-topped table. It had two leaves which were folded down so it wouldn't take up too much space in the small room.

I enjoyed sitting and chatting to Susan. It took my mind of the constant feeling of sadness that followed me around and refused to leave. I knew that, in time, I would come to terms with my broken love affair but at the moment I found that hard to believe. I left Susan's, around an hour or so later, after explaining to her that I had an errand to do before I began my shift and would meet her at the factory gates.

Tiny flakes of snow began to fall as I stepped out of Susan's front door and onto the pavement. I pulled my gloves on and made my way to the police station to deliver my letter. As always, I made certain that no one saw where I was going. I slipped into the narrow alley way and stood outside the door. It took an almost inhuman effort not to knock but I didn't because I knew that would not change the way things were. I pushed the envelope through the letter box and hurried away.

# 39

I walked out of the alley and down the narrow street that led onto the main road. I was thinking that I'd better get my skates on if I didn't want to be late for my shift and almost walked into the car that had suddenly stopped in front of me. I was about to walk around it when a man jumped out of the driver's seat and wrenched the boot open. Before I had a chance to scream or talk, I was bodily thrown into the open trunk and the lid was pushed firmly down. I then heard him locking it.

I was totally stunned for several minutes. I lay in the dark, confined space in state of total shock. I realised that I had been kidnapped and felt terrified. I tried to move but it was impossible. I started to get cramps in my arms and legs and my whole body began to tremble. I wondered if it was anything to do with, Brenda, Harry's wife. Had she found out about our affair and intended to do away with me? I shuddered once more.

Finally, I heard the hand brake being cranked up and the vehicle came to a stop. Now my terror felt like a choking fog that was actually suffocating me. I heard muffled talking and tried to listen to what was being said. Suddenly a smell permeated towards me and I was stunned further still. I could smell the unforgettable aroma of Geoffrey's mysterious after shave. What on earth was happening?

My blood ran cold as the realisation hit me. I was now one hundred percent sure that Geoffrey knew that I'd been informing on him and that he was my kidnapper. I was also absolutely sure that his intention was to kill me before I could reveal any more of his secrets. Why else would he kidnap me? My only hope was to try and talk to Geoffrey. I knew that he must have some sort of fondness for me otherwise he wouldn't have treated me so nicely. The voices ceased and I heard a door shut.

The boot was then opened, and I was dragged out. I looked up to see a well-built man standing in front of me. He was wearing a black balaclava and only his eyes were visible through tiny slits. Not being able to see his face was disconcerting, if he was going to kill me, would it matter if I knew what he looked like? All I could see were two small, black beady eyes looking at me.

I looked around and realised we were in a large barn. I recognised the car I was standing beside as the one that Geoffrey drove around in so that confirmed his involvement in my abduction. There was, though, no sign of the man himself. The unknown man moved towards me and shoved me into the corner of the barn. I fell into a pile of hay that had been spread around the floor. I lay still, terrified at what he would do next. I saw him looking at the top of my stocking and quickly pulled down my skirt.

To my untold relief he simply made a scoffing sound then turned and walked out of the barn. He pulled the door behind him and I heard not only the sound of a key in the lock, being turned, but also the noise of a large bolt being pulled across the door. I waited a while, in case he returned, before I began to look for a way out.

There were no windows in the building and the only door was the one he had locked. I tried to pull it open, but it was hopeless. I looked desperately for a way to escape but there was nowhere. I felt the urge to sob but supressed that quickly, that would not help me get out of the situation I found myself in. I began to shout for help and continued to do so until my throat became sore and my voice sounded gravelly. The barn was freezing cold, it was no warmer than being outside, so I walked around and stamped my feet to try and keep warm.

I have no idea how long I was imprisoned before I heard the sound of footsteps outside. I was sure it was longer than an hour but couldn't work out how much longer. Susan would be wondering why I wasn't at work. I wished I'd confided in her about what I was doing with Harry, because she might have realised I was in trouble, but now it was too late. I looked towards the door and sure that I could hear two sets of footsteps approaching. The sound of the bolt being moved and the key turning in the lock followed.

I looked towards the door and two men walked in. One was Geoffrey and the other was a stranger to me, Geoffrey spoke;

'Joyce darling, my colleague here has told me what you've been up to with your policeman friend, which was a silly thing to do.' He spoke as though he was scolding a small child for pinching some sweets.

'I have no idea what you're talking about Geoffrey darling,' I replied.

'I'm sorry Joyce but sadly, that's just not true,' Geoffrey continued, 'my good man here has seen you going to the back door of the police station on several occasions,' he finished as he moved closer to me. I looked him in the eye and answered.

'That's because I'm having an affair with Harry Shawcross,' I replied, feigning ignorance, 'Why else would I be there?' I enquired.

'Well, somebody's been telling tales Joyce and you are the

only one who's been seen slipping furtively in out the police station,' He replied.

I tried to catch hold his hand. I thought it would remind him of the relationship we had and all the intimate moments we shared but he swatted it away like a troubling insect. The other man then grabbed me by the shoulders and marched me out the door. I stepped outside and the daylight almost blinded me. The snow had stopped and now there was a bright, golden winter sun high in the sky. I guessed that it must about mid-afternoon by the lightness of the day.

My spirits rose and I was about to scream for help when I saw a police car parked on the forecourt a little way from the barn. I looked around and realised that the place might have once been a working farm but now it was derelict. The old farmhouse didn't have a signal unbroken pane of glass in the windows and the whole place was overgrown. It was obvious that no one had lived here for years.

Geoffrey laughed when he saw me looking at the police car. I was puzzled and I struggled as I was manhandled towards it. Looking inside, I saw that it was empty. I then realised that the vehicle was going to be driven by one of the two men. There were no police coming to my rescue. My disappointment made me desperate. I struggled away from my captor and ran as fast as I could away from the place.

It was a fruitless escape attempt. I was wearing heeled shoes and although they were quite low, they dug into the soft earth and slippery snow, hampering my escape. The larger man caught up with me in no time at all. He dragged me back to the car. I looked at Geoffrey and the expression on his face terrified me. I had never seen him look like that. It was like he was wearing a mask of pure evil. He hissed the word 'bitch' then he raised his arm and punched me so hard in the face that I stumbled backwards and would have fallen if his accomplice had not caught me.

For the second time that day, I was jostled into the boot of the car. I lay stunned and bleeding as the hood was banged shut and the key turned in the lock once more. I couldn't believe that Geoffrey had hit me. My nose, cheek and lips were throbbing and I could taste blood in my mouth. I could also feel it running out of my nose. I was now positive that these two men meant to kill me.

I tried to think if I would be missed when I was dead. Thinking intently, I decided that I would be but only for a short while. Mrs Groves would find a new lodger to give her an income and Strachan & Henshaw would soon replace me with a new trainee. I was sure that Susan would probably miss me but that was all. Maybe, this had been my fate all along and that was the reason I couldn't see any future for myself, because I had none. If that was the case, why was I even born? Had I been put on this earth simply to be miserable, I hoped not. The two men began talking and I leaned forwards to try and hear what they were saying.

The car boot was a lot larger than the previous one I had been thrown into and allowed me some movement, I strained to hear the conversation, Geoffrey was speaking.

'Apparently, she's been seen working on an Austin K2 ambulance, load of tosh of course, just something they want the people to believe,' he announced.

There was merely a grunt in reply to Geoffrey's statement.

'So today is D-day,' Geoffrey said and I could hear the glee in his voice and imagined him rubbing his hands together in excitement, ' The weapon you've got will kill her stone dead, the sight on it will allow you to make a clear aim, go for the head, we need her to be dead, not injured,' he explained.

I rolled around in the boot as the car spun around corners. I tried to steady myself as it flew over uneven ground and pot holes along the journey. I was horrified. They were obviously going to kill someone and it was going to be done very soon. It had to be an important person if they were using a police car as a disguise. I guessed that they were going to kill me afterwards and then maybe bury me, and the other unfortunate victim, somewhere no one would find us.

Finally, the car came to a stop. Nothing happened for a while, but I was sure I head the cranking of a rifle clicking into place. Mr Johnson, my old neighbour, used to shoot rabbits, was that why I recognised the sound. I then heard the car door open and slam shut again. I heard the sound of footsteps walking away from the car; this told me that one person had left the vehicle. The car was then cranked into life once more and driven a small distance away before I heard the second person open the car door and walk away.

I was feeling frantic. I had to get out of the car and warn the person who they intended to kill. I banged on the boot and yelled but no one answered my screams. I then tried to kick in the back seat and to my amazement, it gave way. I struggled through the small gap and opened the car door. I felt as wobbly and disorientated as I climbed out and quickly glanced around.

I heard Geoffrey mention an ambulance so scanned the area around me. I then saw a sign above an archway between two large buildings that said *Emergency service vehicles*. I looked around; there was no sign of Geoffrey or his accomplice. I quickly made my way across the road and walked under the archway.

Several vehicles parked up. There were two 'Tilly' light trucks and a Fire Engine at the far end of the courtyard. Three ambulances were parked along one side and there was another one in the middle of the courtyard being washed down by a group of women in uniform. I walked towards them but had no idea what I was going to say. As I did this, my right eye caught a glare of light and I looked up. I could just make out Geoffrey's accomplice on the roof of one of the tall buildings.

It felt like my heart had stopped beating in my chest when I saw he was pointing a heavy looking rifle towards the back of a small, young woman. I thought she looked around about fifteen or sixteen years old. She was wearing an ATS uniform and was laughing and talking to four or five other women also dressed in the same uniform. The young woman had dark brown hair peeking out from under her cap and she was hunched over and deeply concentrating on tightening one of the wheel nuts of the vehicle.

She screwed up her face as she completed the task then smiled and took a cloth, from one of the other girls, to wipe her hands. I was now absolutely positive that this woman was the target. I screamed and raced forward. I can't imagine what she must have thought when she turned and saw me hurtling towards her.

My face was covered in blood from the punch that Geoffrey had given me earlier and I was shrieking like a mad woman. I looked up and saw the gun being raised and pointed in her direction. I was about a foot away when I literally hurled myself on top of her. As we both tumbled to the ground, I heard the noise of gun shot. I screamed at her to 'stay down' because someone was trying to kill her.

All hell began to break loose around me as the other recruits started screaming. Without any preamble, five or six women threw themselves on top of me and the target forming a human barricade. I heard another shot ring out and the then the sound of a woman squealing. I asked the girl beside me if she was all right and she said she was.

I almost cried with relief when I heard the sound of a police whistle being blown frantically and the shouts of several men. A moment later the women all clambered off the would-be victim and I was also pulled to my feet. She was then hurried away by numerous, important-looking men, in smart suits. They all held hand guns and were shooting towards the area where the gun shots had come from.

I turned and saw that one of the girls was not standing but was lying in a twisted heap on the floor. I bent down and touched her head. She looked up at me and was obviously in pain. She pointed onto her back. I rolled her on her side. Some of the other women knelt down too. Blood was pouring out of a gaping wound, like water spurting from a tap.

I quickly pulled my scarf off and put it over the wound. I put as much pressure as I could on it. I had been taught to do this in my St Johns Ambulance classes. I asked the girl her name, she was very pale.

'Rhinna,' she whispered, I noticed that she had an accent and, in an effort to keep her awake and chatting, I asked her where she was from.

'Poland,' she whispered.

She was struggling to breathe, and I was relieved to see a man racing towards us. He carried a doctor's bag and told everyone to let him through. Two stretcher bearers followed and laid the stretcher out beside the injured girl. The medic told me that I had done an excellent job and that he would take it from here. I was afraid to release the pressure on the wound. The doctor gently moved my hand and replaced it with his. He then assured me that Rhinna would be fine, but they needed to get her to the hospital. I nodded then stood up.

I watched as she was lifted into the ambulance which then sped off with the bell ringing loudly. Suddenly, a feeling of sheer exhaustion washed over me. I felt as though my whole body was made of paper. There were three granite steps leading to a locked door to the right of me. I staggered over to them and sat down. All of sudden, I felt the need to vomit and did so. I wiped my face on the sleeve of my coat.

I watched, as everyone raced around the courtyard. I felt like I was watching a film at the picture house. It was as though I was in another place looking at the scene from afar. Then I saw him. Harry was standing just three feet away from me. I could see that he was wearing a holster around his waist and he was holding a hand gun. He began to walk towards me, it looked like he was doing it in slow motion but I'm sure he wasn't.

I didn't have the strength to stand and walk away, even if I wanted to. He knelt down in front of me and held my hands. I wanted him to pull me into his arms so I could cry until all the fear had left me. He took his handkerchief from his pocket and began to wipe the blood from my face. He pushed my hair behind my ears and told me that I should go to the hospital. I shook my head. I just wanted to go home. I was so happy to be alive, but I was also shocked and bone weary.

Both Harry and I turned to the left simultaneously when we heard a commotion coming from the far corner of the yard. I was relieved to see the young girl whom I had saved, walking towards me. She was obviously uninjured. As she approached, Harry jumped to his feet and saluted the girl. Everyone around her seemed to be doing the same thing but I didn't have the strength to move, let alone salute.

The young woman bent down and thanked me; she asked if I was all right, I nodded. Harry then spoke.

'Joyce, may I introduce you to Princess Elizabeth Windsor, Honorary Second Sulbaltern, and member of the Auxiliary territorial service,'

It took a minute to sink in, exactly what Harry was saying and when it did, my jaw dropped open. I tried to get up, but she assured me that there was no need. She then asked Harry if he would take me into the supervisor's office so her personal doctor could take a look at me. Harry nodded and scooped me up in his arms as though I weighed no more than a feather. I wanted to thank the young girl, but I seemed to have become mute.

The person I had saved from being killed was none other than Princess Elizabeth. I couldn't believe it. The doctor tended my wounds and cleaned me up and I felt semi-human again. Harry helped me out of the door. Princess Elizabeth was still there insisting to her courtiers that she needed to know I was all right. She rushed towards me when she saw me come out of the building.

I bowed my head and assured that I was fine. She thanked me once more before she was ushered into large car with blacked out windows. Harry insisted on driving me home. As we sat in the car he began to speak. He told me that ever since I had alerted them about Geoffrey, they had been following him. When I thought I'd seen Harry at The Grange Hotel the other evening, I hadn't been wrong. He'd had to hotfoot it out of the door when I walked down the stairs in case I *'blew his cover'*. I listened as he began to explain;

'We were watching from a small distance away when his accomplice chucked you in the boot of his car,' he explained, 'but there was nothing we could do to stop them, we knew what they were planning and we couldn't let them know we were onto them, we needed to catch them red-handed' Harry continued, 'I saw that bastard punch you in the face, it took four of my fellow officers to hold me back, I wanted to rescue you there and then,' he said.

'Well I'm glad you didn't, it might have cost the princess her life,' I replied. Harry turned towards me and held my hand.

'You're a beautiful and extremely brave woman Joyce,' Harry told me as he kissed my hand.

His touch felt like a tiny bolt of electricity racing through my body. I looked at him.

'I'll wait,' I told him, Harry looked at me with an incredulous expression on his face and starting muttering that it wouldn't be fair on me, it might be another twenty years.

'I'll wait,' I repeated, a little louder this time.

Harry pulled the car over to the side of the road. He then leaned over and gently kissed my swollen lips. He held my face in his hands and said.

'I love you with all my heart and always will.'

'I love you too.' I replied.

Harry restarted the car and headed towards my home. I smiled widely and so did he. Although I was physically in pain, inside my heart was singing. I didn't care how long I had to wait. It would be worth it to be with the man I loved, eventually. Finally, I could come out of the dark and into the light and that was all I had ever wanted.

THE END

I hope you enjoyed my novel. You can meet Joyce again in my other books: *The Enduring Ripples of War* and *Fairly Jane*.

# BY THE SAME AUTHOR

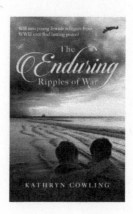

## *The Enduring Ripples of War*

Long before the rest of the world became aware of the terrible things happening in Germany, in 1932 two young Jewish boys have to flee from Hitler's hatred of the Jews.

After a long and challenging journey, they finally arrive in England, to apparent safety. Sadly, their newfound peace isn't destined to last and both of them find themselves fleeing conflict once more.

ISBN 978-1-911546-76-4

Available from amazon.co.uk
www.theconradpress.com and all good bookshops

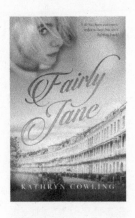

## Fairly Jane

This powerful, passionate, highly emotional novel tells the story of Jane Fairly and her struggle to find love and happiness after being adopted as a baby and then coerced into marriage at the age of sixteen. She only narrowly avoids being killed by her abusive husband and manages to escape to Cornwall, where she tries to rebuild her life. Only after numerous other ups and downs does Jane start to find herself and discover how to be happy.

*Fairly Jane* will move you, shock you, and warm your heart.

ISBN 978-1-911546-42-9

Available from amazon.co.uk
www.theconradpress.com and all good bookshops